Under A Mulberry Moon

Susan Slater

Books by Susan Slater
THE BEN PECOS MYSTERY SERIES

The Pumpkin Seed Massacre
Yellow Lies
Thunderbird
Firedancer
Under A Mulberry Moon
A Way to the Manger (a Christmas novella)

Under A Mulberry Moon

Ben Pecos Mysteries, Book 5

Susan Slater

Secret Staircase Books

Under A Mulberry Moon
Published by Secret Staircase Books, an imprint of
Columbine Publishing Group LLC
PO Box 416, Angel Fire, NM 87710

Book layout and design by Secret Staircase Books
Cover illustrations © Kdshutterman and Zdenat5

First trade paperback edition: August, 2018
First e-book editions: August, 20108

Publisher's Cataloging-in-Publication Data

Slater, Susan
Under A Mulberry Moon / by Susan Slater
p. cm.
ISBN 978-1945422492 (paperback)

1. Pecos, Ben (Fictitious character)--Fiction. 2. Native
American--Fiction. 3. Florida--Fiction. 4. Rare orchids--Fiction.
5. Smuggled botanical items--fiction. I. Title

Ben Pecos Mystery Series : Book 5
Slater, Susan, Ben Pecos mysteries.

BISAC : FICTION / Mystery & Detective.
813/.54

Thanks to my Beta readers—Judi, Sandra, Paula, and Marcia—who now know capitalization and auto-correct are my true enemies. I so appreciate the careful reads!

And a huge thanks to all of Ben's new fans in Florida! Keep on asking me that magic question--
"When's your next book coming out?"
I'll try to make certain I always have an answer.

Chapter One

It was such an ordinary day. Seven-thirty on a Monday morning the first week in May, the last month before summer vacation—*and* the last month before heat and humidity would drive her indoors to air-conditioned comfort. She was a wuss. She admitted it. Sweat was just not her thing but she loved her birthplace, St. Augustine, Florida. Oldest city in the United States, just oozing history, with an ocean and river and knock-your-socks-off sunsets. In all her thirty-one years, she'd never wanted to live anyplace else.

As always, she was right on time. She pulled into her own special slot in the Jefferson Elementary School parking lot—the space right in front of administration, the one headed by a large sign proclaiming her, Maureen Beltzer, as Teacher of the Month. That always brought a smile. She'd had the space longer than anyone else. Three whole months—thanks to a vote by students and faculty combined.

She quickly ran both hands through her short occipital bob, fluffing at the temples. There were times after a good haircut when she could flip her head and every white-blond strand would fan out then settle back, perfectly cupping her face. She turned the rearview mirror toward herself to better apply a swipe of gloss and rub her lips together before inspecting the result. The crease in her chinos was losing its crispness, and she had to roll the sleeves up twice on her wine silk-blend blouse to cover a ball point stain but overall, not bad—if she did say so herself.

She tossed her phone into the glove compartment and locked it, grabbed a roll of posters off the back seat, and she was ready for the day. Her aide, Ginny, caught up with her just inside the front door. "Sheila Watkins in AV wants to know if you need a projector today. She only has two left."

"No. I think I'm down for tomorrow."

"I'll check and pick one up in the morning." A quick wave and Ginny was moving down the first hallway to the teachers' lounge. Starting the day with yet another cup of coffee and a little gossip simply didn't interest her, wasn't her thing. This was the time of day she liked best—the half hour of quiet before her classroom began to fill with third graders. She was by herself and could look at lesson plans one more time and make sure each study table held several sets of multiplication flash cards. This was the hour when a spray bottle of disinfectant was put to good use— chair backs, cabinet pulls, door knobs. Thirty minutes of tidying up and she was ready to begin the day. She always started with math. The class was usually rested and fresh, and concentration seemed easier.

Eight on the dot. She propped her classroom door open, nodded to the teacher whose room was next to hers, and stopped the pushing and shoving at the back of the line. Several times she pointed at the trashcan and watched as wads of gum were deposited. Then a quick reminder—how many had there been during the year?—to put phones in the alphabetized cubbies behind her desk. Ginny stopped to share gossip, but she shushed her—not the place, not the time. Finally. All in.

Twenty-three eight-year-olds fanned out in front of her as she checked roll and entered the total in the computer on her desk, picked up a couple extra pencils and a spare pack of flash cards and walked to the back of the classroom. She announced plans for the day. She'd start by checking homework and do a quick random test of the times tables. She knelt between two students and spread the cards on the table in front of her.

She heard the nervous giggles before she looked up. Or maybe she heard a click, she couldn't say for certain. What she did remember was staring at the revolver as it came toward her—at the barrel before it came to rest against her temple.

Chapter Two

Was the gun real? A toy? Oh God, would this become another story on the evening news? A hundred images flashed through her head before common sense told her she had to take charge.

"Put the gun down, Toby." She kept her voice just above a whisper and didn't move from her kneeling position beside the low table. She was helping the group of boys with math, nothing more, nothing less—she didn't want to put others in danger.

"No," he said, and she watched his thumb draw the hammer back.

"Now. Put it down now." Her voice became adamant, a strident hiss. He was smiling. Goddamn him. He was looking into her eyes and enjoying the fright, prolonging his jollies. Could he do that? He was only eight.

"No more homework?" he asked.

She took her first somewhat steady breath in over a minute. So that was it. A joke. Probably hatched by the five of them sitting around the low table, five pee-wee, inseparable pals. All in hundred-dollar sneakers, punk hair, and posturing far beyond their actual years. Was it Toby's idea? Threaten the teacher, and demand a reprieve from work outside class? Maybe older kids put them up to it. And maybe the gun wasn't even real. She drew in her second unlabored breath. Of course, it was plastic, a water gun, maybe an old cap pistol … it had to be.

"I don't think so, Toby." *Stay in control, I'm the teacher here.*

"Then you'll die." Who did the voice sound like? Certainly not an eight year old. Who was he imitating? Some TV star? Did it matter? The hair on the back of her neck stood straight up. Thank God for a strong sphincter.

"The game's over. I want you to hand me the gun." There, her best no-nonsense voice. But he didn't waver. If eight-year-old eyes could go blank, not register any feeling, then his were two dark brown voids.

"Do it, T. J., blast her." One of his pals leaned in close, elbows next to hers. Tobias Jefferson Wolff sucked his lower lip between his teeth, squinted and pulled the trigger.

There was a moment of stultifying shock, some bit of time during which she didn't breathe or scream or faint. Maybe her mouth was open to shriek to the heavens, but nothing came out, she was sure of that. It took this nanosecond before her brain could process that she was, indeed, still alive, that the click was not followed by an explosion of sound, a burst of light with winged creatures motioning her to join them. She would also swear that her life had not replayed itself in Technicolor wonderment, frame following frame of Maureen, "Mo", Beltzer as child, teenager, and adult.

The breathless moment flashed forward to reality and she grabbed the gun, scrambling to her feet without letting go, pulling it and Toby's hand up into the air, screaming for him to release, twisting hard, clamping down on the slim wrist, bending the arm sideways, pushing him backward. She was on top, holding on as they fell, then banging hand and gun against a nearby chair as their two bodies thudded to the floor in a splintering of wood as the squat table divided under their weight.

Somewhere on the way to the floor, the revolver's cylinder sprang outward pelting their bodies with three fat .38 Glaser bullets, the kind that are encouraged for home-protection because they disintegrate upon impact, scattering bits of metal throughout the body. Death is quick, if not messy.

Suddenly a blind anger flooded all rational systems, and she slugged Toby smartly on the jaw. She had very little leverage, but the gun popped out of his grasp and he started crying, that prolonged wail of the genuinely affronted. She carried his look of astonishment indelibly etched on her brain for a long time. He was shocked that she'd popped him one—followed his actions with some swift moves of her own. But mostly, she knew he was surprised that nothing had happened.

So was she. Simple as that. He looked disappointed. She should have been dead. She knew it had never entered his mind that if he pulled the trigger, she wouldn't have a hole in her head. But hadn't he known that the first chamber was empty? Maybe not. At eight how much could he know about guns? She'd never know. Because what happened after that was the real nightmare.

Chapter Three

"Hey, Short-timer, got just the job for you."

Barely suppressed glee didn't instill confidence. Whatever the job, it was not one he'd stand in line for. Detective Tim Foley was pretty sure of that. And, yeah, the short-timer thing was beginning to feel pretty good. He'd be gone in two months. Off the streets and out of this tourist trap that was beginning to attract gang-crime.

As luck would have it, he'd coast into retirement with a Fed job. In seven years there would be a catamaran secured in a slip on the Intracoastal between trips to the Bahamas. He could put up with anything if the carrot was orange enough. Seven years wasn't that long. Not what he'd planned, but opportunity knocking probably only did happen once.

But, what the hell? He was still on the force. Still a detective, not a special agent … yet. No time to duck responsibility. "Whatcha got, Mike?" He stopped in the doorway of his boss's office. So much for enjoying a Portabella "burger" with melted Muenster in peace and quiet. He idly wondered if mushrooms could be microwaved. He knew it wasn't going to do the Muenster any favors.

"Eight year old takes a gun to class. Teacher says he pointed it at her. A third-grader, for Christ's sake. Parents are on their way over with the kid. Not sure how we want to handle this. The interview will determine if or how much detention time to recommend. Need to know the parent's involvement—you know, was the kid given the gun? Are guns left lying around? Hey, I don't need to tell you your business but just make sure it's recorded *and* you have a witness. Get Randy to sit in or Mary Ellen if she's free. It's short notice, but we better get the kid-shrink over here. Give the college a call. Don't want this one blowing up in our faces once the news hounds get a whiff. Let's keep Channel Two's WESH News on top of checking our fire extinguishers and whether or not we're staffed up for Bike Week and nothing else."

Tim tried to absorb the rapid-fire glut of information. He took the school's report, gave the receptionist instructions to find a child psychologist who could be there in half an hour, then walked back to his office. Head of the school's security had signed the report. It appeared that the student hadn't been questioned. There was nothing more than a brief one-paragraph description of what happened. It wasn't even clear that the teacher had been threatened—only that a student had a gun in class.

The weapon had been given to St. Augustine Police to print. A rooky, Sam Waltham, had accepted it. The report was attached. Fast and thorough, but that seemed to be the extent of their involvement. Tim was wondering at the limited use of City resources. Then it jumped out at him.

The student's father was former School Board Chairman and current City Councilman, T. Jefferson Wolff. That would bring a little clout into the picture. It would be over three hours since the incident occurred if they brought their son in now. Long time between action and reaction. Enough time to "help" a child get his story straight. Tim cursed under his breath. This was most likely an exercise in futility.

Chapter Four

Happy honeymoon and welcome to Florida." Ben glanced at the red-headed woman riding shotgun, "Ever think you'd trade in mountains for an ocean?" He slowed the F-150 and pulled into the middle lane making room for an 18-wheeler trying to merge with traffic from an on-ramp.

"It's difficult to think of this trip as a honeymoon when there's a U-Haul with all my belongings being pulled behind us."

Ben took a deep breath and silently warned himself not to read too much into Julie's less than enthusiastic answer.

"I don't think we're talking more than a year's contribution of time—I'll get the program off the ground, train a replacement and we're out of here. And this summer assignment is just temporary—"

"Oh Ben, I'm sorry. I know we've talked. It's just that we seem to be out in nowhere."

Ben admitted she had a point. Even keeping his eyes on the road there were long stretches of nothingness sometimes blocked along the sides by the tangled greenery of tropical vegetation—and more than one grouping of tall stately pines. Pines and palm trees. This was a real disconnect. Even the scenery seemed at odds with itself.

And wasn't most of the state's sand slated to slip back into the ocean if the global warming trends kept up? By the year 2100, sixty percent of the state was supposed to be gone. No one seemed scared. Population numbers made it one of the most popular states. Growth was skyrocketing. Despite dire warnings, California hadn't fallen off into the Pacific; fingers crossed Florida would follow suit—all conjecture and no reality.

They had cut across the panhandle on Interstate 10, through Pensacola, then Tallahassee, then on to Jacksonville. He'd be dropping Julie off in Jacksonville to catch a flight to Miami. She was spending their first week in paradise interviewing with the Miami *Herald*. He circumvented downtown traffic and found the JAX terminal fairly easily. Sunday traffic beat trying to cross the city any day of the workweek.

He parked in the unloading zone and quickly pulled two fat, square bags from behind the seat. He smiled. Julie always ended up checking "carry-on" sized bags.

They stood on the curb just looking at each other until he pulled her to him. "I love you. I owe you unlimited exposure to sun and sand and margaritas."

"And I'll take you up on that. A week won't be so long; see you next Saturday."

A kiss, a long hug and he watched her walk away, pulling the two wobbly, unbalanced bags behind her, turning once to blow a kiss his way before going through a revolving door. He sighed and stared until she disappeared from sight, reluctant to leave the airport without her. A week was going to be a really long time.

He was startled by an officer on a patrol scooter telling him to move on. He climbed back into the cab of the truck and maneuvered it into the lane that would put him on course to pick up I-95—the north/south artery that took vehicles down into peninsular Florida, his new home.

Did he have any idea what to expect? Not really. Wasn't Florida wall-to-wall elderly and pink flamingo lawn ornaments? How many times had he seen "God's Waiting Room" on bumper stickers? Still, he was going to stay positive and busy. But he knew he'd be counting the days until the weekend.

With Julie, he knew he was trying to put a little country into a city-kid but he could count on her support—once the uprooting phase passed. Their temporary summer home was only fifty miles south. He'd go on into St. Augustine, unload the U-Haul at their rental, return the carrier and get ready for work—a job that maybe wasn't quite what he was used to but exciting all the same. He didn't know much about where they were going to be living. His letter of confirmation described it as "the upstairs living quarters above a 1910 carriage house." But it was in the old, touristy part of St. Augustine—supposedly "close to everything," another quote from the brochure that accompanied the invitation. He just needed to unload, get their things in some sort of quasi-livable arrangement and show up at the local college in the morning. That would keep him busy.

+ + +

Monday morning and Flagler College rotunda was packed. He missed Julie already. She had sounded excited on the phone last night—enjoying the city but looking forward to that promised Florida sand and sea time. She raved about all the fantastic beaches in the area. She couldn't wait for her interview with the Miami *Herald*. The city was close to where they would be landing on a permanent basis and reminded her of home. She even called Miami, Phoenix with water.

This St. Augustine thing was just a fill-in. Indian Health Service loaned him to the Bureau of Indian Affairs for the summer. The Department of Interior was celebrating one hundred years since the founding of national parks. And of the thirty-five original parks, Florida was home to eleven. It made sense to kick off the year-long series of events here.

The centennial celebration would begin with a lecture series at Flagler College and play host to several Washington dignitaries with workshops and tours throughout the summer. University of Florida made certain its sometimes-overlooked research jewel, the Whitney Labs located near Marineland, would partner with the Georgia Aquarium tourist draw. Together, they would showcase national parks with exhibits of sea life from dolphins to turtles to a newly planned exhibit of native plants.

Ben was sharing a class on Native Medicine with walking tours through a couple close-by State Parks. He'd read a thesis a few years back in pharmacology, tracing the derivatives of ancient healing herbs with their modern counterparts. He wasn't sure peyote was a good substitute for Prozac but it would make for an interesting lecture.

He was actually glad he'd been asked—token Indian or not. He hadn't been looking forward to a layoff over the summer. Yes, he needed time to relocate to southern Florida, but not three months' worth. He had been hired by the Seminoles to set up a clinic outside Hollywood, Florida, starting in September. Besides, St. Augustine had always been on his list of places to visit. After he registered and got a catalogue of upcoming events, he'd be free to play tourist. He thought Fort Matanzas would be his first stop.

If he were being truthful, this summer would also give him time to do his homework. It would be difficult to find tribes more different from his own Pueblo background than the Seminoles. Even Seminole was an umbrella, catch-all term for more than one tribe. The Creek, Miccosukee, and Muscogee Creek in the St. Augustine area, and the Cow Creek Seminole from the everglades area, were a few of the tribes he needed to become acquainted with.

"Pecos? Benson Pecos? Uh, Doctor Benson Pecos?" A man with a microphone stood behind the sign-in table at the front.

"Here." Ben waved to get the man's attention before walking forward and shaking the hand of a Dr. Elles.

"I hate to put you to work but I'm in a bit of a bind. The head of our psych department usually offers his services to local law enforcement when needed—when there's a case requiring specialized backup, but Larry's out today."

"Not a problem, I'll help."

"From what I understand, an eight-year-old took a gun to class—maybe even threatened his teacher. Because of his age, they're requesting an expert do the interview."

"Understandable."

"And the kid's one of yours."

"You mean, he's Indian?"

"Yes, uh, I didn't mean any offense."

"None taken."

"Leave your intro packet with me and I'll get you signed in. They'd like you there in the next half hour."

+ + +

At the sound of a buzzer, Tim punched the intercom button.

"Your interviews are in the lobby."

"I'll be out. Oh, can you see if Mary Ellen is free? Ask her to stand by." He guessed the department would be able to do without its office manager for an hour. "Oh yeah, were you able to come up with a psychologist? Great. Tell the Wolffs we'll get started when everyone gets here."

An eight-year-old. Tough to get his mind around. But at least it hadn't turned into a Sandy Hook. The gun wasn't an AR-15 with multiple magazines in the perp's pocket. But what was this symptomatic of? In all his fifty-eight years—make that thirty years on the force—he had never dealt with someone so young. Not on a firearms rap. Maybe he should amend that to read, not a kid that young from a privileged family. But wasn't something like this in the papers almost every day? How many school shootings had there been this year alone? Far too many—up the coast, Midwest, no area seemed immune.

The psychologist had made fast work of getting there, Tim noted. He and Mary Ellen knocked on his door at the same time. But the doc wasn't who Tim had expected.

This man was young, maybe somewhere in his thirties, strikingly good-looking and obviously Native American. It was well known that the elder Tobias Jefferson Wolff was Creek. Was this some setup to get privileged treatment for his son? Just one more thing that Tim needed to keep his eye on.

But the shrink introduced himself as Ben Pecos from New Mexico—one of the presenters in town for the Interior Department's centennial celebration of national parks. Ben also offered that he'd worked with Albuquerque's Child Guidance Agency helping to develop a program to get a handle on juvenile crime there. Tim took a breath. That was encouraging. He didn't need this case to get any more complicated.

Tim motioned to chairs in front of his desk. "I'll give you what I know. The incident occurred at around eight this morning. Not sure about the quality of information we're going to get at eleven-thirty. I obviously don't know how the parents have handled this. But here's our report. One for each of you. Short and sweet—leaves a lot of blanks to fill in."

Ben leaned forward to take the report. "What do you need from me?"

"Assessment, recommendation for what we do next. I'm not big on the D-center. Does more harm than good most of the time but the severity of the situation calls for some kind of action. Of course, we need to find out exactly what happened—did the kid merely get caught with a firearm in class or did he threaten someone? Apparently, the gun was not discharged."

"Sometimes a week in the child's psych ward at UNM hospital was appropriate," Ben said. "Gave us time for observation, at least—made long-term treatment more accurate. Depends, of course, on what happened."

"I like that. Might be low-key enough for starters but impress upon all concerned that there are consequences. And that we know what we're doing." A wry smile. "No one needs to know we're flying blind here."

"And me?" Mary Ellen asked.

"Hate to use you like this, but I thought having a woman in the room might take the edge off." Tim grinned. "Two males could be overkill. The object is to get the kid to talk to us, not scare him. Who knows if he'll open up?"

"I don't mind doing all the questioning. Prefer it, really."

"Thanks, Doc. I'd like to rely on your expertise. Too easy to get in trouble interrogating children. Oh, I might add Dad is City Councilman, Tobias Wolff."

"The asshole that the School Board mutinied against when he was chairman?" Mary Ellen sat forward. "This could be a problem. The man's lawsuit-happy."

"Yeah, I've heard that, too. Any recommendations, doc?"

"First rule is, no parent in the room. One-way glass is fine. Important that they feel involved—fewer problems if they can feel like they're sitting in. And that usually keeps us all out of trouble."

"Good. Anything else?" Ben shook his head and Tim continued, "Why don't you take ten minutes to read through the report? Then we'll get started."

When they entered the waiting room, three adults stood and one child was more or less pulled upward to stand between his parents—his eyes never leaving the floor. Not a good sign, Tim noted. A florid man in a tent-sized overcoat pushed forward, his hand extended. His manner screamed lawyer. Was Tim surprised? No. But he hadn't counted on one. Not this soon. He ignored him.

"Councilman." Tim shook Mr. Wolff's hand and waited until the others were introduced.

"My wife, Lois, and my lawyer, Sigmund Bradley. And, of course, my son, Toby."

Handshakes all around except from Toby who kept his eyes averted and hands in his pockets.

"This is Dr. Pecos, a specialist in child psychology." Tim thought he saw a flicker of surprise when Councilman Wolff turned to Ben.

"Not a local, I presume."

Ben smiled, "You presume correctly. Tewa Pueblo in New Mexico." He then quickly reiterated why he was in St. Augustine.

Tim stepped forward, "Mrs. Wolff, I'd like you to wait here with Toby. I want to speak to your husband and Mr. Bradley, plus the doc and Mary Ellen, before we begin." Tim picked up a set of keys from the receptionist and motioned the group to follow him down the hall. He unlocked two doors then invited the group to join him in the first room.

"Dr. Pecos will be questioning Toby next door. I'm sure you know the drill." This was directed to their lawyer. Tim pulled a curtain aside to reveal one-way glass. "You'll be able to watch and hear the proceedings but not interrupt."

"Sig, is this acceptable?" Mr. Wolff turned to his lawyer.

"Routine. I'm pleased you have a child psychologist here. And an Indian, at that. Good work." The lawyer beamed at Tim.

Patronizing, bordering on racist. Tim was getting close to stepping on the toes of the man who paid him.

He forced a smile. Just another asshole, but wasn't that his view of most lawyers? Still Tim had the distinct feeling that there wouldn't have been an interview if they hadn't been careful with personnel. No, he felt lucky to get Ben Pecos as shrink. Legal posturing was a pain in the ass but just something he had to put up with. He wouldn't miss it when he transferred, but wasn't he being naïve to think there'd be less of it? Yeah, especially at the federal level?

"Then let's get started." Tim walked back to the waiting room and briefly explained to Mrs. Wolff and Toby what would happen and asked them to follow him. Finally everyone was in place. The recorder was turned on and names, dates and location stated for posterity.

Tim sat next to Dr. Pecos who sat opposite Toby. An eight-year-old going on fifteen, Tim mused. Thin, tall for his age, with dark hair spiked across the middle of his head and shaved close on the sides. Expensive haircut. But the bruise along his jawline, a black eye and sling supporting his left arm gave credence to why they were there. Tim could see that Toby's hand was in a cast. Supposedly the work of the teacher, if the report was to be believed. Would the kid look any differently if he'd pointed a gun at me? Probably worse, Tim thought. The teacher was gutsy, he'd give her that. Probably saved her life.

"Why don't you tell us why we're here today, Toby?" Ben leaned back in the straight-backed chair, his hands resting on a yellow legal pad in front of him.

Toby stalled—looked at the table, then the ceiling—and shrugged, "I don't know."

"I think you do. Maybe we should ask your teacher to join us."

Toby looked up quickly and met the doc's eyes. First

contact, maybe this won't be a waste after all, Tim thought. The kid obviously didn't want to face his teacher.

"I was going to get a mountain bike."

"A mountain bike?" Ben made a note on the legal pad.

"Uh huh."

"What were you supposed to do for this bike?"

"Shoot a gun."

"Someone was going to give you a bike if you shot a gun?"

A nod.

"Was this your gun?"

"No."

Well there went any random, found a gun on the way to school explanation. Sounded like the gun had been given to him. The kid is set up and the plot thickens, Tim noted.

"Did you shoot the gun?"

"Yeah. Two times."

"Where did you shoot it?"

"In the woods."

"On the way to school?"

A nod.

"You shot the gun. Did you get the bike?"

Toby looked up, eyes round. Trapped. If he had shot the gun, why hadn't he gotten the bike? Tim almost smiled. The doc was good.

"I was supposed to …" Chin down on his arm, eyes focused four inches in front of him.

"Supposed to what, Toby?"

Silence. No one breathed. Finally …

"Supposed to do something else."

"What was that?"

A shrug, but no answer. The adults froze, waiting.

Finally, the doc changed gears.

"Who gave you the gun and asked you to do these things, Toby?"

"Buckley."

"What's Buckley's last name?"

A shake of the head, another vertical shrug.

"Okay, what does he look like?"

Toby brought his head up. "Like Buckley. Everybody knows Buckley."

"I don't know Buckley. You'll have to tell me."

"He's brown and fuzzy. His head is pretty big … an' he's pretty fat."

Ben looked at Mary Ellen who was sitting behind Toby. "Anyone here familiar with this Buckley?" He twisted to the side to include Tim.

"I think he means the pizza place mascot—the one with the video arcade all the kids love." Mary Ellen offered. All eyes turned back to Toby as he nodded his head.

"Where did you meet Buckley?"

"On the way to school."

"And you didn't find this gun, or bring it from home? This Buckley gave you the gun?"

"Uh-huh."

"Can you tell me what Buckley said?"

Toby studied the table, then pushed upright and picked at a scab on his forearm. "Buckley asked me if I wanted this mountain bike. It was pretty cool, all purple and green, and I got to ride it. So, I said, yeah, I wanted it. An' that's when Buckley said that I'd have to do something for him." Silence.

"And that was?" A gentle prod from Ben.

"You know Miss Beltzer? She's my teacher."

"No, Toby, I don't."

"Well, I had to take the gun to her class."

"Were you supposed to do anything else?"

A pause, head down, then a shake, no.

"Are you sure, Toby? Your teacher reported that you pointed the gun at her. Is that what happened?"

"No." Toby didn't look up. "She just got all mad and grabbed the gun and pushed me over."

"What were you doing with the gun?"

"Just looking at it."

"And you're sure that's all?"

Again, a nod and a shrug.

"Do you know why Ms. Beltzer was so upset?"

"She's afraid of guns."

"A loaded gun is dangerous, Toby. Did you mean to scare your teacher?"

"Maybe, a little bit."

Ben sat forward and reminded Toby that what he had done was pretty serious and his actions had consequences. He told the boy he wanted to meet with his parents for a few minutes. But he would be talking with him again. Mary Ellen took Toby to get a soft drink, and the elder Wolffs joined Tim and Ben in the interrogation room.

"I blame the teacher. I've never liked her—she's far too strict. She brings out a certain meanness in children. And I think she's loose."

"Loose?" Ben turned his attention to Toby's mother.

"Yes. She's maybe latter twenties and already has had two husbands."

Tim looked at Ben. This didn't mesh with his definition of looseness, and from the frown on the doc's face, his either.

"We're due at the school at one. Why don't the two of you join us?" The senior Wolff looked first at Tim Foley, then Ben.

"Now T.J., I don't think we need a crowd." The lawyer intervened.

"Sig, I think it's important to get everyone concerned together under the same roof. No need to draw this thing out. We'll meet with the principal and the teacher and go from there."

Chapter Five

Mo had been suspended immediately after the "incident" as everyone called it—not the next day, or the end of the month, but before lunch. The grapevine had it that this cute kid, son of the former school board chairman, brought a gun to class to show his friends. And then his usually rational teacher just freaked out and tried to grab it, mashing his hand so that he couldn't let go, doubling his arm back, throwing him to the floor, breaking bones, for God's sake—she didn't even call security as the handbook commanded. She took matters into her own hands. That kind of independent thinking seemed to seal her fate. How could she? The fact that no one had been shot apparently didn't count for anything.

Ginny took over her class. Ginny, who pointedly had

not tried to help, couldn't even make eye contact. Mo walked out the door into the parking lot, unlocked her car, got in and just sat there. Completely in shock. The administration building looked misshapen through a mist of tears. She needed a latte and somewhere to sit and think—to make a list of everything that had happened because she would be called upon to give a play-by-play report. Of that she was certain. Starbucks off A1A Beach Blvd. offered just the atmosphere she needed. A feeling of normalcy and no one would bother her.

Now at one o'clock, there was this "formality." When the principal called her cell, he said he wanted her to meet with the parents. He said he'd gotten her week's lesson plans from Ginny. The sub needed to prepare for tomorrow. Certainly she understood. And her grade book, Ginny had provided that, too. He was nervous and talked too fast, every other sentence punctuated by clearing his throat. She could just picture Mr. Blaylock, scarecrow thin, in his everyday gray suit, seams pressed, white shirt and blue tie, one small almost indiscernible splatter of something next to the tie tack, oatmeal, perhaps? And the tie tack worn far too low, so that when under duress he would continually twist it—looking for all the world like he was winding himself up.

So what if he did want her lesson plans? What the hell, surely it would only be for a couple days. The last month of school was always the busiest—testing, checking in equipment, doing a general inventory of books and materials. But under the circumstances of a teacher injuring a child, Mo was well aware that there had to be an investigation and that warranted leave with pay. Ginny was fully capable of copying an entire week's agenda and turning over her grade-book. Mo had another latte and finished her list.

+ + +

They were waiting on her—all squashed into Mr. Blaylock's office, last door on the right, end of the first floor hall—her principal, a detective Tim Foley, a child psychologist introduced as Ben Pecos, a lawyer, and the parents. She had never felt such hostility before, actually tasted it in the air. The room fairly sparked with it.

"Are you going to show her what she did to our son?" Impatient, imperious. No introductions, just get on with it. Lois Wolff's chin jutted forward in defiance. Toby's father oozed upper middle-class righteousness. Indian from the Creek tribe in Alabama, son of the last chief, a lawyer in his own right, former school board chairman, current city councilman—big man on the block. Not being from the area didn't stop the posturing, Mo noted. Real or imagined, it gave him all the clout in the world. At least, all the clout that he needed in that room today.

No wonder her principal was sweating. An incident in his school involving a councilman's child. Only child, if Mo remembered correctly. A thin, damp line stained the top of his shirt collar and there was a sheen to his forehead. Mo found his nervousness comforting. She wasn't the only one on the hot seat.

Councilman Wolff stepped back to pat the shoulder of the woman beside him whose mouth was a thin angry line. Diminutive, honey blond hair expertly streaked, good bone, she simply averted her eyes when Mo glanced her way. Stoic to the max. Had she been in this position before? Some crisis in the family that required her to be supportive—speak up for a family member? That stand-by-your-man, stiff upper lip, stiffer spine effect usually reserved for governor's wives—or first ladies. Wasn't there some tale about the blond cheerleader who ran off with an Indian man much to the chagrin of her circuit court judge father? A long time ago but now, as adults, these two seemed a mismatch.

It struck Mo that the hand resting on the woman's shoulder might be the closest the two of them had been in a long time. The most intimate, anyway. It looked wooden. It shrieked, this touch is for the six o'clock news, then, move over, don't do it again. Every time Mo tried to get a "read" on a couple, she'd imagine them in bed together. And these two just weren't compatible between the sheets. She'd bet on it. It might have been fun and games for a while, but that was a long time ago.

She looked again at the psychologist. Native American. Did that mean he was on the councilor's side? Hired by him—maybe a fellow Creek or Seminole? Mo was feeling decidedly outnumbered.

Her principal stepped forward and cleared his throat. "I think we need to get started. We've determined that there was use of unnatural force, a blatant disregard of school rules—"

"Wait a minute." Mo interrupted, which seemed to irritate the Wolff's lawyer.

And he used her interruption to get his own five cents in. "Miss Beltzer, I'm gonna call this an informal hearing. You have the right to know the facts just as they've been presented to me. There's been a grievous wrong committed here, as your principal acknowledges. Now, you just need to wait your turn, little Missy. Y'all be quiet, just listen."

The man actually put a finger to his lips. What a blow-hard! He wheezed as he talked. And, "little Missy"? Yes, Florida could be considered the South. But "little Missy"? That was just way too Georgian for her. It was all she could do not to grimace as his belly rippled under a custom-made shirt.

Jackets had been discarded by all the men in the room—this jerk of a lawyer, the principal, and Toby's father. Only the detective and the shrink had arrived in short-sleeves. Toby's mother shrugged off a coral sweater dyed to match her coral colored skirt. What a line-up. Even then, it didn't dawn on Mo to demand access to counsel of her own.

The lawyer simultaneously clicked open the two snaps on his briefcase. "Let me show you the result of your attack on an eight year old child. Just a warning, it ain't pretty." He plopped two manila envelopes onto the desk in front of him then shook them from the bottom, one in each hand. Eight-by-ten glossies fanned across polished oak.

"This here's a real good close-up of the multiple bruises inflicted during the alleged confrontation." He casually pointed to blue smudges, smallish, rounded results of fingers dug into flesh.

But *alleged?* She nearly screamed out the word. Yet, she knew where the word came from. There were no witnesses. No one, that is, who would say that Toby threatened her, put the gun to her head, and pulled the trigger. Certainly not the four boys who had encouraged him. They were absolutely mum. And not Ginny. She was too far away, at the side of the room, for heaven's sake. She just couldn't see. Yeah, right. Ginny was a master at not getting involved.

After the incident, as she begged Mo to understand,

Ginny whispered, "I really need this job. You're so smart, you can always do something else. And you don't have children." So there it was. Their friendship was short lived when it came to economics, and child-bearing. But there were fingerprints. Mo had been smart enough to call the cops—St. Augustine's finest, not the pretend security that patrolled the school in pretend uniforms with empty pretend holsters hanging from their belts. She had preserved the evidence and handed the gun over.

So, now she sat back. There was proof—a child's fingerprints on the trigger and hammer. They couldn't hide behind some kind of "no witness defense." She forced herself to look at the photos. There were eight views of the fingernail punctures along his wrist and x-rays of a broken bone in his hand—in addition to a dislocated jaw, a blackened eye and extensive bruising along his jawline and collarbone. At almost twice his weight, she had crushed the child beneath her when they landed on the table.

Her handiwork made her turn away. There's nothing in this life she'd ever wanted to be besides a third grade teacher. She'd guided children for seven years—right out of college, she'd encouraged their curiosity, molded them into good citizens—she didn't harm them.

"Not like I didn't warn you. Not a pretty sight." The lawyer tsked and shook his head, then in one smooth move yanked up the Venetian blinds, higher on the left, and held an X-ray against the light. He seemed to have center stage now, and Toby's father took a chair next to Mrs. Wolff.

"I'd like equal emphasis placed upon the *why* in all this. *Why* did this happen? *Why* are we looking at X-rays. Could we discuss that?" Mo hoped she was imagining the petulant note she heard in her voice.

"In due time, Miss Beltzer, all in due time. It's not your turn yet." Condescending grandstander. She forced herself to look at him as he continued. "The fact remains that you endangered the life of a young person. You did not try to reason with the young man, find out the circumstances before your brutal attack. And there were circumstances, my dear—circumstances that you needed to know about. In fact, you gave no warning to the rest of the class that they might be in danger. You did not clear the room in an orderly fashion. You did not call upon your aide to assist you. You persisted in some superwoman position of strength to overpower, inflict bodily harm—no, maim—let me use the correct word here—*maim* an eight year old. A mere *child*."

How could everyone be ignoring the fact that this mere child was holding a gun—had pulled the trigger of that gun? "I suppose you would have just calmly begun a dialogue—gee, Toby, is there some underlying reason for holding a revolver to your teacher's head? Mom ran out of cocoa puffs this morning?"

"I don't like that tone of voice. You've ruined our son's chances in the Major Leagues."

Major Leagues? *Please.* He's eight years old. Wasn't he barely past the T-ball stage?

"You put our son at a grave disadvantage. We understand that you have a black belt?" Dad weighed in—to keep Mom company, maybe?

"What? That's ridiculous." Four years ago she'd taken a kick-boxing class instead of aerobics. Did that turn into karate's highest achievement? "You are all so off-base. You were not in that classroom. You did not see your son's eyes—at eight years of age, the eyes of a killer."

"Miss Beltzer, I beg your indulgence. You're stretching my patience. It has been difficult keeping this from turning into a lawsuit. Two other parents are particularly keen on it because of the endangerment issue. I think we've persuaded them to rethink, back off at least for the time being. But I cannot absolutely guarantee that. You inflicted trauma this morning on twenty-three third graders." The lawyer perched on the edge of the desk. A pants leg crept above sock height showing the pasty, hairless skin of one who could euphemistically be called mature. Precarious posturing for one his size.

But suddenly, she perked up. Subconsciously, she had expected a lawsuit. But now, wasn't he saying that it wouldn't necessarily happen? She tuned back in.

"No one here discounts the severity of the situation. There was a firearm present in a third grade classroom." Tim Foley stepped forward.

"Brought into that classroom by Toby Wolff." Mo interrupted. "It didn't just drop from the sky."

"Fingerprints seem to indicate that at least at some time during the altercation, the firearm was in the possession of my client's son." A pause.

"I can corroborate that," Tim interjected. "Thanks to Miss Beltzer's quick thinking, we were able to lift two sets of prints from the weapon. A set belonging to the student in question and another set unknown. We've been unable to match those prints in our data base."

There was a subtle turning here. Mo's mind raced to uncover the reason behind it. Wasn't Fatso admitting to wrong-doing by his client? His client's son, that is?

"Have you been in trouble lately? Drugs? Maybe an unpaid loan from the wrong people? In short, little lady, is there a reason that someone might feel the need to threaten you? Give you a good scare?" Their lawyer was actually peering at her, squinting over his reading glasses, a speck of saliva pulsing at the corner of his slack lower lip. Aside from being perfectly erroneous, she also knew these were the type of questions that shouldn't be asked. She had rights, and one was a right to counsel before being interrogated. Wasn't someone supposed to suggest she even had the right to remain silent?

"Is this meeting being recorded?" She turned to look directly at Principal Blaylock.

"Well … I …" His glance darted between Councilman Wolff and the lawyer. "Yes, yes, it is." He opened the top drawer of his desk all the way and pulled out an outdated recorder, the kind used by the school. Pop in a rhythm tape and watch the kindergartners dance around. Old, but sturdy, if not indestructible. "We … the school, that is, has to protect itself. I'm sure you understand."

"That won't be admissible in court," Detective Foley said, giving the two men a stern look. "You didn't inform Ms. Beltzer, or the rest of us, for that matter."

Mo sat up straighter. No one had read *her* rights … unless there wasn't to be any prosecution. This was suddenly a possibility.

Foley turned to Mo. "You can't think of anyone who might want to harm you?"

Threaten had now changed to 'harm,' she noticed. The detective and the shrink seemed laid back—honestly interested in her answers. The Wolff's lawyer, however, seemed hell-bent on proving she had connections to the mob or whatever.

"I understand you've been divorced twice and have no

natural children." This from paleness herself, now leaning forward and looking keenly at Mo. Mo bit her tongue before blurting out something trite about not having unnatural ones, either. But where had this come from? And why? She clearly wasn't keeping up. The players were muddying the field.

"Now, Lois, let's not get ahead of ourselves." The lawyer leaned down and patted Lois's arm.

Chummy group. There seemed to be lots of pats for good ol' Lois. Mo pointedly disregarded her statement.

"There's some indication that young Mr. Wolff was approached by someone who offered to, um, bribe him," said the lawyer.

"Actually, I believe Toby," Ben said.

"Bribe him? Bribe an eight year old to do what?" The shrillness in Mo's voice could shred glass.

"It would appear that the young man was supposed to scare you, possibly threaten you ... I probably shouldn't use the word 'harm'. We don't have all the details as yet." The lawyer wouldn't meet her eye.

Like hell they didn't have the details. The police report. The interrogation. They had talked with Toby. Of course, they wouldn't be giving her this much if it wasn't already known. Toby had been arrested—or whatever you do with a child. They had first called an ambulance and then his parents. After the hospital, she felt certain they had taken him to a station not far from the school for questioning.

She was still in the classroom when they had called his father. She needed to see that report. But what did they want from her now? Why all the veiled insinuations. Unless ... unless they thought *she* might sue. And all this was just peeing off their own positions, marking territory by jumping in first, keeping her off balance—trying to set her up, scare her by recording her answers. Make her slip up, prove she was in the wrong … give them a *basis* to sue. Teacher with mob connections endangers class. It was a distinct possibility.

But a teacher who could prove lax school security, prove that the child in question had had his finger on the hammer as well as the trigger with no fingerprints of her own on the weapon … well, that put a different spin on the story of "kid brings gun to school to show friends" and distinctly gave her a reason to take the gun away. There definitely was more to this story. They knew where he had gotten it. And why.

The lawyer droned on about some injuries not being seen, those deep scars that would continue to surface during the child's lifetime. And who knew how the event had impacted his range of motion and grip. It was his pitching arm. Had she also killed a dream? Ended a career in baseball? A child with so much promise. Toby's mother nodded vigorously and got yet another sympathetic pat from Dad.

How much promise could an eight year old have? This was so stupid. Mo stood and moved to the window whose blind rakishly tilted from being yanked upward. Men were so challenged. Two cords, one up, one down. She evened the upper left side, then lowered the blind slowly. She felt every eye in the room on her back. Had someone hired a child to scare her? To threaten her?

She simply could not use the word 'kill'—not even the word "harm". But she remembered all too well the revolver coming toward her, touching her forehead … A part of her kept saying this was the most ridiculous thing she'd ever heard of. In her classroom, third graders. But a certain numbness had leadened her feet. She felt her Pollyanna view of eight-year-olds eroding. Could Toby Wolff have betrayed her love of being surrounded by small chairs and tables and blunt-tipped scissors?

As a child she'd glued her pumpkin-man's feet on backwards so that the tracings showed and Miss MacDonald, her second grade teacher, had berated her in front of the entire class. But not once, for so heinous a crime, did Mo think of blasting her away. Had times changed so drastically? Yes, they had, and she hadn't wanted to admit it.

"Aren't background checks mandatory? I can't believe that you'd let her in the classroom. Two former husbands and the one, well, with a rather questionable reputation."

Mo didn't turn around; she didn't need to look at Toby's mother to imagine the sanctimonious, overwrought expression of concern as she leaned toward the principal, maybe even with a barely concealed smirk. Mo fought the inclination to slap her. For someone who even saved the lives of spiders, she was becoming rather violent.

Mo kept her back to the group and quickly flashed to each of the infamous former husbands. Toby's mother was wrong. Neither one had any reason to threaten her. The first had remarried and gone into the service. She hadn't heard from him in five years. She was paying alimony to the last, for God's sake, until he got through school—he wouldn't kill the golden goose. A good Hispanic mama's boy who just needed to be taken care of. Maybe a little slothful, but nothing 'questionable.'

"The point is that this woman has led parents to believe—may I go so far as to use the word *assure* parents—

that she is capable of keeping our children safe. Then, in a crisis, fails us." Lois's voice wavered at the end. Mr. Wolff quickly offered his wife a handkerchief.

"Well, let's hear it for melodrama." Mo swung back from the window and applauded smartly. She was feeling stronger. She had some leverage here.

Toby's mother shrank back into the chair and pulled her sweater around her shoulders—to ward off the chill in the room? There was certainly that. Or was there fear? Afraid of what Mo would say? Do? Blondie was not a woman who could handle a challenge.

"There's no reason to be snide." This seemed to be as far as Toby's mother would go with an attack.

"No? Well, I happen to think differently. This is all lies. Lies to cover up, give a reason for a child not having been taught right from wrong—making excuses for a child who takes his father's gun to school—"

"I don't own a gun." Councilman Wolff turned to face her. "Someone gave Toby that gun. He said so and I believe him."

The lawyer quickly asserted himself. "Look, there's some questions out there. Miss Beltzer, the Wolffs have graciously, and I must add against the better judgment of their counsel, decided not to pursue this matter further. It is, however, their recommendation that you not be reinstated for the fall term. At least not in a classroom. Yes, there's summer vacation coming up, but the situation would be difficult for your students to forget in a couple or so short months. A new attitude is needed here, a strong guiding personality that the students won't fear. I know you'll agree with me that it would just be too awkward for young Toby even after a break—"

"Not go back to the classroom?" Had she heard correctly? Was she being replaced? Could they do this? She felt numb.

"Yes," Principal Blaylock paused to clear his throat, "I'm sorry, Maureen. I think in the best interests of all concerned, well, surely you understand?" The tie-tack was getting a workout. Maybe his ass would fall off—it would just unscrew and slip to the ground. Maybe if she just ignored him. But that was difficult. He was in a straight-backed chair between the flag of the United States and the red cross on a white shield with the seal centered on the flag of Florida.

"Of course, I'll try to find something else for you—it'll be difficult so close to the end of the term; decisions have already been made. In the meantime we'll just call it 'leave' until the board decides about a position for next year." He couldn't meet her gaze but hovered over the tape recorder when he wasn't fiddling with his clothing.

"And Toby?"

Ben stepped forward, "I've recommended a one week's suspension with hospitalization for observation— for starters. I will also be following up with several weekly sessions."

That seemed to end things. There was a shuffling of chairs and Mo headed to the door. Somehow she'd had enough of Jefferson Elementary for one day.

"Miss Beltzer? I know how painful this day has been already, but we really need to talk. Any chance you could stop by the courthouse later. My office is in the basement. Let's say in an hour?" At Mo's nod, the detective held the office door open then turned back to speak with Principal Blaylock.

Once again, Mo was in the parking lot with the dregs of a cold latte. She tried to imagine how things could have been worse. She could have been charged with assaulting a child. But still—not teaching anymore? Her dream career—would this be the end?

It had been a horrible morning, and her stomach was in a knot, but she knew she should eat something. Maybe a burger at the nearest drive-through and then she'd go on to Detective Foley's office.

Chapter Six

Mo watched Detective Foley walk toward her. For the first time, she really noticed him. He looked young, but was in his fifties somewhere, she'd bet. Over six feet, a body straight out of Gold's gym, dark hair, deep tan, and dimples that accompanied a ready smile. Absolutely no spare tire. No sweet-tooth or simply no riding around in a cruiser all day. This cop oozed action. She realized she was staring and turned to thank the man at the desk for paging the officer.

Suddenly, she knew it had been a good idea to swing by the station. She needed to know what the Wolffs knew. Leverage? Perhaps. She wasn't sure a lawsuit wasn't in order—with her as plaintiff. Shouldn't she do *something*? Suspended. Probably fired. How would that look on her resume?

"Let's go down to my office."

Again, that ready smile. She relaxed and shook his hand. Up close, lines around his eyes supported her guess on age. He held the door open to a narrow, sterile room across from a coffee station and moved behind the desk that squarely faced a glass-partitioned east wall. The metal, prison-issue-gray hulk held a doodled blotter, and phone with intercom—the only two things that proved human occupancy. No touches from home here. Moms must not be allowed.

"Have a seat. I've asked Dr. Pecos to sit in with us."

The psychologist offered his chair and then pulled another metal folding chair around to face the desk. "Please, call me Ben. I'm glad it worked out to talk today without the crowd in the principal's office, earlier."

She appreciated his thoughtfulness.

"We interviewed Toby Wolff earlier this morning and we'd like to hear your side of the story." Tim smiled.

Mo felt herself relax. She started at the beginning, added facts about having gone to Jefferson a year out of college—eight years ago to be exact. And then launched into a passionate account of her dedication to learning and concluded with a play-by-play report of the incident with Toby. She sat back.

Tim paused, fingers drumming on the blotter, a breath, then, "Miss Beltzer, I'm going to come right to the point. Toby admits having a gun in your classroom. He doesn't admit to aiming it toward you or pulling the trigger. But he does say he was given the gun to scare you. Perhaps, harm you. Actual intent is unknown, however ..." He looked at her a moment before continuing, "I think you need to be alerted to the fact that you may be in some danger."

A tiny shiver prickled across her shoulders.

"Toby Wolff maintains that he was approached by Buckley Bear—"

"The pizza restaurant's mascot?" Her laugh sounded a little maniacal. But this was absurd. More fabrication. Why had she ever thought there would turn out to be a plausible explanation for all this?

"I know what you're thinking. Sounds a little fantastic. But I believe the kid. Who else to better earn Toby's trust? Kids react to stuffed animals. They can interact—what's the phrase? A willing suspension of disbelief? It comes naturally to kids. Besides, we're a little far from Disneyworld. Maybe this stuffed animal costume was the best St. Augustine had to offer."

She couldn't help but laugh. Mo liked his sense of humor.

"Anyway, supposedly Buckley gave him the gun with explicit instructions to—" another pause, "to scare you, but I'm not sure there wasn't more. I suspect the scare part was due to coaching before we were able to question him. Your side of the story corroborates that—it would appear he was set up to kill you."

"Kill?" Not scare or threaten or harm, and this wasn't just a touch of melodrama. The police didn't waste time with glossing over facts. They believed her; they knew she had been in mortal danger—believed her without Ginny backing her up or any of the students, for that matter. The prickle was back, this time running down both arms.

"Yes. I think Buckley's directions were quite specific on what was supposed to happen, but Toby showed off on his way to school, fired the weapon a couple times for friends then managed to give the cylinder a turn or two—all in your favor, I might add." The smile was rueful.

"Kill." There was a broken-record repetitiveness to the way her brain was working. For some reason she needed to say it again out loud. "So? Get the guy who was wearing the bear outfit. There can't be too many of them running around this town." She stood and leaned closer to his desk. "In the old days we worried about adults who tried to lure kids into cars with candy—now they're giving them handguns. It's bad enough that they have little parental guidance when it comes to watching violence on television. They see everything. You can't imagine the things I've heard from eight year olds. It's disgusting. Sometimes, I have a real problem with humanity."

She looked up guiltily. She hadn't meant to pontificate but her nervousness seemed to encourage a certain loquaciousness. She stepped backward and sort of plopped back down into the chair.

"There was a new mountain bike in the deal if he succeeded."

No wonder the Wolffs' lawyer wanted to get to her first, show her photos of her supposed abuse. Play on her guilt. Make her admit to something. Anything. And all the time the little bugger had been angling for a new bike. And they'd set him up to lie. She could have a lawsuit ... "Any leads?" Her hands felt like ice. She rubbed them against her thighs, willing circulation to kick in.

"I think you can help with that. Who might want to kill you?"

"I am so ordinary. My life is so uncommonly—" She stopped and shrugged her shoulders, "common."

"I've done some checking—"

"And you're about to remind me that I have two, yes, count them, two former husbands as you heard earlier?"

"Some wouldn't consider that ordinary."

"Well, the first is best remembered for his antics in the front seat of an antique Buick. I was young. I got an abortion but he left anyway. The second left because we *didn't* have children. He finally sensed a career as house-husband wasn't in the making ... I'm paying him two hundred dollars a month until he gets out of photography school." She paused. "I got the house." Then defiantly, "My second marriage lasted seven years."

"I see."

No, he didn't "see." Seven years wasn't exactly a record but it didn't make her a candidate for total failure either. But hadn't she probably just volunteered too much information?

"Any other possibilities? Run-ins with neighbors? Fellow workers? Disgruntled parents of a student—maybe you held someone back last year?"

"Nothing. Teacher of the month, three months running. Students and faculty vote to choose the recipient."

"What kind of kid is Toby? Good student? Makes friends easily?" Ben leaned forward. "Have you had any other interaction with his parents?"

"Leader of the pack—that about sums up Toby's social skills. He's bright but often holds back so as not to show up his friends. And, God forbid, someone would think he's a nerd, but I've caught him reading during recess—books with a scientific bent. Rockets, for example, and not at an elementary reading level either. He tested at a seventh grade level at the start of the year."

"And his parents? Overly protective? Any siblings at the same school?"

"No siblings. He's an only child and, I guess, everything

that goes with that—expensive sneakers and haircuts, for example."

"Spoiled?"

"Yes, definitely. The one problem I have is with homework not being turned in on time. Of course, I've found that he'd completed it, but because it wasn't cool to be teacher's pet, he'd bring it to me later—when no one was looking. Maintaining one's position in the pack starts at an early age. Being popular is everything—even at eight."

Ben smiled, "You sound like a great teacher. I think those were the only questions that I had. Back to you." He turned to Detective Foley.

"I can't help but think there might have been some warning. I'd like you to give this some thought. Sometimes it's an incident we've forgotten, doesn't seem important at the time but in retrospect, it's out of the ordinary."

"I hate to disappoint you but there isn't anything." She knew she was beginning to sound cranky, but she was feeling cranky. This wasn't her fault. Plain and simple, it wasn't.

"Then indulge me in this. Have you been home yet?"

Mo shook her head. "I've been a little busy." Oops. Don't be snide. Detective Foley was trying to help.

"Could we follow you home? Make a quick run-through of your apartment?"

"House."

"Yes, of course, house. I want to make certain that everything's as it should be. Ben here can ride shot-gun." The smile was genuine but he was scaring her to death.

She nodded. She hadn't been home, she hadn't had lunch. There was a very cold hamburger and fries on the front seat of her car that she hadn't been able to make herself eat, she wasn't in school, and she couldn't go back … her life was a time warp.

Chapter Seven

By the time she pulled the Volvo into her drive, clicked the Genie, and rolled to the back of the garage, she was in terror. She waited until Detective Foley and Dr. Pecos got out of their car before she opened her door. The garage was detached and the fifty feet of garden between could have been a minefield, her heart was racing so fast.

"We can go in this way." She gestured toward the back door.

Their steps sounded hollow on the flagstone walk. She hoped they weren't looking at her backyard. It was a mess. The grass needed mowing—St. Augustine grass, no less, that favorite turf for warm climates. Soon it would need mowing twice a month, sometimes more. And she'd been meaning to repaint the patio furniture. Rust ate its way through everything metal. The ornate iron gate was probably a total loss.

"Did you leave your door like that?" The three of them stood on the bottom step of her back porch.

She jerked back to the present. The screen was pulled to one side and the door was ajar.

"Looks like it's been jimmied. Actually, you might want to replace the entire door with something metal. Old wooden ones like this don't offer much resistance. Let me go in first. Doc stay close. Ms. Beltzer, wait here until I say it's clear."

As if she was going to bound in front of him and go charging in. She knew the ragged breathing she heard was her own. Detective Foley drew his gun and Dr. Pecos motioned her to step to one side of the door. No, she wouldn't wait out there by herself. It was her house—"I'm going to follow you."

"Stay out here," Foley said.

"No."

"Sit in the car, go next door, a neighbor's—"

"No." She was hugging her sides and shivering.

"Then stay behind me." At least, he knew when to give in. "Doc? You ready?"

Her house was a Victorian bungalow, a fixer-upper about a hundred years old right off the plaza—maybe four blocks from King Street. The fixer-upper part had been the second husband's passion. A passion that never materialized. Talked to death, planned to death, and finally spoken of in the past tense. But she had stayed and he had moved. Other than tourists parking in her driveway every once in awhile, living here had been uneventful.

They entered through the kitchen, a high ceilinged room with open-faced white cabinetry and a Boos butcher block island. That had been her idea, but the craftsmanship of a handyman and not husband number two.

"There's a draft—" A distinctly cool breeze brushed her cheek.

"Quiet."

He stood listening. She thought she heard it, too. An intermittent flapping sound. Then it stopped. This time she stayed rooted to the oak plank floor and only watched as both Detective Foley and Dr. Pecos inched along the white plastered wall leading to her bedroom.

"Hands behind your head." Detective Foley boomed it out.

She jumped and realized she was waiting for a shot with both her hands crisscrossed over her heart. As if to slow the thumping? Or just make sure it stayed in her body? Probably the latter. Then there was silence. She didn't dare call out, but she couldn't just stand there either. She slid one foot in front of the other and propelled her way to the bedroom.

"Any doubts now?"

The detective stood beside the enormous head of Buckley Bear, in the middle of her bed resting against her pillows, bedclothes pulled to his chin. She heard her intake of breath, more of a gulp. She walked to the edge of the bed. Her mind was racing. She'd burn the linen. And fumigate. Those pillows were toast. And she'd never sleep in that bed again. She'd—without warning, she sank to the floor.

"Hey, hold on. I've got you. That's right, sit here." Ben helped her up, held her steady, then guided her to a settee. Her knees had done a noodle-number and were refusing to bear weight.

"I need to get the lab boys here. I want that window

dusted before we shut it." A breeze continued to keep the curtains in motion, which explained the flapping noise. "I think this … costume … was placed here after the gun incident with Toby. In other words, if you were dead, finding Buckley here would corroborate Toby's story—someone wanted you killed and, indeed, Buckley was involved. If you weren't dead, finding it in your house would put the fear of God in you."

They'd done a good job of that. She couldn't stop shaking. Her teeth chattered in an uncontrollable dance macabre that kept her from speaking.

"Stay with me now. I hate to scare you but I don't want you to take this lightly. We still don't know that this isn't just some prank. But I doubt it—too much planning, too many details." Tim moved to the foot of the bed. "What do you think that is?"

She stood, holding tightly to the edge of a dresser. He was pointing at something on the bed. She leaned forward. "Phalaenopsis."

"Huh?"

"Orchid—a moth orchid—the flowers look like moths. Sort of. The spray was cut from a plant in the living room."

"Are you sure?"

"I can go check but I know my own plants." She bristled. People who didn't know plants wouldn't understand, but they did not all look alike. "But what's that—that thing with the flowers?" She was clutching the foot of the bed now. "It looks like a baby's head that's been boiled, my God, the flowers are sticking out of the eye socket."

She felt the floor sway just as her knees buckled and once again, Ben caught her. "I think you need to stay put." He eased her back down on the settee then turned to look where she had pointed.

"Not yours?" Tim asked.

"Hardly. What is it?"

"Looks like a shrunken head, but I'm not an expert."

"A real one?" Mo leaned forward, curiosity almost overriding fear.

"What do you think, Doc? I can't tell. I'd have to have experts decide that. Sure looks real though. No way to tell if it's old."

"Buckley Bear, a shrunken head, and a spray of orchids. Do you think there's supposed to be a message?" Ben leaned in to take another look.

Detective Foley just shrugged. "Hard to say. If it doesn't mean anything to Ms. Beltzer, it could be just another scare tactic—a way to cement the horror factor in place."

"Nothing. It means nothing to me. But it is frightening."

"Then you stay there while I finish the room." He pulled white latex gloves from a back pocket and put them on.

He was keeping an eye on her as he worked his way around, checking the open door of the closet, then a fallen throw pillow, before coming to a stop in front of her dresser.

"Do you think you could tell me if anything's missing?" He indicated the top drawer that was open an inch.

She nodded, stood to see better, and reached forward.

"Careful, don't touch, I'm the one with gloves here, let me pull it out. Now, can you see well enough?"

Again, she nodded. She knew the contents by heart. These were all her important papers, mortgage, service agreement on her car, insurance papers, will, transcripts, computer printout of the contributions to her retirement plan—he was picking up each item gingerly by an edge and placing it on top of the dresser after she'd acknowledged it. Two rubber-band bound stacks of old photos, unused airline tickets when she hadn't reconciled with husband number one. And that was it.

"Wait."

"Is something missing?"

"Did you find a passport?"

"No. Let me check again." A sweep of Tim's hand to the back of the shallow drawer yielded nothing but two bobby pins.

"And there should have been a packet of snapshots, blue envelope."

"Not here. Is it possible you put them someplace else?"

"No. I know they were here."

"Odd. What were the snapshots of?" He was trying to catch her eye.

"Not what you're thinking." Then she blushed. She knew he'd thought porn. The type of thing every woman is supposed to do once, according to some magazine she'd read. *Cosmo*, maybe?

"My mother's birthday dinner at my sister's house last August. Just Mom and me". Not a very happy event, Mo reminded herself. Claire had made a big deal about how ragged and faded her plaid shirt looked—literally made her change and drop the shirt in the garbage. "Claire's husband took the shot, plus a couple of the cake." Mo shrugged, "Someone's going to be disappointed if they were expecting their teacher to be in the buff."

"So, you think this could have been done by some of your students?"

"Maybe. Maybe they found the Buckley suit, left part

of the costume here to back up their story to you. The gun could have belonged to someone's father. The shrunken head … Who knows? But it would appeal to a child …" She let the sentence trail off.

"Any explanations for the passport? Or the pictures? Or the flowers?" He pointedly left out the shrunken head.

"None. Maybe those articles were taken at random. The flowers—" She shook her head, "Maybe it's not supposed to mean anything."

"I may not be as certain as you are. I don't think we can discount Toby's story about someone bribing him. You've got to consider that it could be truth and act accordingly. I've got to call this in and wait for the fingerprint guys. Do you think you could come up with a cup of coffee?"

"Sure." It would keep her busy, but she found leaving the two men and going back to the kitchen by herself daunting.

"Don't touch the screen door."

She yelled back, assured him she wouldn't, and then went about dismantling the coffee maker, rinsing it, finally finding a new box of filters in the cupboard, measuring coffee and water, and turning the switch. The instant gurgling was soothing.

She waited for them to join her but curiosity won out, and she took a quick look in the living room. Lined up to capture north light, all ten Phalaenopsis looked perky, with only the far plant missing its flower spike of bright hot pink "moths." The plants were her children. This was a first-time flowering for the one missing its crowning glory. Who would do such a thing? And why?

She walked back to the kitchen, leaned against the sink, took a deep breath and let her mind stray to what-if. What if it was true? An eight year old had been bribed to kill her? If so, what now? She could feel her stomach tighten. Would she ever be able to go into a classroom again? Even if they would let her? She didn't think so. But, where would she work? There was a mortgage, a student loan, car payment, alimony …

"You okay?" She hadn't heard Ben come back and wished she hadn't jumped.

"I think so." She knew she didn't sound convincing but busied herself with getting mugs out of the cupboard and setting out Half & Half next to sugar. She hoped she had two clean spoons in the drawer. "I checked on the orchid. Someone cut the spray from my plant." She placed three water-spotted spoons next to the mugs just as Detective Foley entered the kitchen.

"What's the next step?" She scooted the Half & Half closer.

He seemed reluctant to comment and busied himself pouring a mug of coffee and doctoring it.

"After dusting for prints—and I don't expect there to be any unless they belong to an eight year old—I'm afraid it's wait and see." She started to protest. "I know. That's not comforting and there should be more, but we can't make a move until the perp makes a move."

She nodded. She knew this. The crime had been minor—breaking in, taking a few items, leaving others—not a murder, at least. She was supposed to be dead, but wasn't—and that didn't count. She feared this would be the end of it until something else happened. Something far more drastic. She didn't trust herself to hold the coffee mug steady. She put it down on the counter.

"I'm sorry I can't promise more."

She nodded. He was trying to be honest and seemed to genuinely care. "Would either of you mind checking the house before you go? I mean, like in the closets … under the beds?"

"No, not at all. Doc, I'll take the bedrooms."

By the time they'd bagged the weird evidence, the fingerprint team had gone, and Detective Foley and Dr. Pecos were preparing to leave, she was feeling better— maybe not really measurably so, but calmer. The shrink had even checked the attic and the crawlspace. At that moment, they were the only human beings in the house. She was certain of that.

"You have my number but let me leave another card." Tim placed his card on the table.

Ben followed suit. "Here's my card. An old one, I'm sorry—I'm the new kid in town—but I'm putting my cell number on the back." Ben took out a pen, scribbled on the card then put it on the kitchen counter next to Tim's. "I'll check in when I can, if that won't be intruding. In fact, why don't you stop by this Friday? I'd like to complete a profile on Toby and I think you'd be a great source of information, if you don't mind? I've been assigned a room at Flagler College to use while I'm here. I just don't know where it is. I'll let you know when I find out."

"I'd like to help with Toby. See you Friday. Thanks to both of you for all you've done." A few more amenities, a handshake and they were gone.

She immediately locked the screen door, pushed the old fashioned carved wood door shut, and dragged a chair to balance under the knob. New locks. That would be a priority, hefty deadbolts which would be discouraging, if not downright impossible to kick in. She went around the house checking every window and the other two outside doors, walked back into the living room, sat on the nearest couch, stared at the defaced orchid, and couldn't stop shaking.

Chapter Eight

"Pizza for M. Beltzer."

"Black olives, extra cheese?"

"You got it."

"Leave it on the porch."

Mo was squatting in the hallway, talking through the mail-flap cut below the center of her front door. "Here's a twenty. Keep the change."

She couldn't decipher the muffled reply but the bill disappeared. There was the sound of something being dropped, then scooted forward to bump against the jamb. She stood and peered out the fish-eye. The porch light illumined an eerie world slightly oblong. The small pickup pulling out of the drive way had Domingo's Pizza in red caps on the side of the silver camper top and a lighted tentlike sign above the cab—she would never order another one from the place with the Buckley Bear mascot. She waited until the truck turned the corner. And continued to wait, hand on the doorknob. Then in a rush she opened the door, crouched, grabbed the pizza box, turned it sideways, dragged it inside, then slammed and locked the door in one, almost fluid movement.

Paranoia. And pizzas that had more toppings on the top of the box than on the slices. She knew what was wrong but couldn't control the shaking and clamminess, the thump of her heart, irregular breathing, which she had to force back to calmness. Anxiety attacks. She hadn't been out of the house in five days. But, likewise, she hadn't been the target of some maniac wanting to kill her. She had been safe. If the tradeoff was a few lukewarm dinners, then it was worth it.

Detective Foley had been great. So had Dr. Pecos. Both had called several times—even offering to come by. Maybe she'd like a cup of coffee some afternoon? She declined, of course. Just too busy. She thought she had them fooled—at least, she'd put on a good front, assured both she was keeping her eyes open, staying alert. Staying petrified was more like it. But she reassured Dr. Pecos that she would be in his office Friday morning at ten. She just didn't know how she was going to get there if she still couldn't walk from the house to the garage.

Last week at this time she'd been a sane, normal woman. Now, she was unemployed. Now, there were night sweats and the thump of her heart every time the phone rang, or a branch rubbed against a window, or a solicitor came to the door. Wasn't there a short story about man as trophy kill—human beings who were periodically released into the wild to be hunted down? Maybe, her number was up in some great lottery in the sky. It was her turn to run through the woods looking over her shoulder.

Tonight she didn't even go into the kitchen to get a plate or utensils. With her back against the door, she slipped to the floor, tore open the box and groaned. Pepperoni. The kid had delivered the wrong pizza. And she couldn't do one damned thing about it. She picked off the thin red slices and ate the underlying, greasy mozzarella with her fingers.

The door chimes above her head sounded like an air-raid siren, and she wished she hadn't shrieked and flipped the pizza box upside down when she jumped up.

"Maureen, it's mother. I've brought soup."

Mo could hear her clearly. She must be yelling with her mouth pressed to the door.

"I know that you don't want to open the door, dear. But we'll just stay a minute."

We? Shit. Claire was with her.

"Your sister and I are worried, dear."

Damn. Damn. Damn.

"Marjorie, she has every light in the house on, for God's sake. I tell you we need to get professional help in here." Claire's super smooth alto drifted through the mail-slot.

"Claire, please, just this once, try to understand your sister and what she's been through."

"Are we talking about the disappearance of *numero dos* or this thing at her school?"

They were talking as if Mo wasn't there. But how could she hear Claire so clearly? Was she leaning over, mouthing her words into the mail slot?

"Either one. I've never thought Maureen was as strong as you. Maureen? Answer mama now. We're here to help."

Sweat. Never let 'em see you sweat. Who said that? Well, if it was true, good ol' Mom and Claire would be out there a long time, because Mo couldn't stop the mist that clung to her forehead, wet her upper lip, and left a clammy swath between her shoulder blades.

"I told you to just bring the police. They'll break a door down if you suspect injury to the person inside."

"Break a door down? There's no need for force here. My baby will come to herself and let us in. Maureen? Hear that?" If possible her mother's voice rose an octave and gained several decibels in volume. "Claire thinks we should call the police. Now I know you wouldn't harm yourself."

The woman was yelling. Every neighbor within a mile would hear.

Mo jerked the door open. "Mama. Claire. How nice."

"Well, don't just stand there. Let us in, Maureen."

Mo stepped back just as her mother gasped.

"Oh, my Lord, what happened here?"

"Pizza, Mama, a spilled pizza, just step over it. Claire, how nice you could bring Mama over." Withering looks had never worked on Claire, nor had sarcasm. Not at age four, or ten, or now. But it was always worth a try.

"You'd think your sight was failing. This place is a floodlit fortress. Let me turn off some of these lights." Claire reached for the wall switch.

"Don't touch the lights," Mo hissed.

"Whatever." Claire held both hands in the air, palms outward, and sauntered into the living room.

"Maureen where do you keep the sponges?" Mo could hear her mother opening and shutting drawers in the kitchen.

"Under the sink, but leave this mess to me. Let's go into the living room. I'll make coffee." Now she was yelling. They had her doing it, too.

But she had to admit it felt good to walk upright in front of the windows and not scurry along the floor, bent double, risking permanent disc problems. She waited in the kitchen as the coffee maker chirped along. Dear ol' Mom and Claire were huddled in the living room. Mo could detect urgent whispering every now and then. There would be some plot. Something hatched by the two of them to "save" the youngest sibling. She was tired of being saved. But what the hell, a killer wouldn't dare come bursting into the house with a crowd like this.

She emptied the coffee, piñon nut, into a carafe. She even had biscotti. Loading a tray with matching cups and saucers—she always saved the good stuff just in case her mother showed up—she marched off to meet the troops.

"They look good." Claire indicated a cluster of *Paphiopedilum*, lady slipper orchids, on a shelf below the *Phals* and to the right of a large west window. "Do you mist?"

"Of course."

"*Paphs* are not supposed to like misting, you know. Soft foliage." Claire picked up the plant nearest to her, inspected a leaf and put it down. "I think you'd get bigger flower size if you used a pesticide. There's mealybug on that plant," she nodded in the direction of the one she'd inspected. "Are you still dabbing at the little devils with rubbing alcohol?"

Claire, the expert. Claire, the obnoxious.

"It's against my religion to use toxins. The fewer poisons we put into the atmosphere, the better." Mo turned her back and placed the tray on an end table. If she didn't give Claire an audience, sometimes she'd just shut up. Mo fussed with the coffee and handed her mother a blue demitasse cup and saucer—not dirty and not cracked. Whew! That ought to be worth extra points or prove she wasn't crazy.

"It never ceases to thrill me to look at my two girls." Marjorie had settled into an overstuffed chair but not before she'd picked something off the arm.

An inward groan, this could be worse than she imagined, good old Marjorie was about to wax poetic about her two greatest achievements in life. Hadn't Mo heard that one before? Many, many times before? Well, maybe the older one was a wonder—the PhD botanist, a tenured professor at the University of Florida in Gainesville. The one who wowed the world at age twenty-five with the discovery of a hitherto-unknown species of orchid in some God-forsaken rain forest and then cloned it for all posterity.

"You're both such beauties. You could be twins. No one would ever guess there's even four months difference in your ages, let alone four years. Remember how Grandma used to say 'Claire got the brains, but Maureen got the angel hair'?"

"Give it a rest, Marjorie." Claire flipped up the top of an expensive-looking gold lighter and held it to the end of a stylishly slim cigar. "Sorry, Toots, but this is for the mealy bugs. I'll just woof a little smoke their direction. You can chalk this up to crop-dusting."

Mo didn't say anything. She hated smoke. She hated cigars. She hesitated, waiting for what? Her mother to intervene? Marjorie hadn't been good at keeping Claire away from her for thirty-one years, so why would she now?

"House rules say no smoke." Mo moved to stand

directly in front of Claire. Usually, she'd just let this sort of thing go, then sleep with the windows open all night. But not any more. Life was suddenly too short—and she was very tired of being taken advantage of.

"Whatever." Claire simply handed Mo the cigar and walked to the sofa.

Shit. Now what was she to do? Walk to the door, open it, risking all kinds of unknowns in order to get rid of it? Was that a smile on Claire's lips as she tucked her long legs under her and casually picked up a magazine?

"Can't you two be civil for five minutes?" Her mother sounded peevish.

Mo shrugged. She didn't think it was up to her to make the first move. But she did make a decision to dump the smoldering cigar in the hall toilet.

"Maureen, come back in here and listen to Claire. If I didn't know there was just a river of love flowing along between you two—I don't know what I'd do. Maureen, your sister has just knocked herself out to get you squared away."

Mo wasn't certain what "squared away" entailed, but she'd bet her life on the river of love not being much more than a trickle—a seasonal stream that dried up for most of the year.

"So, whatcha got?" Mo flopped down on the wide arm of the overstuffed chair that held Mom and had been picked clean of lint. It always felt better to have someone between them even if Mom couldn't keep Claire controlled.

"I've found someone for you to talk with." Claire had unfurled a leg and was leaning forward.

Her words focused Mo's thinking immediately.

"It's such a good idea. Listen to Claire, Maureen."

Mom settled deeper into the blue denim slipcovers but kept a hand on Mo's knee.

"My friend graduated in August—"

"Ol' what's-her-name, the shrink?"

"Janice Eldridge. Yes, a psychologist. I've made an appointment for you tomorrow morning at ten."

"Maybe you haven't heard. I'm not working. I can't afford expensive introspective jabber at two hundred an hour. Plus, I'm already seeing someone. Someone provided by the school." A bit of a lie but Dr. Pecos had set up an appointment to talk. Maybe it was for help with Toby, but Claire and Mom didn't need to know that.

"That's a lie. I've done some checking. I called your principal and you are not seeing anyone or, at least, have not registered that person with the personnel office. I don't know why not, your insurance will cover everything. This is a clear case of post-traumatic stress."

"Wait. I'll give you the name and number of who I'm seeing." Mo quickly walked to the kitchen and picked up Ben's card from off the kitchen table—if you never put things away, you never lost them. "Here. Call him. He's a psychologist, Native American and working on the case. I have an appointment at ten tomorrow morning."

"We'll see." Claire briefly looked at the card then handed it back. "It doesn't say here that he's board certified. And Indian Health? Since when did you qualify for IHS care?"

"This is a case involving an Indian boy. I'm involved. Dr. Pecos is involved. I'm seeing an Indian shrink to give me better perspective on what happened." Another fib.

Mo thought Claire seemed irked that she wasn't funneling a patient to her good friend. "You know, I got the idea your principal is afraid you're going to sue them."

"On what grounds?"

"Oh, lax security for starters. Mishandling of the entire situation. Trust me, any medical bills you might have will be taken care of. And just for peace of mind, we'll have an alarm system put in here."

The "we," of course, meant dear ol' Dr. Roth—orthodontist, moneybags husband of Claire, and employer of their mother. Gainesville's finest—cream of society. But Mo had to hand it to her, she was taking care of Mom. Something Mo was not willing to do. Claire had even gotten the ritzy sounding married name. The only names Mo had gotten were "Smith," for God's sake, and a two-foot-long Spanish thing that was about fourteen syllables. Beltzer was comforting, even if it did sound like warm beer.

"So, you'll go?" Marjorie patted Mo's knee. "To see Claire's friend?"

Where had her mother been? "No, Mom, I'm going to continue to see Dr. Pecos."

"I'll pick you up." Not even an edge to Claire's voice. It would be easy to believe she really cared. But why was she ignoring everything about seeing Dr. Pecos and trying so hard to steer Mo to Dr. Eldridge? Because Claire was nothing if not in complete control of every situation. Couldn't stand it any other way. Had anything changed since childhood? Mo, wear the brown skirt, no, don't cut your hair, a B+ in math? I bet you could bring that up in summer school ... the bane of her existence, a brilliant older sister who had all the answers. Yet, even Mo knew that life couldn't go on with locked doors and home-delivered pizzas. And if Claire picked her up, it took care of the problem of opening the door and going outside.

"Okay, my darling girl. If you're seeing this Dr. Pecos,

then we are both pleased. Aren't we Claire?" A nod and a roll of her eyes but Claire stayed silent.

"But there's more good news. This is really why we came. I mean we didn't drive all the way over from Gainesville on a weekday just to make sure you see a doctor—even though that's a worthy cause. No, if anything will make you well, this will. Claire, tell Maureen the good news. Oh honey, wait 'till you hear." Marjorie squeezed Mo's leg and bounced forward in her excitement.

Looking down at the top of her mother's head, Mo could see the separation of hairpiece from scalp—black curls, each anchored to a circular wire meshed with hair drawn up through the center of the ring. Mo would rather have studied this somehow-riveting phenomenon but forced herself to look at Claire.

"I want you to consider something. It's an opportunity that's just presented itself, but I think it would be perfect for you." This was Claire's no-nonsense voice. Mo leaned forward, intrigued in spite of herself.

"A job?"

"Yes, honey, can you imagine?"

"Marjorie, let me handle this." Claire frowned at her mother and paused before leveling her gaze at Mo. For effect? Mo thought so. "I've been contacted by the Botanical gardens at the University. They need someone—"

"*Please*. A ten- year- old minor in botany and the culture of a few orchids doesn't qualify me—"

"Let me finish. What they want, you *are* imminently qualified for—a photographer. A photographer of flowers."

"I'm not moving to Gainesville."

"That's the great part—it's right in your own backyard.

The centennial for the National Parks begins this month. The Department of Interior is adding a display of native Florida orchids to the Whitney Labs at Marineland. They've built three greenhouses on the premises, and they need to begin a pictorial record-keeping of species from acquisition through blooming cycle. And any other ceremonial pictures that they might ask for. They need someone familiar with tropicals with a specialty in orchids, who also just happens to be an ace at taking pictures of flowers. Your college work in botany is just icing. And it's a mere twenty minutes away."

Claire sounded triumphant. Of course, if the job were for real, then it would be a feather in her cap for having found the perfect match. Because, yes, it did sound like it was tailor-made. Mo was familiar with the general project—it had been well publicized. Bond money and a general election had provided St. John's County with the impetus to build, sharing the cost of clearing the beach along the Atlantic for extra parking with Georgia Aquarium, owners and operators of Marineland. Then on the Intracoastal side of highway A1A, they would construct three commercial-sized greenhouses behind the Whitney Labs. The land was on some kind of permanent government "loan," and the plan included a laboratory and research center—a combination of Whitney Labs and the University of Florida—bioscience meets Plant Science.

Two greenhouses had been completed—each at least two thousand square feet. The third was under construction, and Mo wasn't certain how far along the lab was. Upon completion, matching funds would come from a federal grant and continued fund raising. The exhibit would be permanent, an exciting project added to an established park and recreational area, and a great way to celebrate the Centennial. There was even talk of expanding Georgia Aquarium's tourist attractions.

"You need to be able to travel. Don't quote me, but foot loose and fancy free is a prerequisite."

Travel? Some steamy island or shrouded rain forest dripping with mist? At this point an air-boat ride in the Everglades sounded exciting. Could she be so lucky?

"This is just going to turn out perfect. Sometimes things happen for a reason—haven't I always said that?" Another bob of her mother's head and her curls slipped further to the right.

Mo smiled. Truly the woman wanted her youngest to succeed. Mo gave her a hug. Maybe this family was on her side after all.

"I've taken the liberty of presenting your name and forwarding copies of that slide presentation you did for me last year. If that doesn't get you in the door, nothing will."

Mo started. Seriously? The infamous slide project had almost drawn blood, emphasizing that the sisters could never work together. Yet, now Claire was all praise. Oh well, go figure. It *was* some of Mo's best work. And it never hurt to get the drop on other candidates—wasn't it always who you knew? Nowadays, lovingly referred to as networking?

"I'll pick you up at 9:30."

Mo opened her mouth to protest, then closed it. Quarter of ten would be sufficient. They were only going a few blocks. After all, Claire had been a life-saver, that is, if the job came to fruition. Maybe a few extra minutes together was a small price to pay for Claire's generosity and thoughtfulness. The job was such a plum. She could put up with a lot not to have to worry about next month's mortgage payment.

"It's settled, then." Marjorie bounced up from the armchair and smoothed black polyester over ample hips. Anymore, Marjorie's office attire seemed to work for every day. As office manager for dear ol' Dr. Roth, she chose what she called "nurse-like" clothing—flared polyester tops over fitted slacks. More like leftovers from a Supercuts hair salon. Mo always half expected her mother to grab a broom and sweep around the edges of her furniture.

Stop it, she chided herself. Be appreciative. She felt like a corner had been turned and life was going to go on.

Chapter Nine

For the first time in almost a week, Mo didn't think of guns or third graders or stuffed animals. And she slept—even after a jolt of piñon coffee and two biscotti. No pills, no TV half the night, just the drugged slumber of the sleep-deprived.

Only the phone encouraged her to acknowledge the daylight that pushed through shutters she'd forgotten to close. She rolled over to the side of the bed and grabbed it.

It was Marjorie. One, to wish her well—advising her to just empty her heart out to the doctor 'cause that was going to be the only way she'd get well. And two, reminding her that she didn't have tea towels. Tea towels, at seven a.m.? If Mo's cardinal sin wasn't the lack of a dishwasher, then it had to be this other missing implement. Not to mention that she used a pair of her ex-husband's shorts as a dishcloth. They had been washed to within an inch of their combed cotton life, and anyway, "Waste not, want not." But that sounded exactly like her mother, so why didn't they get along? She thanked her mother for the best wishes and was truly thankful the call was short. She stretched and put two bare feet flat on the floor.

Ah, the luxury of time. Claire wouldn't be there for another hour and a half or so. A pot of coffee—this time it was Guatemalan—and a read-through of yesterday's local news-rag, *The Record*. Just to dawdle, mist her plants, read—this was heaven. Then a shower. Thirty minutes beneath the water and she didn't once hop out to listen for a strange noise or look out the window. She pulled on jeans and a short-sleeved sweater, ran a comb through her damp hair, slipped into clogs and grabbed her purse. She'd heard the first honk from the drive. She'd best not keep Claire waiting.

"You might be out of work but you don't have to look the part."

"Good morning to you, too, Claire."

"Is your hair wet?"

"Damp."

"Well, don't touch the leather."

Mo made a face, scrunching up her nose, but Claire, as usual, was oblivious. The dove gray leather was warm to the touch and Mo folded into its depths—keeping her head upright. The black Mercedes was a little too funereal for her tastes but what the heck, she wasn't looking gift horses in the grill this morning.

Mo had swiped a bag of bagels off the counter on her way out the kitchen door and now pulled one out. Stale.

And what was that green stuff around the edge? How old was it anyway? She'd toss it before Claire could comment.

Mo pressed the electric switch, waited for the window to silently sink into the door then tossed the bagel, bag and all, onto the compost pile next to the hostas. Not everyone kept a pile of decaying matter so close to their house, but it was convenient. She'd been known to twirl a cantaloupe rind all the way from the back porch and land it in the middle. She idly wondered who might need that kind of talent. Fruit Frisbee. Would it become an Olympic event? Humor. Her sense of humor was coming back. Getting out of the house and facing her demons must be a cure.

The few blocks' ride was uneventful. The morning was warm with just the tiniest bit of humidity. Claire simply bubbled over with details about the job. Mo braced for more criticism. Claire had been known to pick up where their mother left off. But none came as Claire expertly maneuvered the Benz between a bus stop and the corner.

"Promise me you'll be on your best behavior during the interview tomorrow." Claire turned toward her and handed her a copy of the posting. Here's the nitty-gritty. Not one thing you're not good at. If you have questions, think of something later, call me. After I take you home, I'll be in my office this afternoon from three on."

What did she think Mo would do? Wipe her nose on her sleeve?

"Best behavior? What kind of request is that?" Mo felt anger tiptoeing just beneath the surface.

"Mo, I don't want to fight. I just want this job—this opportunity—to work out. You deserve this kind of break. I don't want anything to ruin it." Claire pleading? Mo almost jumped as Claire touched her arm. "You're too good to waste your life on eight-year-old ingrates. Don't look back. Just think how rich life can be in the future."

What was there to say? She'd always loved teaching and never thought of the kids as ingrates. But did Claire really care? Maybe she did. Maybe this was an important new step forward in their relationship. Then she realized that Claire was opening her car door.

"Hey, I can make it in on my own. But I really do appreciate your help."

"Good. Now, it's not that I don't believe you, but I want to meet this Dr. Ben Pecos of yours. Just going to say hi and then I'm out of here."

Claire was out of the car before Mo could protest further. She wasn't lying and it irked her that Claire felt this need to check. The minute Mo started to believe Claire really cared, she'd pull something like this. It was like being taken someplace by your mother.

Still, Mo didn't lag behind. At least walking side by side, it gave the sharpshooters of the world duplicate targets. And then they were across the lobby, out the double doors, and into the office area.

"Ms. Beltzer. Good to see you again." Ben was standing in the doorway of a small but serviceable room. Well, the word 'closet' came to mind. Borrowers couldn't be choosers, Mo guessed.

"Dr. Pecos, my sister, Claire Roth." She and Mo were the same height but *willowy* had always been applied to Claire. In fact, wasn't that her mother's favorite word? Her first born was just all legs. But Mo had gotten the boobs. And there were few times when Mo didn't think that she'd come out ahead.

"May I speak with you alone?" Claire put a hand on Ben's arm.

Mo started to protest. Why hadn't she seen this

coming? Just one more example of Claire the know-it-all … Claire in control. Would Dr. Pecos tell Claire that the appointment was only to go over information concerning her student? She hoped not.

Claire followed Ben into a room to their right and closed the door, while Mo took a seat in an alcove off the main hallway. Claire was probably giving Dr. Pecos a play-by-play report of the last five days. But Mo didn't care. Maybe this would help. Maybe it would help to talk with Dr. Pecos about her fears. She was willing to try. It wasn't her nickel.

Mo thumbed through a few year-old magazines and settled on a copy of the *Journal* but had barely read the woman's side of "why my marriage failed" when the two returned, laughing. Was that a good thing? Hard to tell.

"If anyone could put Humpty-Dumpty together again, it's you." This as Claire shook Ben's hand. "I'm glad she has this opportunity to meet with you."

Mo stood but, as usual, thought of nothing clever to say. If she hadn't felt dowdy before, she did now.

"I'll be back in an hour." And then Claire was gone in a whirl of tweed pantsuit and perfectly understated cloud-gray silk blouse, dark blond hair slicked smartly back by a paisley scarf tied to cover just the tips of her ears, bouffant curls escaping to cascade across her shoulders. They had both inherited their mother's hair color—maybe a shade or two different. Mo's, the attention-getting platinum white "angel's hair" in a smart short bob and Claire's with honey golden highlights, exploding in natural curls. Only when Marjorie's locks had started to turn gray had she dyed her hair black. She had become the Elvira of the dental clinics. It made her look harsh and added to her almost-sixty years.

But who was going to tell her? Hair aside, no one spent the time on wardrobe like Claire.

Now there was a reason to start driving again—so she wouldn't worry about her chauffer out-dressing her. Mo resolved to at least back the Volvo out of the garage when she got home. Maybe roll back and forth to the street a few times until she felt certain—

"Mo, are you feeling ill?"

Dr. Pecos stood in the doorway of the tiny office, quizzically eyeing her. Mo did a quick inventory. No, she wasn't ill. She was tired. She needed to collect her thoughts, stay on subject. And now that she was here there was no reason to put off talking about "the incident"—again.

"Mo?"

"I'm sorry, what?" Of course. No wonder he was staring. She'd forgotten mascara. It was amazing what a seeming lack of eyelashes would do. For one thing, it gave her a distinctly alien look.

"You really don't look well. Should you even be here?"

"No eyelashes and no liner." Mo pointed to her face and grinned. She batted her eyes and watched Dr. Pecos fasten on the white hairs that framed her eyes but were almost impossible to see.

"Of course. I see. This is new territory for me—I'm not an expert."

Mo had looked into permanent liner, but the ink didn't come in a color that would work. Everything seemed too harsh with platinum blonde hair. Her mother could do Elvira, she couldn't. She shook off the thoughts. Was she stalling, thinking of makeup and hair to avoid her real problems?

"Let's get started, then. Sometimes retrospect offers

perspective in addition to distance. How are you doing?"

Ben stepped back into his temporary office, holding the door for Mo before squeezing his six-foot plus frame sideways between wall and desk edge, exhaling as he turned to plop into a padded, and surprisingly new, swivel desk chair. Must be borrowed—someone trying to make the visitor feel more comfortable, Mo thought.

She had followed Ben into a room made even smaller by the sound-proof acoustic tile that decorated ceiling and walls. The room really could have been a custodian's supply closet at one time—in fact, she was sure of it and now it had been brought into use as an office for visitors. With storage cabinets removed, there was room for a desk and two chairs—one behind and one in front. But no room to move the chair Mo sat in, so her knees touched the cold metal of a modesty panel.

"I'm doing better … really." Mo continued to take in the sparseness of the pretend office. She wasn't sure whose nickel was paying for her visit but she was grateful. And it certainly wasn't being wasted on plush office space. She was certain Dr. Pecos had any number of other pressing assignments that needed his attention and probably didn't spend a lot of time cooped up in a windowless cubby.

"First of all, your sister seemed to think there might be some things we should talk about. She seemed worried that you've had a rough week. Let's start there."

"Are you asking if I looked for a job?"

"Is that what you did?"

"No."

"Then let's talk about what you did do."

"Let's see … I organized my closets and took a load of clothing to Goodwill. Baked three dozen cookies for a church bazaar …" Lies, but she wasn't ready to admit to hiding in the house.

"Claire seemed to have a different picture. She seemed to think that you've been having panic attacks and haven't been out of the house. Whom should I believe?"

"Maybe … me. Okay, okay, her." Why was she doing this? She had a feeling that this man really cared, really wanted her to get better. "I can't seem to move on. I haven't been out of the house and probably wouldn't have come today if Claire hadn't driven me. But Claire is so critical."

"Has Claire been critical recently?"

"When hasn't she been? The latest? She's disappointed in how I'm handling the incident. She thinks I should sue the school district for—I think she refers to it as 'emotional damages' in addition to back wages and lost retirement."

"What do you think?"

"I don't give a rat's ass. I mean, excuse me, but I don't. Maybe I have been wasting my time in an elementary classroom. This whole thing has made me reconsider what I want to do—when I grow up." A wan smile.

There was silence. Ben made a note on the pad in front of him. "I don't think one incident should define parameters for your career and make you walk away without some soul-searching. And I don't mean to belittle it. It was shocking, mind-numbing, but you can work through it. I don't want to see you jump to conclusions and do something that you later regret."

"Just because someone tried to kill me and I don't know why? Plus, I don't know if they will try again. I have little or no control and it's my life. Last month, even two weeks ago, no one on the face of the earth could have been happier with her job. Last Monday started out as a great day—"

"Tell me about that. I know you have before but you might have remembered something new. In fact, if you can, why don't you start at the beginning—what happened that morning?"

"Even before class started?"

"Yes, if you don't mind. Maybe something will stand out—a clue, a warning—something that should have told you that the day wasn't ordinary. And if it was just like any other, you need to see that, too. There are lots of things that are just out of our control. There is no warning for them. We're left dealing with the aftermath."

Mo thought for a moment. The morning had seemed completely ordinary. But if the good doc thought it would help …

"I always get to school on time—sometimes early. I have my own parking spot—teacher of the month—and I had just entered the Administration building when this whiny voice called out for me to wait up. It was my aide, Ginny. I guess she'd been trying to get my attention and I was pretty preoccupied."

"With?"

"I don't know. The day's schedule. I'm a Virgo, I plan and then plan some more. That sort of thing. I loved that place so much. When no one was looking, I'd even pat the brick walls and say something totally inane like, 'Stand tall, you hear?'" She felt a catch in her throat, but continued. "I always felt a rush of pride when the smells from the hallway assaulted me—lunchroom leftovers, a backed-up toilet from a wad of paper towels. Everything overlaid with the BO of burgeoning bodies racing toward puberty. It was my cologne, Eau de Pre-teen." She looked up. At least that had gotten a laugh from the doc.

"Ginny has been my aide for over five years. We make

a great team. She was still disappointed that I preferred reading over playing bridge at lunch but I held out hope that she'd get over it. That morning it was her turn to pick up messages and she went on to the principal's office and promised to check on my AV order for the next day. I remember seeing a notice on the electric sign board that there would be an assembly at eleven.

"I walked past the rows of lockers, secretly proud of how many children spoke to me. Teaching isn't a popularity contest, but I'd probably win if it was. I loved what I did—that was the simple truth. My mother always said thank God I wasn't religious or I'd be a nun. I was that devoted."

"What do you think prompted that devotion?"

"I saw progress. I could excite children to learn. I introduced them to worlds they hadn't known existed."

"An example?"

Mo laughed as she remembered a favorite. "I had sprung for a subscription to *National Geographic*. One morning during free reading, a group of five or six boys gathered at the back of the room and were snickering and pointing at something and cuffing each other on the shoulder. Well, I knew in an instant that the object of so much glee was the two-page color foldout on various tribes in Africa—the women sans clothing to the waist. You know, bare mammary glands swinging freely. So, I immediately strode to the back of the room, stern look—my no nonsense look—took the magazine and then couldn't help but laugh out loud. It was open to the foldout on sharks—over a hundred species. I should have known that that was far more titillating in the third grade."

Ben smiled. "Good example. Let's go back to that morning."

She was talking too much—too much detail. Maybe

because she had had little or no interaction with people during the week. Mom and Claire, but the pizza delivery boys didn't count. No, she was definitely starved for human company. Mo collected her thoughts. "On the way to my room the teacher in the room next to mine said good morning. She always stands outside in the hall. I opened the door to my room and remember making a note to wipe a set of incredibly sticky fingerprints off the knob. In fact, I went to my desk and pulled out the Lysol spray. I tried to do little chores like that before class. And they always needed repeating after class."

"I can imagine."

"When Ginny came in she said something like 'Guess who's got a hair up his ass now?' I reprimanded her. I really kept an eye on the language—the kid's and mine."

"You didn't reprimand a child?"

"No, not that morning. It was Ginny hoping to draw me into a little principal-bashing. Referring to him as Barney Fife." Mo paused. "There may be some truth to that characterization, I just didn't want the kids to hear."

"What was her problem with the principal?"

"A mandatory two-weekend conference on reading."

"Was that unusual?"

"Not really. We were expected to get recertification points. It was just short notice. I think Ginny might have had plans."

"Did you say anything to her other than the reprimand?"

"I ignored. Ginny can get a little melodramatic at times."

"Would you describe her as a close friend—someone you did things with after school? Happy hour sort of thing, maybe?"

"No. She was a single mom, money was tight. She'd been on her own for a couple years with two preschoolers. She lived with her mother."

"Do you think she could be bribed? Offered money to get involved—involved in setting up what happened?"

Mo could feel her hands growing cold. Ginny? An accomplice? "I suppose so, but I don't want to believe it. She was always helpful."

"How did Ginny help you? Did you give her directions or did she volunteer her own variations on classwork?"

"Of course, she had a copy of my lesson plans. And I always asked her for input. But, yes, the day's lessons were up to me."

"How often did she contribute?"

"Not often. This was a job, only a job for her—but one that allowed her paid vacation, a health plan, and all the holidays off to be with her kids. Single mom syndrome, you know?"

Ben nodded, but Mo wasn't sure he really understood.

"How many students in your class?"

"Twenty-three."

"What was the first lesson that day?"

"Math."

"Did you give any directions to Ginny?"

"I wanted the two of us to work individually with every student before the end of the hour. Check homework first. Give out as many happy-face stickers as we could. I remember Ginny opened her mouth and pointed a finger down her throat."

"How did that make you feel?"

"She was grinning. I know I get to her sometimes. She thinks I'm a little goody-two-shoes. But it's just that I don't want some stymied seventh grader to suddenly decide that his math anxiety was born in the third-grade class of Miss Maureen Beltzer. For example, I was determined that everyone would have the chance to just love the multiplication tables. Each student had a set of elaborately designed flash cards provided by money from my own pocket. Batman and Mighty Morphin Power Rangers graced the backs, as did Snow White, Cinderella and the Minions. They were a success until trading at recess hopelessly muddled most decks. So, it was back to the plain vanilla cards provided by the school.

"You know, that morning I surveyed the room of heads bent over papers spread across small tables and felt a surge of honest-to-goodness love for those children. Hands were waving and there was a chorus of 'Miss Beltzer'. I shushed them and explained how we'd start our day. I always did that. I thought it modeled organization. Anyway, I instructed Ginny to check their work and start the last two rows along the side on flashcards."

Mo paused.

"What happened next?"

"I moved toward a group of boys in the back by the windows. They had been clustered together and broke away guiltily when I walked up. I had expected to see something alive, a frog or toad. Maybe the elusive *National Geographic* showing the tired, overworked mammary glands of a Zulu matriarch. I don't know. They were acting guilty."

"Do you think they had been looking at the gun?"

"I suppose so—no, now that I think of it, I'm sure it was the gun. But it wasn't behavior out of the ordinary. Huddling together, whispering … Secrets are a big thing at that age. Secrets and pranks. I still wouldn't have had a reason to frisk five eight-year-olds."

"I can see that. But wouldn't your aide have been aware of something going on?"

"Ginny wasn't really good at getting involved. Discipline wasn't her thing. You're asking an awful lot of questions about Ginny. You don't think she—"

"No conclusions, but someone had to have singled out Toby and set him up." Ben quickly inserted. "I just want you to reconstruct the morning, and that includes information on your aide. So, she started several tables of students on their multiplication tables, what did you do?"

"I asked if anyone had questions about the homework and Toby Wolff pushed a crumpled but entirely blank piece of paper toward me with just the hint of defiance. I knelt by the table between Toby and his friend, Asher. I told him it looked like he hadn't even tried to work the problem. Then he pointed at a spot in the upper left corner where something had been erased so many times, the paper looked scrubbed. I leaned in and squinted at the supposed problem and asked Toby to help me decipher it." Mo stopped and stared at the floor.

"And that's when it happened? When he held the gun to your forehead? I want to remind you that he tells a different story—that the gun remained on the table; it was never pointed at you."

"Yes, I know our stories differ."

"I want you to carefully talk me through what exactly happened. I want to know your thoughts."

Mo swallowed and waited a second then began and left nothing out. She was amazed that, in retrospect, she wasn't frightened when it was happening—that came later. She recalled how intent she was on not injuring anyone. And she remembered thinking it strange that Ginny wasn't there to help her. But that in itself wasn't necessarily unusual. Ginny was good at not putting herself in danger. One sign of a cold or flu, and she wore a mask. The entire morning in question, save for the gun, was not different from a hundred other mornings.

She briefly touched upon how she felt about the meeting with the parents, the meeting with the detective followed by the Buckley explanation and finding the head of the costume in her bed but, of course, the doc knew about all that. The skull, the spray of orchids. She still didn't have an explanation. When she'd finished, she just sat there. There was a feeling of relief … a feeling that she'd put it into perspective. That, oh so carefully, she'd coaxed the monkey off of her back. Mo knew, at some level, it was inevitable she'd tell the story so many times it would lose its punch. But today somehow a revolver pointed at her head didn't sound so menacing. It didn't sound like something she couldn't handle—wasn't already handling, in fact.

"Isn't it possible that Toby thought up the whole thing? Make himself look like the big man—I use that term loosely."

"But how does that explain the gun? It wasn't his father's. And I assure you, he knew it was a very real gun with real bullets. And then there's this Buckley head … in my bed."

"Perhaps, he, along with his friends, found the gun, or stole it. Children can be very imaginative. I know I don't have to tell you that. The gun could have belonged to his friends' parents. Maybe they stole the costume or found the head. When Toby realized he was in trouble, he fabricated this person in a Buckley costume who wanted him to shoot you. I think they could have found the head of the costume and broken into your house to plant it. Keep anyone from blaming him."

"That's a lot for eight year olds to think up and do, don't you think? And it would mean that Toby wanted to kill me. He first indicated the gun was only a threat to get out of homework."

"I'm not an expert on eight year olds. But the understanding of death is not a developed concept at that age. Have you checked with Detective Foley? Followed up, found out how his investigation is going?"

She hadn't. Not after the first nerve-wracking interview when Dr. Pecos and Detective Foley dutifully crawled around and checked under her beds. And she was curious, just a little anyway, about the thing that looked like a shrunken head. Was it real? She didn't have any good reason for not at least calling to inquire about the investigation. Detective Foley had called once to check on her. He hadn't offered any information and she hadn't had the presence of mind to ask. There was a very big part of her that didn't want to know. But that was then.

"I guess I thought they'd get back with me."

"I don't want to sound pessimistic, but sometimes when there's been no major crime—"

"No bloodshed."

"Exactly. They put these cases on a back burner."

"So you think I should call?"

"I think, Maureen, that you should take control of your life. There's something about thinking and acting like a victim that makes you become one."

Mo sat there. What the doctor said was true. Whoever

was behind all this—and that was plural because not for one second did she think Toby was the sole perpetrator—was enjoying her fright, a fright that had brought her life to a standstill. Yet, certainly nothing had happened in the last few days to cause her any worry.

"I know what you say is true. I've allowed myself to become a victim and that lets the other side win."

Ben nodded, "Think about it. We don't need to go further today but I think you're on the mend. That's not a promise that you won't have relapses—incidents that bring it all back, usually without warning."

Mo smiled. "I know. I think I'm prepared. Can we talk about something else?"

"Sure."

"Well, I think I've found a job." That wasn't entirely a lie. Claire seemed certain, anyway. Hadn't she handed her the posting from the University when she'd gotten in the car this morning—had reiterated all the good words she'd put in, insisted Mo take it seriously and look into it?

"That's great. I sense this isn't a teaching job?"

"No. I have mixed feelings, but it's something that might be better in the long run—certainly something that I need right now. Claire's recommending me."

"That seems like a very supportive thing for her to do."

"I know." Mo didn't go into how she suspected this sudden altruism. She'd expect something in return. That was just Claire.

"So, share. What will you be doing?"

"Photography. Pictorially tracing the blooming cycles of various flora. Florida flora. It's part of the centennial celebration. I'd be keeping records, arranging plants, caring for rare species. Designing displays—all things I love to do.

I'll let you know how the interview goes."

"That's terrific. Looks like we'll be working in the same program." Ben quickly filled her in on his lecture series topic. "I'll be headquartered at Whitney Labs. I hope you get the job."

The interview was the next day. A Saturday, but it allowed University profs from Gainesville to spend time on the new project without disrupting their own schedules at U of F. And any students or student interns interested in a job just had to show up. Mo was excited. Who knew? With Claire's input—she could be a shoo-in. What was amazing was this excitement. The real thing? Or just a reaction to what had happened? Did she care? It had been a long time since third grade lesson plans had given her such a rush. Maybe she wasn't the type to hide her head in the sand forever.

"You seem pretty excited about this interview." There it was. People obviously noticed.

"Yup. I cannot tell a lie." Mo gave a mock Girl Scout salute.

"Good luck. Sometimes a change of scenery can work wonders. I have an interview with Toby set up for this afternoon. I'll let you know if I find out anything new."

Ben finished the last fifteen minutes of their appointment by having Mo reiterate how she would handle a panic attack if she had another one. Somewhere during the session, Mo's abject fear of someone stalking her, the fact that someone tried to kill her had been reduced to that. A panic attack. But Mo knew there would not be any more pizza with money exchanged through the mail slot. When she stood up, she could feel the difference. God, that monkey must have weighed a hundred pounds.

"Well, how it'd go?" Claire was in the hallway—all smiles with just a touch of concern wrinkling a smooth brow. If Claire didn't own stock in Lancôme, she should. But Mo was taken with the solicitousness of her sister. Anyone who didn't know their history would believe them to be best of friends. Could Mo be wrong? Was she being unfair? Had something changed with age?

"It went well." Mo said.

She saw the relief on Claire's face and didn't have to turn to know that Dr. Pecos was nodding in agreement.

They headed across the rotunda. "I need to stop for pantyhose." As long as they were out, there was a Walgreens on the way to her house.

"Oh, sweetie, I don't want to disappoint you, but I'm dashing. I'll drop you off at home. Maybe you could walk down to the 7-eleven. Better yet, just skip the panty hose. I don't know anyone who wears them any more. Just use a good spray-on tan."

One more thing Mo didn't have, and the store in question was some ten blocks from her house. Obviously a ploy to get Mo to drive. And pantyhose or even spray-on tan at the 7-eleven? Mo didn't even comment. In truth, she was a little tired of being chauffeured. And she felt good. Whole, whatever that meant, and totally disbelieving in broad daylight that anyone could wish her harm.

Claire dropped her off at the curb in front of her house and was gone with little more than a wave. Without giving herself too much time to think, Mo walked up the drive, silently beeped the garage door open and climbed into the Volvo. My God, the keys were in the ignition. Had they been there for a week? Probably. Wasn't this proof that no one was out to do her mischief?

She adjusted the rearview mirror and checked the side mirrors. Not that they needed adjusting, no one had touched the car. She turned the key in the ignition and turned to back down the drive. She paused before entering the street; checking to make sure her path was clear, she entered the street and accelerated. And then exhaled. She'd done it. She was on her way to recovery.

Mo laughed out loud for the first time in a long time and allowed herself to think of the new job. Something was telling her to wear the demur little jacket that just happened to have the slinkiest and shortest of dresses that matched. Yes, she'd wow 'em. This job was hers. She felt it. She gave the horn a punch—two longs and a short. Could life get any better than this?

Chapter Ten

Ben needed more information on Toby. He'd heard Mo's side of the story, but her aide and other students had remained quiet. Chatting with witnesses would help explain who was telling the truth—did Toby point the gun at his teacher and pull the trigger or was the gun simply on display being admired by Toby's friends? It made a big difference in how Ben would approach therapy.

He pulled up to the front of Jefferson Elementary and found a parking spot marked 'visitor.' The complex included a single-story, sprawling series of portable buildings to the side and back of an extensive cement block structure with a low, pitched roof. The parking lot fronted the building and a soccer field encompassed the rear. It was barely ten o'clock but there were twenty-five to thirty adults carrying signs and either walking back and forth in front of the main entrance or huddled in small groups. Ben walked around Keep Our Children Safe, Metal Detectors for All Schools, Teachers Teach—Criminals Kill … and stepped through the double doors into the information/check in area. Handing over a picture ID and proof of credentials, he signed in. The receptionist entered pertinent information into a machine on her desk that whirred out a temporary paper, glue-backed badge.

"All set, just wear the badge at all times. Of course, you'll need to meet with Principal Blaylock. I can't authorize you to enter the school grounds. I'll see if he's available."

The principal didn't keep him waiting but just poked his head in to ask Ben to follow him back to his office, which, as he remembered, was at the rear of the building. A little small talk as Ben followed him to the last door at the end of the hall.

"It's quiet back here. Fewer interruptions." A quick smile, almost apologetic, Ben thought. "Now, take a seat and tell me why you're here. I don't think I have to tell you that we need to down-play the incident—don't need any more news coverage."

"Of course, I understand. But I'm also certain that you would want to be supportive of my evaluation and recommended treatment for Toby Wolff. It's of utmost importance that we get this right. His age makes our decisions all the more critical. Councilman Wolff is counting on the school to be cognizant of just how much hangs in the balance." A little heavy handed but name-dropping never hurts, Ben thought.

"Oh, yes. I'm fully aware of the parents and their concerns. Tell me how I can help."

"I'm putting together a profile on Toby. There are

conflicting stories about what actually happened. I'd like to chat with Miss Allen, Ms. Beltzer's aide, and maybe a student who was in the room at the time—perhaps, a friend of Toby's."

"Ah, that would be Asher Compton. Those two boys are never apart. First, let me send someone to get Miss Allen. For obvious reasons I'd like to sit in on your interviews."

"That won't be a problem." Ben could only hope having an authority figure present wouldn't skew the information he'd get.

Ginny Allen didn't keep them waiting. She was one of those people who appeared to bounce instead of walk, and she entered the room a little out of breath.

"I can't stay long. I have Ms. Dixon keeping an eye on my class—it's my reading hour so there shouldn't be a problem." She turned to look at each man in turn. Ben sensed just a touch of a seductive smile when she turned his way. Dark brown eyes, thick lashes, almost black hair cascading down her back ... this was a woman used to attention.

"Tell me about Ms. Beltzer." Ben began, turning over a fresh sheet in his notebook.

"This is difficult for me."

"Why is that?"

"Well, I want to be fair and I certainly don't want to get anyone in trouble ..."

"How could you do that?"

A shrug, deep breath, then, "Mo means well. Don't misunderstand, but she's been under a lot of stress lately—with the leaving of her second husband. She took it as a failure on her part and I think that's impacted her teaching."

"How?"

"She's much more strict—more likely to act first, question later. She doesn't want anyone to doubt her authority. Mo knows best—that sort of thing."

"Can you give me an example?"

"Well, that morning is perfect. It could have been handled very differently."

"In what way?"

"She was way too demanding, actually threatening—'give me the gun, Toby', 'put the gun down, Toby'—that sort of thing. Then that awful attack, an attack on a child."

"Tell me about that."

"First of all, I didn't really see anything. My line of sight was blocked by students. And I needed to protect my own group of students. I immediately had them get under the table."

"So, you did not see Toby hold a gun to Ms. Beltzer's forehead?"

"Oh, good grief, no. I don't think that happened; that's just more of Mo's overkill crisis excuses—she had to have a reason for the physical abuse. For overreacting like she did."

A dead end. No new information to be gotten here. He handed Ginny one of his cards with his cell on the back and asked her to call if she thought of anything else.

Asher Compton was waiting in the hall and Principal Blaylock ushered him in.

"Asher? I'm Dr. Pecos. This won't take long but I'd like to ask you some questions about your friend, Toby Wolff."

"Okay."

"Have you been friends for a long time?"

"Yeah."

Another reluctant talker, Ben almost groaned out loud.

"What's your favorite thing about your friend?"

"He's good at sports."

"Soccer? Basketball? Baseball?"

"Baseball, mostly."

"What did Toby tell you about the gun he brought to class?"

"That Buckley gave it to him and he was going to get a bike."

"Were you with him when he shot the gun?"

"No, he shot it on the way to school."

"Did you see Toby point the gun at his teacher?"

"No, it was on the table. He didn't pick it up." Averted eyes, staring at the carpet. He's lying, Ben thought. Another dead end. He *still* didn't have a clear picture of that morning. He thanked Asher and Principal Blaylock, and walked out to the parking lot.

Eleven o'clock. He Googled the councilman's office, got the phone number and placed a call.

"Councilman Wolff, I know this is short notice but I'd like to ask you a few questions about Toby if you have the time. I'll be meeting with him at the hospital later this afternoon and I want to make certain that I have a solid profile."

It sounded like the councilman was relieved that he'd called. He immediately invited him to his house, gave him directions and promised to meet him at the gate to his community in fifteen minutes. Ben crossed his fingers that this meeting would be fruitful.

+ + +

The mansion in the gated community had pretentious columns that would make Tara look like a shack. Ben followed the councilman's Mercedes up a winding front drive and parked in front of a detached 3-car garage.

"Let's talk in Toby's room. My wife has her mahjong group coming over for lunch later."

The councilman pushed open the front door, and Ben followed him up a center staircase to the second floor. There was nothing common about Toby Wolff's bedroom—for starters, it was a gym, a movie theater and a computer room all rolled into one. Over a thousand square feet that also included an indoor shuffleboard, three oversized TVs, a miniature railroad and a rack of sports equipment. The walls were covered with memorabilia—posters of American Indian leaders, a shadowbox display of arrowheads, a floor-to-ceiling feather and bead headdress, maybe Kiowa, Ben thought, and a collection of old musket-loader rifles. Wow. Who would have thought the kid could have been tempted with a dirt bike?

"Here, have a chair. There's something I need to get off my chest. I trust I have your confidence?"

Ben nodded.

"I'm afraid I've asked my son to lie." The councilman waited for Ben's reaction.

"Go on."

"My son has handled guns since he was five—pellet guns, BB, .22 rifle—you name it. I've taught him to respect weapons. He's not afraid of a gun because he knows how to use it—and how not to." A deep breath, "I know he pointed the revolver at his teacher and pulled the trigger. I also know that he knew that the first two chambers were empty. He emptied them himself by shooting the .38 in the woods. He was being careful; he was not going to kill his teacher. I knew no one would believe him so I told him to lie—tell everyone that he was asked to bring the gun to class only to scare Ms. Beltzer, not harm her. He was only showing the firearm to his friends. That wouldn't be such a big thing."

"What happened next got a pretty good teacher basically fired—removed from the classroom anyway."

"Not saying I'm proud of any of this. A kid with everything says he'll do something like this for a dirt bike?" A wave of his arm took in the largess surrounding them. "I just need to keep him out of serious trouble when nothing overtly dangerous was intended."

"I'll admit it gives me some structure when working with Toby the next few weeks. I'll want to include you and your wife after we get a few sessions under our belt. Any problem with that?"

"No. We went to see him yesterday and other than missing his family and friends, he's doing well. Doc, I appreciate the care you've shown. Just keeping him out of the detention center has earned our gratitude. I mean that. Let me know if you ever need anything."

Chapter Eleven

The children's psychiatric wing of Flagler Hospital was on Highway 1 North, on the south side of St. Augustine, behind the four-story hospital itself. Ben would visit Toby today and would come again next Friday for a second meeting. Ben had reminded the boy's father to phone the hospital to put Ben's name on the allowed visitors' list.

Even with his father's admission, this wasn't an easy case. Why did Toby do it? There was nothing on the surface to indicate any of the usual reasons why an eight-year-old would be tempted to knowingly go against rules and bring a firearm to class—even if he decided to only scare his teacher. Why did he tell "Buckley" that he would shoot her?

There was no history of sexual abuse or violence, no anger issues or extreme sibling rivalry or bullying at school—this was an only child of an affluent family with a doting mother and a high-achieving father. Toby already had three bicycles and several guns. Other than showing off for friends and wanting to appear "the big man," there was nothing more concrete as to motive.

A plus was that the end of the school year was near. Toby was passing and, with a little tutoring, he could be taken out of school now and have the summer for continued therapy. Ben was going to recommend a supervised summer camp with specialized child counseling. He hoped he could convince the parents. Ben would rely on his own training to 'read' the situation and make adjustments to his recommendations as needed.

This first visit would be, for the most part, just talking to gain Toby's trust. Toby met him in the lobby and they walked outside to feed the ducks on a pond and then played some video games—Toby won and not because Ben let him.

"I almost forgot. I brought you a present."

"What is it?"

"You'll find out if you unwrap it." Ben handed Toby a gift sack stapled at the top.

"It's a book." Ben probably imagined a hint of disappointment—a game would have been better received. "Can you read the title?"

Toby gave him a look. "Yeah—it's *Whispers of the Wolf.* Hey—just like my name."

"Exactly right. It's a story by a Pueblo author."

"Are you a real Indian?"

"Yes, I'm Pueblo."

Toby frowned, "What kind is that?"

"Pueblo means town and I grew up in my grandmother's house on a reservation in New Mexico."

"In a Chickee?"

"No, in a house made out of dried mud." The look of incredulity on Toby's face said it all. Ben took out his phone and pulled up pictures—he needed to save his reputation here. There were pictures of the village in the snow, others of trees along the river and then workers in the fields. There were several of the schoolhouse and church, more of childhood friends.

"A mud box all stuck together with a bunch of mud boxes. That's pretty cool. Did you have a horse?"

"No. My tribe is mostly made up of farmers—we grew corn and squash and melons."

"Where'd you go to school?"

"There." Ben enlarged a photo of the one-room parochial schoolhouse to the right of the rectory.

"It's not very big."

"It used to be just one big room. If you were in the third grade you might be in this corner, in the sixth back here along the windows, a fourth grader would sit with others in front of the bookcases." Ben pointed to various segments on the photo. "Today there are portable buildings behind, over here." Ben pointed to the back of the parking lot. "Five buildings in all. Now pretty much every grade has its own room."

"Did you have a car?"

"Didn't need one. We walked everywhere, even up to the top of mesas." Ben pointed out another photo of a flat-topped mountain behind the pueblo.

"Looks like a big table."

"It does, doesn't it? And see here? In this photo there are huge white puffy clouds above the mesa. My people would say 'the grandfathers are coming' meaning there would be rain. In the desert, rain is sacred. Let's take a look at your book. I'd like to find out more about the wolf whispers."

+ + +

In hindsight that first visit had been a good one. Ben purposely skirted any reference to Jefferson Elementary or the incident. There would be time for that and today was the day. He would begin to question Toby about that morning—more in depth about Buckley, for example. Ben liked a good puzzle, but this one had him stumped.

For the life of him he couldn't find a reason for anyone to want to kill or even just scare this third grade teacher—a teacher of the month, no less. A new bike seemed a little flimsy if for no other reason than his father said he had three others. Peer pressure and wanting to show off might remain top of the list of possible motivators.

After some opening questions about how he was doing, and a promise that they'd feed the ducks before he left, Ben pulled a chair up to a low study table and indicated a spot for Toby.

"What are these?" Several 8 ½ X 11 inch sheets of construction paper and a stack of white typing paper littered the top, alongside a box of glue sticks and a box of crayons—sixty-four count.

"Some art stuff. This other doc who comes to talk to me makes me draw things."

"What sort of things?"

"Oh, like what Buckley looked like an' the bike. Here's Buckley." Toby pulled a piece of white paper from the stack in front of him with the cut-out of a brown construction paper figure pasted in the middle.

This was pretty good. There were ears and large paws and shoes and maybe a tie and pants—it was hard to tell. The tie alone was just a guess at what that red smeared line might be around his throat and down his front. But overall, it was a decent rendition.

"This is good, Toby. You're good at art. When Buckley told you about the bike, what did he sound like?"

"Regular, I guess."

"Did he ride the bike up to where he met you?"

Toby burst out laughing. "That's funny. He's too fat. He got it out of the truck."

"Buckley drove a truck?"

"Yeah."

"What did the truck look like?"

"Big and white with sides on it so you couldn't see out."

Must mean a panel truck or van of some kind, Ben mused, maybe a delivery truck. "Was there any writing on the sides of the truck?"

"Yeah, on the front."

"The driver's door and the passenger's door?"

"Yeah."

"Do you remember what it said?" Fingers crossed that a third grader could read the inscription.

"It was a picture—with an Indian."

"Do you remember anything else?"

"The tag had oranges on it."

Florida tag—standard, not personalized or one of the hundred special issues with golfers or dolphins or turtles.

"So, the bike was in back? Did you see inside the truck?"

"It was all empty, 'cept for the bike."

"Was the gun in the back?"

"The gun was in Buckley's pocket. He had to take his hands off just to get it out. The paws are just big mittens."

"What did Buckley's hands look like?"

"Like a girl's."

"I don't understand, Toby. What made Buckley's hands look like a girl's hands?"

"Cause he *is* a girl." Said with not a little scorn, Ben noted. Obviously there were things that Ben was supposed to know.

Ben paused. This was off the wall and might change a lot of things—at least, who the cops were looking for. "Inside the Buckley costume was a girl?" A vigorous nod. "Do you think this girl was your age?"

"No, she was old, like my Mom."

"Why do you say that?"

"Cause she had rings on, like my Mom."

"Wedding rings?"

A nod.

"So, Buckley or this girl drove the truck?"

Toby shook his head. "Some guy did."

This was getting interesting. "Did you know this guy?"

"No."

"What did he look like?"

A shrug. "The truck was parked pretty far away."

Possibly a married couple preying on children? He couldn't even begin to get his mind around it, and now, more than ever, he believed that Mo Beltzer had no idea why she had been singled out for death because he certainly didn't.

"I brought some Romaine lettuce. Let's go feed those ducks."

+ + +

"Okay, Doc, let me get this straight—Buckley Bear is a married woman who is driven around town by a man in a white van or paneled truck with Florida plates and has a picture of an Indian on the cab's doors. That about right?"

"You've got it." Ben had taken a chance that Detective Foley would be in his office when he left the hospital, and he wasn't disappointed. He had the detective's direct number and he'd answered on the first ring.

"Do you believe the kid?"

"He has no reason to lie, that I can see. And I'm convinced he was never in possession of the Buckley Bear head—the one found in Ms. Beltzer's bed. He didn't find the costume. It, with an occupant, came to him. He has no idea where his teacher lives. After Buckley gave him the gun, he, er, she left—head intact."

Ben heard the detective take a breath and let the air out slowly. "You know I can't give the incident priority; it's what I call one of my 'spare time' cases. Councilman Wolff has a few enemies in the area—I'm not ruling out he's somehow involved. Someone could set his kid up in something serious, embarrass the father, cause family hardship ... I know the name Wolff has been tossed around for the upcoming Senate race. And her aide, Ginny, I think she might know more than she's sharing. Anyway, if you find out anything else, let me know. And, hey, thanks. I appreciate the heads up."

Ben clicked off the call. He needed to put Buckley Bear

heads and errant eight-year-olds out of mind for awhile. Julie would be there by five. She was flying from Miami to Daytona, renting a car and driving up the coast to St. Augustine. He was still enamored with the idea of there being a Mrs. Ben Pecos and could hardly wait to see her again. He was pretty certain that she'd love the Bed and Breakfast accommodations—an entire top floor of an old carriage house just a couple blocks off of George Street, St. Augustine's prime tourist thoroughfare. Easy walking distance to just about everything in town. Flowers, a good bottle of red, snacks … he didn't plan on going out the rest of the day. Maybe not for the entire weekend. He didn't even try to stop the grin from spreading across his face.

Chapter Twelve

The interviewer met Mo at the door. A secretary ushered her in, separated her from fifty-some applicants eagerly sitting in chairs crammed along the hallway outside the office on the main floor of The Whitney Lab for Marine Bioscience, University of Florida's research institute on Highway A1A. Had Claire's pull moved her to the head of the line? Mo hadn't had to wait long.

"Miss Beltzer? Geoff Mitchell, here. Come in."

She caught her breath. He was gorgeous. In her four-inch stilettos, she was exactly his height maybe 5' 11". And with that wiry build? He was either a rock climber, a cyclist or a runner. Great hair, a sort of dirty gold that fell over one eye. He'd perfected the one-hand brushback and as she watched, he absently finger-combed both sides. An olive and gold striped Henley blended perfectly with a sage herringbone jacket. Impeccable. With a man like this, that word worked.

"Maureen, isn't it?"

"Mo, actually."

"Mo?" He blankly stared at her and then repeated, "Mo?"

He just wasn't connecting. Already he was thinking The Three Stooges, Mo could tell.

"Short for Maureen."

"Oh, of course, silly of me. It's pretty—Maureen, that is."

She smiled. He gave it two drawn-out syllables like her mother. "Mo-reen," Marjorie would say. Mo had asked her once why she didn't have a middle name like Claire did. Claire Ann Beltzer. It was pretty sounding, no hint of a stifled belch. And her answer? "Why, honey, Mo-reen already sounds like two names. Whatever more could you want?" And that was that. Mo shortened it as soon as she could but not until she'd answered to "Mo-reen" for seventeen years.

But, for once, she didn't care how it was pronounced, not when Dr. Geoffrey Mitchell uttered it. She gazed into light hazel eyes, grinned, and took the chair he offered.

"This is a new career for you, I understand. Claire—Dr. Roth," he amended and looked down at her from his perch on the edge of his desk. Should she nod? He continued, "She told me you'd recently given up teaching? Some nasty little incident at your school?"

If he was trying to get her to say that she'd basically gotten permanently replaced even before the end of the year for belting a pee-wee Billy the Kid, she wasn't biting.

She'd made up her mind. That was definitely a thing of the past, and it was going to stay that way. Taking the initiative she changed the subject.

"I was interested in the requirements for the position. Frankly, the posting reads like my resume. My BS is in fine arts, emphasis photography, with a minor in botany. Photography has been a hobby since I can remember." She smiled up sweetly. She probably didn't need to say more. If Claire was on her toes she'd already given him the run-down. And Mo knew what her sister would say. She'd use words like "perky, trustworthy, thorough, superior drawing ability… excellent photographer." Claire could rattle off the awards received over the years better than Mo.

It was the "perky" Mo objected to. Not that she wasn't. The description probably fit most women with bobbed hair and an upturned nose. But would she ever be able to outlive it? At fifty would there be another word? She could only hope.

"Dr. Roth forwarded a copy of your resume. You're quite right. Your background is very interesting to us. The project is in need of talented, dedicated individuals—with the credentials to back up the talent, I might add."

As she listened to him speak about the project, she realized that this job might not be without its perks. She was already fantasizing about putting bare hands on his deeply tanned chest, if she could trust the tiny sliver of a V revealed by his two undone buttons. She was amazed at how taken she was with this man. It was difficult for her not to just stare at him. Was that in itself proof of recovery? Or just more of the weakness that had gotten her two ex's before the age of thirty?

"Dr. Roth sent me some of your work, a slide

presentation you did for her, last year wasn't it?"

Mo nodded.

"I have to say, it's exceptional. Your series on Guatemalan Phragmipediums was just outstanding." His smile backed up his admiration. She returned the smile. "She's assured me that you aren't a stranger to orchid culture, either."

This time her smile was demure, modest even, but she had to say something. He was waiting.

"I've babysat Claire's collection often enough. And I dabble a little on my own. I have a small grouping of phals that are coming along. I'm only a windowsill grower." She didn't add that some of hers had earned the privilege of being with her just because they were pretty. That wouldn't have a place in his thinking. It was specimen plant or nothing, with guys like this.

"I don't want to lead you astray."

"What?" She really needed to pay attention. Hadn't she just been hoping that he would?

"Well, I mean I want to be perfectly clear that there would be a bit more to the job than just the photography end of things."

"I would expect there to be other duties." Maybe not what she was fantasizing unfortunately. It was certainly not a requirement of this job to fall head over heels in puppy love. And that was the *last* thing she needed to do.

"Yes, good. We need someone who's plant-savvy. I would expect a report on the condition of the plants you work with—each greenhouse taken separately. You'll be handling the plants, staging them for photographs. I hope it would be simple to also inspect them. It's important to hire someone who can spot a problem—knows what a problem is." He'd finally stopped staring at her and moved to stand by a window. "We've had an outbreak of soft-shell scale in the third greenhouse. Obviously, brought in an infected plant and no one noticed. I'm afraid now no one's gotten around to keeping it from spreading. We're a little understaffed at the moment. But what's new for federally funded programs that also rely on handouts?" His smile was rueful. "I won't be much help to you. My time is taken up with breeding." He moved toward her and a tingly lime scent floated between them.

A shiver skipped across her shoulder blades. She couldn't stop herself. The thought of him spending his days introducing pistils to stamens was incredibly sexy. After all, wasn't the very name 'orchid' Greek for testicle?

Maybe she should discuss her sexual urges with Dr. Pecos. No, she told herself. Mo was smart enough to figure out that her sudden preoccupation with Geoff Mitchell was probably a result of her near-death experience—we have to propagate before checking out, that sort of thing. Plants did it. Saved themselves from extinction by gathering all their energy and blooming. Hence, seed; hence, survival. Had she given herself away? He was looking at her strangely. She tried a demure smile but felt her neck grow warm. She only hoped the heat wouldn't creep upward.

"Do you have any questions?"

"Not really. Claire's kept me up-to-date on the scope of the Gardens and future plans. It's exciting." Which was true. Like it or not, she'd sat through hours of tedious monologue. Claire had called to reiterate the positives, the negatives, the background info she thought would be useful. The Botanical Gardens were a first for Whitney Labs—the baby of the University of Florida folks, as well as those hired in, such as Geoff Mitchell. The Department of the Interior's Centennial celebration project was truly a shot-in-the-arm for this park. It meant extra money for a plan already in motion.

"Well, then I'd say we're finished here."

He stood and offered his hand. Mo stood, too, and slipped a not–too-damp palm against his. Geoff Mitchell seemed reluctant to let her go. She saw his gaze dip down to chest level for the teeniest of moments. She should be more thankful that the great boobs hadn't yet sagged. The good Prof certainly gave them the once-over.

He cleared his throat when he caught Mo's eye and a tiny spot of color appeared along each cheekbone. Embarrassed at being caught in the act? She thought so.

"Well, if you don't have any questions, shall we say you show up Monday morning ready to work?"

"Are you giving me the job?" To her embarrassment the word 'me' seemed to have two syllables.

"Yes. I can't believe that we could find anyone better suited. I'd say you were exactly what we were looking for." He frowned. "I suppose we should discuss some of the particulars? Maybe you have questions? I'm sorry if I'm rushing things. I'm usually not the one doing any hiring at the University." He finger-combed his hair and looked earnest, then laughed. "I'm sounding a little desperate, aren't I? In order to be a success, the program needs good people. I really sense that you're one of those. But that doesn't excuse my not giving you a chance to voice any concerns." A sheepish look, "I think I flunked basic HR rules. Sorry."

She laughed, assured him he was doing fine and that she couldn't think of any questions. She knew the salary.

Claire had talked non-stop on the phone yesterday. The job was part time, twenty-five hours a week—at least, for now. But Claire warned that it could turn into something full time if the money came through. The institute was paying forty-five thousand with full benefits for someone to come in to photograph, sketch, and catalog all its Florida tropicals, orchid species included. It was a special set up, botanical gardens and research lab would continue after this celebratory year endowed by the Federal Government and supported by the rich until it could support itself. If the project was successful she assumed it would expand, turn into a full-time job that might lead to travel, some steamy rainforest on another continent that would offer a little hammock time, but she didn't want to give the wrong impression by asking about travel the first thing.

"I think I know the particulars." She smiled.

"Well then, that's that," he said, and smiled back.

It wasn't Mo's imagination. They both seemed reluctant to end the meeting. Another smile on his part, looking down at her through those dusty brown lashes. A little squeeze to her hand. Finally, he moved to open his office door.

"Thanks for coming in, Mo. I'm sincerely looking forward to working with you."

"Monday morning, then." Mo said, and this time turned and walked down the hall and out the front. His eyes never left her backside. She could feel them, along with a little hostility from the two rows of hopefuls who would soon be disappointed.

Chapter Thirteen

Monday already. The alarm pulled her from deep sleep at five forty-five. A hop on the treadmill for a thirty-minute jog, and there was still time to get there early. It was always best to impress the first day. She showered, allowed another thirty minutes for makeup—no lack of eyelashes today—and pulled on what Claire would surely consider "casual chic." An understated dusky pink silk canvas shirt and rose-brown cords, brown Mary Janes with a one-inch heel. A single pair of gold hoops swung from her ears—there were holes for three pairs but best to be conservative—at first.

He met her at the door of the conservatory. Seven-thirty and it seemed he'd spent the night there. Maybe he had spent the entire weekend there and not gone back to

Gainesville. He looked mussed as only a Brad Pitt lookalike could and still be incredibly handsome. Plus, he was out of sorts. Brusque with his greeting. Was she late? Maybe her day really started at seven. Or earlier? She hadn't asked. Her heart sank. She'd thought of nothing else but Dr. Geoff Mitchell all weekend. The smiles, the squeeze of the hand. What had happened? He seemed to not even see her. He motioned to two large greenhouses behind the Ocean Cliff house and began walking toward them.

"We'll start there."

Terribly curt, Mo thought as she fell in behind to single-file past a thirty foot cascading waterfall. So much for color coordination, she could be wearing sackcloth.

"We don't have an office for you yet. This was all such short notice. I mean suddenly there was this extra money and we felt it necessary to act. If you've identified a need and don't act immediately, you might not get more funding later. Some sort of government rule."

She wasn't sure what her response was supposed to be. Was this a nice way of saying she wasn't on a tenure-track?

"I don't have to tell you that this whole thing is a first for our area. The opportunity came along to establish a native plant research wing of Whitney because of the Centennial and we're making up the rules as we go." This time there was a quick smile as he turned to acknowledge her. Better. Whatever seemed to be bothering him was fading.

"As far as an office goes, the space isn't important as long as I have a safe place for my cameras." Surely Claire could help her with that. Pull a few strings.

"Yes, of course. We'll see to that. I could always get a locker stuck in somewhere."

There was an air lock on the first greenhouse, a space

that allowed visitors to close the outside door and seal out insects or changes in temperature before exposing delicate, tropical foliage. The first blast of warm, moist air was a gentle reminder that the cords were overkill.

"Well, welcome. I feel like I should carry you over the threshold. This will be your home for awhile."

Cute. Definitely losing his testiness. She laughed and felt relieved that he was loosening up.

"Listen, I'm afraid we're on stage for a big fundraiser three weeks from Friday. I know it wasn't something I mentioned in the interview, and I don't want to derail your getting started on the cataloging. We've put it off too long as it is. I tried to get out of it—your being new and all—but I pissed off two dowagers in the trying this morning. Money-makers are important. Especially at this stage. The Government has a tendency to help those who help themselves. 'Matching' is some magical word to Washington. So, some glamorized show-and-tell is our life's blood at the moment. I'd just thought we could get through the summer, let you get your sea-legs before becoming a mendicant.

"The project has worldwide appeal but it's especially important in North and South America—we're on a path to lose thousands of native plants, mostly orchids, in the next fifty years. Saving them involves growing them in a laboratory—some we can clone—but the goal is one million orchid seedlings, alive and thriving in five years."

He paused to look at her. "I'm going to need help with this event. It's the last week in May, a black-tie gala at the Casa Monica Hotel, highlighting the very new botanical gardens—I should say the yet-to-even-be-established botanical gardens, laboratory, and greenhouses. I'll offer select, guided tours of our progress here at the Whitney Labs in the afternoon, followed up that evening by several presentations at the Hotel. In the next two weeks, I expect two semis of native plants from around the state and Central America. Some from private collections will be brought separately. The bulk will come from the Everglades. All need to be entered, catalogued, photographed—well, I think you know what's expected. Usually, we have some time off after the regular school year. Think you could pitch in? It'll require some overtime—make that a lot of overtime—that I may not be able to compensate you for— at least not fully for starters. But I should be able to make it up."

So that's what was behind the testiness. Getting slammed with work but then it looked like some of that was dribbling downhill. Overtime wasn't a problem but speaking in front of an audience was.

"On stage? How do you mean that?" Claire hadn't mentioned this either. Mo feared public speaking right after thunderstorms—actually, most of the time the two were equal. Florida was known for having the most deaths by lightning. That almost drove her crazy. Even a hint of a thunderstorm and she was under the bed. "I'm not really a performer." She shrugged her shoulders and tried a rueful smile.

"Nor am I. But every once in awhile we need to pass the tin cup."

"Sans monkey?" Another one of Mo's little phobias.

"Absolutely." He laughed. "It'll just be me. Dog and pony shows are a part of my job. This place eats money. We still have one greenhouse to complete, and we're already about five hundred thousand delinquent. That is, if we intend to follow the board's suggested budget. You didn't catch the fine print in your contract about ass-kissing duties?" Another laugh.

Politics. Wasn't it everywhere? Mo relaxed. It was good to be a confidant and certainly Dr. Mitchell seemed to need one.

"I'd be uneasy with any speaking role, but maybe I could wear something skimpy and hand you things—I could practice my flourish. Maybe a Vanna White approach to horticulture?"

He laughed. "I like the skimpy part. But let's try to keep you off stage. I'll need you to put the cataloging on hold and help me put together a display that'll knock their socks off. At least, loosen some purse strings. Like the slide-show you did for your sister. We'll have an outside display, as well as inside. I thought I'd hang a number of *Oncidiums* on the hotel balcony near the side door. Lots of night bloomers are also heavily scented. There should be ample natural light that night—a full moon, the mulberry moon."

"The mulberry moon?"

"Creek Indian calendar. There's a wind moon, a harvest moon, a frost moon, and so on. The full moon in May is the Mulberry."

"Sounds like a night to remember. And don't worry about the overtime. I'm the committed type—I'd like to help."

"Let's see how eager you are after you see your office."

He had continued to walk down a ramp leading behind the displays and across a catwalk to a windowless 10' x 10' room that housed plastic display shelving. "Well, it's not much. But until we can find something else, think you can make-do? It can be locked."

And to think she'd made fun of Ben's back-of-the-building cubbyhole at the college. This was abominable. But would she be here very much? And it looked safe for camera equipment.

"Of course." She smiled and watched him sigh.

"I wasn't sure we'd keep you a second day after I showed this to you."

"I won't be here much of the time."

"True. Did I mention that there will be travel involved?"

"Claire did."

"Oh, good, then. No additional surprises. Once we're set up here I'll need someone to spend time in the Everglades—mostly collecting—but we need to know first what we're missing."

"Sounds like fun."

"Well, swampland, mosquitoes, alligators, unbearable heat—maybe not 'fun' exactly."

"I've read about the 'living dead.' The plants simply not strong enough to propagate and continue."

"Ah, the Florida Ghost Orchid and several others. Precisely the plants we hope to save and clone. Unfortunately, there are far too many on their way out. There are roughly twenty thousand species of orchids in the world—over fifty here in Florida. So many are in danger. This mission is critical but it will take money. So, first things first. It may be that you'll be working full time at the gardens in the very near future. I feel this project will be recognized for the value it offers the world of botanicals and will fast become more than a just showpiece part of the centennial activities." He beamed at her. "So, you won't be adverse to a little swamp time? Especially if it's part of a fulltime job?"

Hot and sweaty. But she'd be working with him. "Not at all." She beamed back.

The rest of the day was taken up with in-depth tours of each greenhouse, then a review of the paper work attached to all acquisitions—the few in place and the lists of those to come. He was most proud of the miniatures—a collection that included several endangered species. She didn't have to pretend; she was enthralled.

Many the size of her thumbnail—plant and all—produced jewel-like flowers of intricate color and form. Mauves, deepest purples, golds—if she were a collector, this would be it. She took the magnifying glass he offered and leaned over several tiny plants in bloom. Remarkable. Superb color. They sparkled like tiny gems.

"I've never seen a collection quite like this."

"Took half a lifetime to put together. You're looking at some prize winners. Not all of these are native but we've been able to introduce them to Florida's ideal climate and save a few lives. The University of Florida works with several botanical gardens throughout Mexico and Central America."

He turned and pointed to a row of look-alikes. "And I've been able to insure that many of the old specimens will be around for awhile. We almost lost the *Paph's Winston Churchill*. But it's back to being a staple." He paused and smiled, "I was always that geeky kid who'd rather play indoors. These are like old friends—we grew up together."

She was trying to imagine him as geeky—even putting an imaginary pair of black horn-rims on him didn't work. They moved on. The species collection was going to be vast—one entire greenhouse—and nothing less than spectacular. Several micro-climates existed in one huge domed laboratory. Delivery of hundreds of plants was due next week.

"Eventually we'll be taking some of these back to their original habitat."

"I didn't realize you replaced plants."

"Part of the current grant—that's why the emphasis upon having several laboratories. A lot depends upon our ability to not only preserve, but propagate."

They walked on in silence. The collection already set in place was really not to be believed. She hadn't been certain she'd get a chance to get her hands dirty, but she offered to tackle the repotting of the "big boys"—*Cattleyas* that had outgrown their pots and were stacked against the south wall of the third greenhouse.

"That's fantastic. These were delivered three weeks ago. One of those jobs that I never get around to. And I'm always reluctant to let student interns take a whack at it. I guess I'm not very trusting."

"Then I'm flattered." And she was. She smiled up at him. "I noticed bags of bark, some cutting tools, and disinfectant in the second greenhouse. May I help myself?"

"Anything you need. If you're missing something, use the intercom. I'll be in the office—gives me a chance to catch up on paperwork."

"What about dividing the pseudo bulbs? I don't mind making duplicate tags."

"I leave it up to you. Those guys have been ignored for a long time. They're going to need some pretty serious trimming back just to get control again."

The hug before he left was heartfelt and he added, "I've needed you. *We've* needed you." His gesture took in the greenhouse around them. "I'm really glad you're here."

She watched him walk back up the cinder path between the houses to finally disappear into the first building at the edge of the parking lot. She felt good. Suddenly life had promise. Purpose. And she hadn't thought once about lesson plans or small people with guns all day.

First misting and fertilizing and recording that data along with other statistics then finally the twenty, once ungainly, pot-defying Cattleyas were placed in new bark and clean containers, separated, staked, tagged and watered. She hadn't noticed the time and was startled when Geoff stuck his head in the door. "Hey, don't you think it's about time to call it a day?"

"It's five already?" They'd decided that three eight-hour days would comprise part-time.

"Five-thirty to be exact. Everything looks great. Good job." He started to close the door, then stepped back inside. "I was going to grab a bite in town. How about The Ice Plant? They have great drinks. Want to keep me company?"

"Perfect. My favorite place. Give me five minutes to clean up."

She followed him north on A1A . The drive along the ocean was always her favorite. The water was calm with a few whitecaps and lots of people fishing from the Matanzas Inlet Bridge. Offshore shrimp boats dotted the horizon. Suddenly the normality of it all sunk in. Life was good. Once again.

Chapter Fourteen

They were seated in the back, behind the enormous two-sided brick and wood bar that stretched across the room. Loft-high ceilings added atmosphere. Yet, it was cozy and warm and relaxing. It had been a long time since Mo had found herself enjoying being with another human. She could get used to this. She ordered a Paloma—grapefruit and tequila—and he had a craft beer. They toasted the project then dug into a fish dip with homemade chips before their Caprese salads arrived.

"Sorry about being out of sorts today. I hate being told what to do."

"The dowagers?"

"Yeah. I remind myself fifty times a day I wouldn't have a job without them—that usually puts things in perspective." He grinned. "Still, the soirées are really just a barely disguised staged event to show off their money. A little one-upmanship. A lot of people retire around here so that they'll be big frogs in a little puddle."

"But the cause is worthy—as you said. I used to overlook a lot of my principal's foibles just to stay at that school."

He nodded and sipped his wine. "Are you okay after the attack? Your sister filled me in on the particulars. I can't even imagine what it would be like to be threatened by an eight-year-old."

"Tough. But I'm getting there—moving on." Damn. She'd given him an opening to ask about what she'd really been trying to forget.

"It's going to be a hell of a transition—but I've never known a Phal to pull a gun. And I know they don't dress up as stuffed animals."

"I'm counting on that." She smiled. He was being sweet and he was studying her. It was all she could do not to squirm.

"What are the police saying?"

"No leads. At least none that go anywhere or even make sense. Appears to be a dead end. If one is going to commit a crime, it's probably not a bad idea to enlist kids—they have awful memories when it comes to details and usually a real fear of adults. Though the detective did tell me that the kid swears it was a woman in the Buckley suit and that she had a male accomplice—some guy driving a van."

"Wow. A woman? Is he certain? That's not the usual M.O. of felons."

"I know. But Toby wouldn't have a reason to lie. One

hypothesis is it was a random attack—gang related. It could have been any teacher. Maybe initiation rites, set up a kid to do a killing. In the old days, they used to just steal a car." She paused while the waiter placed their two salads on the table. "No one's questioning the involvement of adults—the whole thing was just too sophisticated for eight year olds. But the police would like to think I was chosen simply because I give homework."

"What do you think?"

"That theory is as good as any. Except that my passport was taken, and packet of family pictures from my house. I don't think a child did that. But who? And why?" She added the bizarre touch of an orchid spray sticking out of the eye socket of a tiny skull, then shrugged, "Nothing about it makes sense."

She was saved any other comments when Geoff excused himself and hailed a waiter for two glasses of wine—a New Zealand white, Flight Song, that he wanted her to try. The break was just what she needed to change the subject. Further conversation and questions between bites centered around his life … only child, deceased parents, best schools, an overriding belief in saving the planet. Never married. Yes, a trust baby. He was forty. She tucked every nugget of information away. Nine years difference in their ages. Wasn't that perfect?

She passed on getting a drink after dinner. The Paloma and a glass of wine were her limit. She was driving. And there would be time for drinks later. Now, she needed to keep a little distance between them. Not appear too interested—if that were possible. He walked her to her car, opened the door, gave a quick hug then turned to go, but first another thank-you for saving the Catts' lives. They could offer a few of the duplicates for sale at the soiree. Always an eye on making a dollar. The part of his job that he admitted to not liking. She adjusted the rearview mirror and watched him walk to his car. A superb restaurant, great glass of wine, good conversation—she could get used to this.

Going home now wasn't a problem. Mo sensed, somehow, that the "incident" truly was behind her. She had made real progress. A little over a week and her life had changed forever. And an exciting new job, to boot, with a man of interest … It didn't keep her from checking the doors and windows, however, and setting the new alarm the minute she got in—the gift promised by Claire and the good doctor. But she could sit in the kitchen in front of the windows, sip a cup of coffee, read the paper, and not jump at every sound or fear an intruder lurking in her closet. Tonight, she microwaved a cup of this morning's coffee, added cream, pulled a stool up to the butcher-block island, opened the paper she hadn't had time to read earlier, dug her phone out of the bottom of her purse and checked messages.

A call from Detective Foley—just checking in, he hoped she was doing well. A brief message from Mom, someone else checking in; and lastly a hang up. But not before the sound of a shot. She flinched and dropped her phone.

Not a firecracker. A single shot. And not the ping of a BB gun either. This was the explosive concussion associated with something high caliber. She sat upright, then leaned over, picked her phone up off the floor, and willed her heart to stop thumping. She tried to take a sip of coffee but lowered her cup to the table. Coffee sloshed on her hand as the cup chattered against the saucer.

She had to get control. Deep breathing. A help, but still the shakes. Could she have been mistaken? She wasn't going to play it again just to be sure. The call was made fifteen minutes ago. Someone who followed her home? Or one who had driven by her house and knew she wasn't home because she'd stopped leaving all the lights on? Or was she supposed to have received the call while driving? Maybe run off the road? Hit someone?

This was ridiculous. Was she going to overreact to every threatening sound the rest of her life? Maybe. But the sound of a shot slammed her right back to the "incident." Didn't someone know that? Of course. Wasn't it intentional? Or could it be some copy-cat follow-up? But by whom?

Dr. Pecos had agreed with Claire and had briefly touched upon Post Traumatic Stress Syndrome. Warned her that it could be a possibility with reoccurring bouts. And he'd stressed the need to have countermeasures firmly mapped out—the reaction to panic-attacks they had discussed. He'd assured her that he would be available to talk whenever she felt like it—it might not be such a bad idea now. A live, honest-to-God gunshot was a live honest-to-God PTSS trigger. And she better reiterate how to deal with it. She'd make an appointment in the morning.

Chapter Fifteen

Ben had left his phone on vibrate but the thing had just jiggled itself off the nightstand and onto the floor.

"Ben?" A very sleepy Julie turned over in bed. "Was that your phone?"

"Yeah. Not sure who's calling this early." But he'd already seen the caller ID—Tim Foley. What could the detective want at six-fifteen on a Tuesday morning? "I'm going to take it out on the balcony, go back to sleep."

"Hey, Detective Foley." Ben stepped out into the sunshine and closed the French doors behind him.

"We've got a new twist. Toby Wolff is missing. Local news is just breaking the story—thought you needed a heads up."

"Toby ran away?" Ben was wide awake now.

"I wish. That would be simpler. There's proof of abduction. No one discovered it until about a half hour ago. Looks like it happened late yesterday afternoon or early evening. Kids usually have an escort to the dining room. Apparently the usual escort took him to the dining room, but someone impersonating an orderly met him after dinner and failed to get him back to his room. The real orderly was found this morning bound with duct tape in the Pharmacy, which is locked up tight after four-thirty and doesn't open until six. Apparently the guy took a nasty blow to the head, so not a lot of help there."

"No one saw anything?"

"Not that we know of. Did Toby say anything when you met with him? Friday, wasn't it— just before you called? Nothing about visitors?"

"Nothing more than what I told you. He didn't even say anything about wanting to go home. Or missing playmates. He mentioned another psychologist who came to see him but that was all." Ben's thoughts flew in a hundred directions as the situation sank in. "Whoever took him has a twelve-hour lead."

"Don't remind me. But I think this turn of events points a finger closer to home—talk about a disruption to the upcoming Senate race. The parents are hysterical, as you can imagine. Puts any stumping and pressing of the flesh on hold."

Politics? Really? But when he thought about it, Ben had to agree. If someone wanted to keep a very viable, probable candidacy in check, this would be the way to do it. "Where are you even going to start?"

A short laugh. "That's the problem. I'll make sure all the players have alibis, but we don't have a person of interest, yet. I'll spend some time at the hospital, check visitors' lists, see if personnel noticed anyone hanging around. I'll talk to the shrink the hospital assigned. There should be tape from surveillance cameras—hallways and parking lot. Sure moved this case off the back burner in a hurry."

"Let me know if there's anything I can do."

"Will do. Thanks."

He turned back to the apartment to find Julie smiling at him from the bed, the sheet enticingly draped just below her waist. Her index finger beckoned him.

"You're distracted," she said, getting little reaction when she flung the sheet completely off.

"Yeah, sorry. My young patient was kidnapped."

"Oh, God, Ben." She pulled a silk wrapper around herself and followed him to the living room.

Ben flipped on the TV and started coffee. Pictures of Toby, then pictures of Toby with his parents, the hospital, interviews with personnel. Nothing new—nothing that Tim Foley hadn't just told him. He muted the TV and moved to his worktable to gather his notes. He'd goofed off all weekend and even yesterday. But who could blame him for a little sight-seeing with his new wife—well, not a lot of sight-seeing, more like a lot of togetherness behind closed doors. He glanced longingly toward the bedroom door where she'd gone to get dressed, but couldn't allow himself the luxury of following right now. Now, he needed to get some work done.

His first presentation would be on a timely, even popular, topic—the breakout berry—Saw Palmetto, the prostate healing drug known and sought after worldwide. Florida was a major contributor and legitimate farmers as well as those who deal in contraband flocked to Volusia and Flagler Counties every fall for the harvest. Of course, bears and other wildlife who made the berries a staple of their diets, combined with rattlesnakes, wasps, and bees competed with harvesters and made the work dangerous.

Ben was looking forward to this presentation. It would be interesting. He was scheduled to be part of the roster for the Whitney Lab's big fundraiser. He'd probably need to rent a tux. A night at the Casa Monica Hotel sort of dictated that. Just a little pressure—it was coming up in three weeks. He'd need pictures and the actual berries. Perhaps, he'd ask Mo Beltzer for help.

He'd just opened his laptop when his cell buzzed. Not a number he recognized but a local prefix.

"Dr. Pecos? Tobias Wolff here. I think you've heard from Detective Foley that my son has been abducted. I want you involved. Toby trusts you—he likes you and you have my total confidence. I had wanted to share once again that I appreciate your seeing him. He needs role models. He doesn't interact with many professional Indian men. And I want him found."

"Mr. Wolff, I'm sure Tim Foley will do everything in his power, use all available resources—support the Feds in any investigation."

"I don't share your enthusiasm or certainty. You forget, I'm a public servant. I know how thinly stretched those resources are. I'll pay you for your time. Keep track of it, plus mileage and meals—anything incurred in a search. I'll email my office address; send everything to my attention."

"I'm not sure I can be of help."

"You know the key players. I'm convinced that this episode with the teacher is somehow connected with his disappearance. Maybe you just need to keep an ear to the ground. His mother and I are frantic. It will mean a lot to us to know that you're helping out."

Another call coming in for the councilman, a quick

good-bye and Ben was left holding his cell phone, wondering what he'd just agreed to.

Chapter Sixteen

"Would you feel better if you carried a gun?" Dr. Pecos was watching her intently. Mo had gone into work at six Tuesday morning, worked until ten, left a note for Geoff —who was in meetings all day—that she was taking early lunch and then dashed downtown to Flagler College. They'd just spent fifteen minutes discussing the phone call where she'd heard a gun being discharged.

"I've thought about carrying."

"Are you comfortable with firearms?"

"Husband number one used to target practice. I'd go with him. I've killed a few beer bottles."

The doc didn't seem to find that funny, "I'm asking about you. Are *you* comfortable? Could you kill someone, if threatened?"

"I think so."

"I'm not convinced. But one positive step might be to buy a gun and take a course on handling it."

"Is that what you recommend?"

"It's just one possibility. It might give you a sense of protection."

"I need more than a 'sense.' What's an alternative?"

"I'm assuming by now we agree that locking yourself in the house and dining on lukewarm pizza is out." He was smiling.

Mo nodded. Was that an attempt at shrink humor? Or a way of reminding Mo of how far she'd come and making that comparison humorous? She guessed the latter. And realized the gun idea had some merit. Control. She would be in control. Alternatives seemed lame in comparison.

"There's something else we need to talk about. Detective Foley called this morning. It seems Toby Wolff was abducted last evening." Ben pointedly didn't mention Toby's father and how he'd been recruited.

"From the hospital? Abducted or did he just walk away?" Had she heard correctly? Toby? Who would take a child?

Ben told her what he knew. He hadn't heard anything more from Detective Foley but assured her that her case was now getting a lot of attention.

"So, it would seem there's some connection? Some link between what happened in the classroom and his being abducted? There would have to be. This just couldn't be random." She answered her own question. "I'd thought this would be over. I don't see any reason behind any of it. But to take a child—that's doubly criminal—I don't care what he's done."

"I agree. And leaving the sound of a shot in your voicemail seems to be some effort to prolong what happened to you. Keep you on edge. I'd like Tim Foley to help you find a firearm and instruction. And, please, tell him about the shot."

+ + +

She got back to the laboratory at twelve-thirty, a tuna sub in tow and bottled green tea with lemon. She chose the species greenhouse next to the waterfall for a lunch spot. Geoff's office was at the far end separated by a double thickness of Plexiglas. That's why it startled her to hear yelling. Angry yelling.

She left her sandwich on the bench and started toward thc office just as the outside door banged open and two men left, headed toward the parking lot. One was Geoff but the frosted glass window panels distorted a clear view of the other. There was a lot of arm-waving on Geoff's part, and she heard him yell, "Just do it."

But he stopped short at the edge of the walk and stared off to his right. Her car? Had he just realized she was back from lunch? She thought so as he turned and stared back at the buildings. After a quick visual sweep he was apparently satisfied that she hadn't heard.

The man walking with him had kept going and climbed into a dark pickup—without so much as a good-bye, as far as Mo could tell. The man was Hispanic, Mo thought. His truck with extra chrome had that south-of-the-border feel complete with mud flaps. Dr. Mitchell stood in the drive, fists clenched, arms at his side, before gesturing palms up, then turning and walking back to the first greenhouse.

How odd. This was a Dr. Mitchell she hadn't seen before. Was the other man a worker? Someone on contract to finish the laboratories and garden? She knew they were behind schedule but chalked it up to the time of year—building was always in full swing in the spring and summer. More beach houses, shops—Palm Coast, that bedroom community to the south was a contractors' and landscapers' paradise. Summer should be the perfect time to build but a couple hurricanes within a year's time had slowed construction in several states, in addition to Florida because construction crews were stretched thin.

"Sorry you had to see that." Geoff stepped through the vacuum door. "Seriously, I seldom lose it. I think the pressure is getting to me." A rueful smile.

"Construction worker?"

"Yeah, the foreman. Supposed to be overseeing everything from building to deliveries. A semi full of orchids from the Hollywood area was going to be delivered today. It's been scheduled for a month. Now he says he can't find a crew. He has access to illegals, which I finally told him to just hire—we'll worry about any consequences later. It's trouble if we get caught by the University— hiring unlicensed workers who are obviously not bonded. We have a list of suggested contractors but we've got a deadline that's fast approaching. I don't know what else to do. Listen, I'm going to be in a meeting all afternoon. There should be a couple interns to help you if you need them. I'll see you later."

She shrugged off his long-winded explanation, finished her sandwich, and decided to complete repotting the Cattleyas—she had found a few more that needed attention. If they were to be offered for sale, she needed to make certain the transplants were neat and inviting. She worked until four-thirty and then cleaned the repotting area and put her tools away. Geoff had not returned. In fact, the only company she'd had were two interns who said 'Hi' and wandered off. She was glad she hadn't needed them.

Tomorrow she'd get started on the presentation. She checked her camera equipment. Batteries were charged and flash attachments were in working order. She locked her office and made a mental note to bring her computer in.

She hadn't received any phone calls during the afternoon. She'd half expected Detective Foley to call, saying that Toby had just wandered away from the hospital after all and had been found safe and sound. But no such call, and it still wouldn't have explained the orderly who had been beaten unconscious and drugged. She put her phone in her pocket. There had been no other calls or voicemails.

She wouldn't have listened to them even if there had been. One discharged gun only meant it could happen again. Remembering Dr. Pecos's advice, she pulled her phone out and dialed Detective Foley's office. Besides being anxious to hear something about Toby, she needed to tell him about the phone call and follow up on Ben's advice—ask Foley if he could recommend classes on gun handling. She was serious about getting a gun. The more she'd thought about it the better it seemed. It was a chance to feel in control.

"I was just walking out the door. If you haven't eaten, why don't you join me? I'm going to stop at Gas."

She hadn't really thought about dinner, but she needed to get some food and the mention of the Gas restaurant sounded perfect. A refurbished gas station, with a sign a half a block from the restaurant admonishing, "You've just passed Gas!" Yeah, corny, but the restaurant was terrific and close—the other side of the Bridge of Lions—*and* they had comfort food. She instantly had visions of a heaping plate of "Not Your Mama's Meatloaf" with a side salad, or maybe just a little extra dollop of mashed potatoes.

The wind subsided to a slight breeze the minute the sun went down and less than forty-five per cent humidity. May and October—Florida's perfect weather months. Maybe she could get in some Sawgrass, Everglades time before it got too hot.

Detective Foley was already at Gas when she walked in and had snagged a booth near a window—no mean feat. There were six people waiting to be seated. He must have come straight here after they hung up. She almost didn't recognize him in civvies—jeans, black turtleneck sweater. A really good-looking man, dark brown hair short and combed straight back. Great eyes—dark as his hair but still expressive. But even taking into consideration his age—absolutely no comparison to Geoff Mitchell. There she went again—thinking of her boss … romantically. Mooning over something that wasn't. That couldn't be. And it was senseless to torture herself with 'what ifs' but it was that 'sense' thing again. There was a very real possibility she didn't have any.

The restaurant smelled like heaven—her mouth was watering. It had been far too long. Her mother was always yammering at her to cook for herself, think of the money she could save, but she knew she could never equal the meatloaf she was about to enjoy. Never. Not in this lifetime.

He got up and pulled out the chair opposite him, "Doing okay?"

"Pretty much." They ordered drinks—a couple craft beers and went ahead and put in their dinner orders. He was right about meeting here—this was far better than a cold metal folding chair in his office … in a basement.

"Please tell me you've found Toby." But she knew instantly before he shook his head, that the answer was a negative.

"I think we have half the force on it. And kidnapping always involves the Feds."

"But security on the grounds, surely there's footage of what happened—of Toby leaving or being lured away?"

"I had counted on it. But it's as if we're trying to track a ghost. Two south parking lot cameras weren't working, and that would seem to be the entrance and exit of the kidnapper. I should add they were electronically put out of commission. Nothing is as simple as cutting wires anymore."

Then she told him about the gunshot phone call.

"Time of call?"

"Here, let me check." She took out her brand-new iPhone—yes, an extravagance but the camera was exceptional—and put her purse back under the table. "I'd just gotten home so, maybe eight. Yes, seven fifty-five." She handed him the phone.

"May I play the voice mail?"

She nodded and willed herself to not put her hands over her ears.

"Forty-five."

"What?"

"Caliber."

"Oh." She looked up. She hadn't realized that she was braced for the shot; she forced herself to let go of the edge of the table.

He pressed replay again and then saw her flinch. "Sorry, I should have asked. I just needed to make certain there was nothing before or after."

"There's only the gun shot."

"I'm not so sure. There's a sustained one-decibel horn sound, a faint background white noise—actually like a foghorn. I think the call was either placed off shore or very close to the water. And when caller ID comes up 'no number', a giveaway that it's a burner."

"So why me?"

"To throw us off. Take time away from finding Toby—dilute forces. Keep you off balance. Take your pick."

"You think the two incidents are connected?"

"Yeah, I do. I may be alone in that and I can't prove it, but let's call it a hunch."

She took a sip of water. "Dr. Pecos seems to think I might feel safer carrying a gun."

"What do you think?"

"I've made up my mind to try it. I thought you might be able to suggest someone who's a certified instructor."

"Yeah, I can. Dave Colbert. Former cop, retired. Good rep—I think you'd like him." He pulled out a card and wrote a name and number on the back and handed it to her. "Let me know how it goes."

"I will."

"Do you own a gun?"

"Not yet."

"I might be able to help you out. Give me a call when you're ready to shop. It's seldom a matter of buying the first little chrome beauty you see. Let's see your hands. Right handed?"

She nodded and held her hands in front of her. He

reached for her right hand, turned it over palm up and spread her fingers.

"First off, you're probably going to need oversized grips."

She yelped and grabbed her hand back. Shades of her first date. The same thing had happened to her in Junior High. Then the boy had dropped her hand and said that under the circumstances, because her hand was so big, she could hold *his* hand. She refused. Only as an adult did she begin to appreciate pragmatism in males.

"Hey, why so sensitive? You have great hands."

She mumbled through the first date fiasco, then apologetically added, "Sorry, guess I'm still a little self-conscious."

"Trust me, the guy's a loser—then and probably now." He was grinning.

She was saved any further conversation by a waiter putting a steaming plate of meatloaf and mashed potatoes in front of her and a chicken pot pie covered in gravy in front of Detective Foley. Conversation was kept to a minimum and consisted mostly of raves about the food. Another beer and Mo found herself relaxing—probably tough to stay hyped over .45 caliber shots with what looked to be a double helping of garlic mashed potatoes.

"Coffee? Or dessert?" The waiter was busy clearing their table.

"Not for me." Not after the mashed potatoes, Mo thought. She needed to feel virtuous about something.

"Going to have to pass, too. I have an exam in the morning at the academy and need to run. I know you know what I'm going to say—call me, day or night, if you see anything out of the ordinary. Nothing is inconsequential.

At least, let me decide that. You're being stalked and harassed. Don't take it lightly."

He must have sensed her resignation. But maybe it wouldn't just go away. "I want you to make that call to Dave Colbert. Get enrolled as quickly as you can. I'll send you the paperwork for concealed carry."

"Thanks."

He touched her on the arm, "I want you in that class. Promise you'll give it a try?"

She nodded. "I promise."

"Good." He stood looking at her, "You know, next time, I'm having the meatloaf.

I think you're on to something." A wide grin as he paused by the cash register. "This is my treat."

He walked her to her car and again asked her to not buy a firearm without him.

Chapter Seventeen

Sometimes Mo just needed to give herself a little pep talk—a reminder of what was what. These talks usually centered around the opposite sex. And she needed one of those talks badly. She couldn't believe how in 'Wow' she was over Geoff Mitchell—she couldn't stop thinking about him. She hadn't missed having a man in her life.

Claire gave up on fixing her up after the first six months sans husband number two. So, what made this thing she had over one Geoff Mitchell different? How could she be so star-struck? But wasn't it more? She thought so. They shared so many of the same interests. They enjoyed talking. They laughed easily. They were comfortable together. There, the word never to be uttered in a relationship. Comfortable.

And wasn't there a saying about keeping one's genitalia out of one's salary? She was smarter than this. She wanted this job; she needed this job. Wow. She sounded just like Ginny. But it was true. Because she had as much as quit the career of her dreams. Blaylock's turning the decision over to the school board would, no doubt, result in a long commute to a bad neighborhood, *if* she even got a classroom assignment. Mortgage be damned. Well, maybe not, but wasn't the job Claire found a godsend?

But even with a couple dozen pep talks, she couldn't keep things from just happening. She and Geoff made it until the following Wednesday working together, having lunch a couple times. She knew he had lots of other more pressing duties but he'd hang out with her, watching her stage his miniatures for the camera. Little looks and "Oops, sorry, didn't mean to bump your arm," finally led to a plain old-fashioned kiss. Well, maybe not so plain. She'd just stood up from using a toothpick to stake a tiny dendrobium against a wine cork when he'd put his hands on her shoulders and turned her to him.

He brushed her hair back, looked into her eyes and traced an outline of her lips with his index finger, then leaned in and softly, at first, kissed her, then pulled back only to lean in again and with a moan—hers? his?—nibble at her bottom lip before tracing the outline of her lips with the tip of his tongue. She honestly thought her knees would give way as he pulled her to him and with lips parted, both covered the ravenous hunger of mouth upon mouth, tongues teasing, her fingers digging into his shoulders then arms coming up to wrap around his neck.

Reluctantly, they parted. Not sated, but appeased. Both a little breathless; she tried to even out her breathing but still couldn't bring herself to look in his eyes. Was this for real? Was he really feeling the same way?

He looked pensive, kind of shrugged and sighed before sitting on a potting bench, leaning back, and looking up at her.

"You know this is dangerous." He suddenly seemed somber like good sense had reared its ugly head.

She only nodded. She was frozen in place. Why did she expect it—whatever 'it' was—to just go poof? It was insane to feel this way. *Too much, too soon. Back off,* screeched the good angel of her conscience. But when had she ever listened?

"Because federal grants are such fragile things and because I was stupid enough to only interview *you* before hiring, a relationship could get us into trouble … could lose us the grant. At the very least cost us our jobs. There are always people waiting in the wings to blow the whistle."

Again, a mute nod.

"That doesn't negate my feelings. I tell myself that I chose the best qualified—and I know that's the truth—but then I think of that body. I wanted to jump you the minute you walked through my office door. Okay, okay, I like your mind, too." He laughed, brushed his hair back and looked up at her. "I've grown to care about you, Mo. Really care." Then with a shake of his head, "This is insane."

Her words exactly. She took a deep breath and swallowed hard. "I didn't plan on this."

"Nor did I. But I suppose the question is, what do we do now? Under any other circumstances I'd spend every waking minute with you—and more than a few when I wasn't awake. This is becoming painful. I don't want to sneak around. I want the world to see how I feel."

Again, she just stood there. What would they do? How could they walk away from each other? She waited. Wasn't it up to him to define how they would continue?

Finally, he sat forward, "I value my job and my reputation. I value your reputation. We're doing important work here. I want us to act professional and pretend this never happened."

"You expect that to work?" Frankly, she was shocked. Could he just turn off his feelings? And what about hers? She hadn't initiated the kiss.

"I expect you to make it work … and me, of course." Just a touch of testiness. He really was distraught.

"Of course. You have my word." Frosty. But she was ticked.

"Mo, please—"

"No, it's all right. I understand. Now if you'll excuse me, I need to download these pictures."

"Mo, I'm sorry. I shouldn't have overstepped boundaries. Mo?"

She turned, didn't answer, and didn't look back—simply picked up her camera and walked out the door. She knew he just stayed seated and watched her go.

Chapter Eighteen

A m I in jail?"
   "No, Toby."
"Is my dad gonna come pick me up?"
"Not today."
"Why not? Does he know where I'm at?"
"No, he doesn't."
"I need to call him. Can I have my phone?"
"I don't have your phone, but it wouldn't work real well out here anyway."
"I don't like this place. I want to go home. I want to see my friends."
"No can do, little man. Come on, finish your hamburger."
"I don't like McDonald's."

"There's even a toy. Drink your apple juice."

"That's for babies."

"Okay, I'll get Whataburger tomorrow."

"Does that hurt?" Toby pointed to his arm just below the elbow.

"My tat?"

Toby nodded.

"No. Well, maybe a little bit when I got it. A tattoo is done with needles and ink. Do you know what this is?" The captain pulled his shirt sleeve up further and held his arm out.

"Yeah, it's an anchor. Like on a boat."

"Right."

"I want to watch TV."

"No TV out here. You're in a boat—a boat on the ocean."

"This boat stinks."

"Stinks like money." The man laughed. "You know what shrimp are? Well, this here's a boat that we use to catch 'em. I'm going into town tonight. You got a bunk here and a sleeping bag, and to make sure you stay put, I'm gonna lock that door. This is a nice cozy cabin, you'll be fine."

"Why can't I go with you?"

"Gotta keep you safe."

"This boat doesn't have lights."

"That's right and it's going to stay that way." The man walked to the door, turned and locked it behind him. As he lowered himself into the power skiff moored on the backside of the trawler, he could hear Toby yelling and kicking the door.

Well, maybe he'd tire himself out. He listened for a

couple minutes. Kid was determined, not one of those whiners, he'd give him that. But kidnapping? And a killing? He been told to get rid of him. But he hadn't signed on for any capital offense.

He'd killed before; it wasn't that. It was the fact that it was a kid. A stupid innocent kid who probably knew more than was good for him. He figured the kid could just disappear and he'd decide what to do with him. Later. Nobody needed to know. In the meantime his part of the take just went up a couple hundred thousand. And if nobody wanted to pay, then a nice tidy ransom from the kid's parents would make up the difference.

Chapter Nineteen

Staying in bed until ten, then a coffee and croissant run, or maybe a walk down to the Casa Monica for breakfast on the balcony—not bad. Ben could learn to live like this. Problem was, however, he wasn't getting anything done—research, pictures, a visit to a couple parks—all on the back burner. Now he'd also agreed, or at least didn't refuse, to help search for Toby. He sighed. Time was becoming a scarce commodity.

There had to be limits to the honeymoon phase, as Julie liked to call it. He was afraid to ask what came after this "phase." He just knew he had to get to work. First on his list of stops would be Marineland and Whitney Labs. Julie would love it. Who could turn down a tour of the place where *Creature of the Black Lagoon* was filmed?

"You're kidding, that old 50's classic?"

"Scout's honor, one and the same. Plus, I'd like you to meet Mo Beltzer."

"The teacher who got bounced over the gun incident?"

Ben nodded. "Yeah, a really bizarre bunch of circumstances. And the kid who pointed the gun hasn't been found."

Channel Two had kept the story front and center for three nights now on the evening news— fueled, no doubt, by the notoriety of the family, Ben thought. He was truly interested in how Mo was doing, but he also needed to ask for help. Before he started collecting items for his 'show and tell' presentation, he needed a corner of a greenhouse to keep them. He'd lined up a potted Palmetto Palm and been promised several stalks of berries. Thank God, he owned a pickup. But maybe, on the way out of town, he'd stop at the hospital. There was a chance the psychologist who was seeing Toby might be able to tell him something.

+ + +

Ben had called ahead and Dr. Hardy met him at the information desk. After promises to Julie that he'd only be ten or fifteen minutes, at most, Ben had asked her to wait for him. He needed the doc to feel comfortable sharing information, which probably dictated a chat just between the two of them.

"Let's take a walk." Dr. Hardy signed out and pointed to a door at the end of the hall. "All right with you if we go watch some ducks swim?"

"I think I'm on a first-name basis with those ducks." They took a graveled path that led away from the hospital and the surrounding parking lot.

"How about the bench to your right? Toby and I spent some time out here. It's also where he visited with his parents."

Wrought iron and wood didn't exactly make for the most comfortable seating, but it was a quiet area shaded by live oaks and magnolia and only about twelve feet from the edge of the pond.

"Thanks for meeting on such short notice. I've been asked by the family to help find Toby, and I'm at a bit of a loss. There doesn't seem to be any clear-cut place to start."

"I'm going to share with you what I told the police and it could be something … or absolutely nothing at all." A pause, Dr. Hardy appeared to be collecting his thoughts. "I think the first time I noticed it was two days before Toby was abducted. We were sitting here. It was just after lunch—maybe one o'clock—and I noticed Toby tense, go perfectly stiff actually, and I realized he was watching something out on the road." He pointed some two hundred feet to the road that bordered the pond on the north. "There was a slow-moving white van that actually rolled to a stop as we watched. No one got out. It just sat there, but Toby was clearly scared to death. He insisted on returning to the hospital—ran ahead of me in his haste to go back in."

"Can you describe the van?"

"It's amazing how nondescript a white van can be. Paneled sides, probably double-door opening in back, though I couldn't see from this distance."

"What about markings?"

"Again, distance was a problem but there appeared to be signage on the passenger-side door. No making out what it said but it appeared to be a delivery van. The interesting thing is, it was also here the next day—the morning of the day Toby was taken. I had walked down to the pond on my way into work, looking for a favorite pen I'd misplaced, and there it was again—parked in almost the same spot only this time someone inside appeared to see me and took off."

"Believe it or not, this is a big help. It would seem to conclusively tie together the incident of receiving the gun from people in a white van and his abduction. Can't be a coincidence that someone in a white van seemed to be casing the hospital and someone in a white van singled him out to shoot his teacher."

He wondered what the police were doing with this information. And it gave Ben something else to ask Mo Beltzer and the Wolffs about.

+ + +

A1A was fast becoming his favorite diversion. He used every excuse to drive along the ocean highway. Yeah, the mountains of New Mexico were pretty impressive, but the Atlantic was absolutely awe-inspiring. Mesmerizing, actually. Evenings weren't complete without a walk on the beach, and Julie agreed.

The cab of his truck was full of sand and there was a treasure trove of mismatched, scruffy, chipped shells— calico scallops, oysters, jingle shells, keyhole limpets ... maybe three or four in the hundred-fifty or so littering the floor boards were real keepers. He just didn't have the heart to tell Julie. Anyway, wasn't beauty in the eye of the beholder? Or however that old saying went.

Mid-week and there were only a half-dozen cars near the two-story research lab and office complex, because over half the parking lot was taken up with an eighteen-wheeler and an ant-perfect line of people unloading it. Overlooking the Intracoastal waterway, the building housed a four-hundred-seat auditorium and ample foyer, in addition to lecture areas, labs and rooms of holding tanks containing every aquatic specimen imaginable. There was even a nationally recognized sea turtle rehab center within the complex.

The newly erected greenhouses towered over the parking area at the north end of the lab's property, behind and to the side of several low-profile, single-story offices. The lab's location, a couple blocks off of A1A and another half block from the ocean, was perfect. The true tourist attraction, Georgia Aquarium's Marineland, complete with gift shop and housing for several dolphins, had its own parking facility ocean-side.

Julie leaned against the wooden railing along the walkway leading to the ocean. The day was perfect, a light breeze fluffed her shoulder-length, strawberry blond hair, blowing an errant strand across her cheek. The air felt fresh and spring-like. For someone from Arizona, the ocean was a treat.

"I love it out here," she said.

"I thought you might. Did you know that before there was a Sea World, there was a Marineland?"

"Seriously?"

"Yep. Used to be a big tourist attraction. Only place you could get up close to dolphins. You can even sign up to swim with them today. It's still a big draw."

"I think I just added something to my 'to do' list."

The semi was almost empty before Mo joined Ben and Julie at the entrance of the first greenhouse.

"Tell me Toby's been found," she asked eagerly.

Ben shook his head. "Not yet." He quickly introduced Julie and shared the information about a white van. "Mean anything to you? Know anyone, any business that uses one? Maybe made deliveries to Jefferson Elementary?"

"Not that I can think of."

"Have you talked with Tim Foley about a firearm class?"

"He recommended someone. I'm going to call this afternoon."

"Could you reserve a place in class for me, too?" Julie asked.

Ben was surprised but didn't show it. In fact, it was probably a good idea. There were lots of lonely stretches of roads in Florida. Someone out researching a story might not always be near civilization. A gun for Julie made sense.

Chapter Twenty

S elf-protection—don't leave home without it, Dave speaking." He'd answered on the first ring.

Mo name-dropped Tim Foley and asked about classes. Dave Colbert invited her to stop by that Saturday and sit in on a class. It was the first in a series of eight. If she liked it, she could join. They met at the Armory on San Marco Avenue.

She said she'd be there. And, oh yes, there would be two of them; she gave Julie's name. Dave made a point of ten sharp—door was locked at one second after. Hadn't Tim said he was former military in addition to his work on the force?

Oh well, it wouldn't cost her anything to visit and it would be fun to spend some time with Julie. She missed interacting with friends. A beer after work, a dinner out … she'd been isolating herself, hiding from reality. Maybe that's why dinner with Geoff had meant so much. And why his dumping her hurt. She really was ready to rejoin the human race.

+ + +

Eight women and two guys. What did that say about the interest in self-protection? Of course, if Mo were really looking at the total picture, what guy would admit to needing a class on shooting? She looked closely at the two men. A computer dweeb of about twenty—bet his parents wouldn't even let him have a BB gun growing up—and an older man, maybe seventy, retired professional of some kind. Probably just wanted to be able to fast draw a little something out of the glove box if accosted on a camping trip. But it was hard to say. There was a heavily chromed six-shooter poking out of a sack at his feet.

The women were another thing. Easier to read. Young, old, middle-aged—they covered the gamut. And probably every one of them had a story to tell. Something threatening or frightening—certainly Mo fit into that category. The older ones hugging purses on their laps, afraid to relax— they weren't here to enjoy themselves. The younger ones chatting and laughing—one twenty-something was showing off a derringer. Derringer? Did they even make those things anymore?

She and Julie chose two seats down front—a row in front of the dweeb and next to the Roy Rogers wannabe. There were three presenters but Dave was in charge. The first hour was lecture. Dave trying to intimidate. If you owned a gun you better be able to use it. And be able to kill. Some stats on how many are killed by their own guns just because they couldn't pull the trigger.

Not Mo. She was certain she could kill—not that she wanted that tested, but she knew she could. Dave zeroed in on a cute blond in the front row who finally burst into tears with his badgering, blurting out she only needed a gun to scare her ex, not kill him. Dave suggested she find a school that specialized in scare tactics and stock up on pepper spray. The blond left class.

What an asshole. But he was probably effective, and what he said was the truth. She could give up eight Saturday mornings for peace of mind. She briefly looked at the agenda. Four in-class activities—Basic overview introductory lecture (that was today), choosing your weapon (this included a field trip to a local gun shop), cleaning your weapon and trouble-shooting mechanical problems (apparently handgun to cannon), discussion and test over what constitutes a 'legal' kill and related issues (if you shoot him and he's going out the window, drag him back in), and the last four sessions would be on the range (bring your own weapon). That's what Mo looked forward to.

Mo picked up two applications during break and handed one to Julie. "What do you think? Are you in?"

"The instructor leaves a little to be desired—personality-wise. He was a little rough on the girl who wanted to scare her ex. But he has a point. I'm in."

At the end of class, Mo handed Dave the two applications and checks for two hundred dollars each and turned to leave.

"How do you know my friend, Tim?"

"He's working a case I'm involved in."

"Murder?"

"Not yet." She thought she saw the beginnings of a smile but then it was back to business.

"Nice to have you with us, Ms. Beltzer and Ms. Pecos. I look forward to working with you both."

Mo waved good-bye to Julie, then started the Volvo but reached for her phone. She needed to set up a time to pick out a gun. She had to admit she was really getting into this.

"Detective Foley? Just thought I'd give you a report."

"So, you sat in on a class?"

"Yep. And I think I'm going to like it. Oh, and before I forget, Dave Colbert says 'Hi'." A bit of a fib but she was sure he wouldn't mind.

"He has some real asshole qualities but he knows what he's doing. Did you sign up?"

"Paper-work and money already handed in."

"Great. Under the circumstances, I think it's the best thing to do."

"Are you still up to helping me find my weapon of choice? In fact, I should invite Julie Pecos—think you can handle two of us?"

"Absolutely. I have some time off over the weekend. I'll give you a call."

+ + +

What to do with the rest of the afternoon? Grocery shopping, never a favorite, still had to be done. And the dry cleaners—this would be a perfect time to take those slacks in to get them hemmed. Another thing her mother thought she should be able to do herself. She'd grab a quick lunch at the house and then start on errands.

Toasted cheese and a cup of tomato soup—and she was out of there. Only she just remembered; she'd written her last check to Dave Colbert and had left the box of new checks at the office. Damn. She had thought she was being so smart having the bank bypass the house—not trusting that someone wasn't watching her mailbox out front. Oh well, not a problem. She'd run by the office first.

The parking lot was empty but for the same black truck she'd seen the day she'd overheard the argument. Working a weekend? He must have access to overtime. She unlocked the first greenhouse and pushed through the vapor-locked outer entry locking the door behind her. Her office was in the second greenhouse just inside the door, but it was easier and warmer to walk through this way. Besides she'd use any excuse to look at the species—so many were in bloom right now.

But the minute she opened the second greenhouse, she knew something was wrong. Two Hispanic men, one on a twenty-foot aluminum ladder were picking orchids off of corkboard and tree trunks and dropping them into a huge burlap bag. They were half the length of a football field away but she knew beyond a doubt they were stealing, and being discriminate. One of the now-empty spaces in the corkboard had held a very rare miniature.

"Hey!"

Both men turned at her yell, and the taller one steadying the ladder pulled a gun from his belt, took aim and fired.

The bullet went wild nicking one of the metal support poles to her right. She knew the shooter would adjust and the next one would hit her. She saw him already moving toward her at a run, slowed only by the rows of seedling trays on high stand-alone shelves which he pushed out of his way.

She was literally six feet from her office. She bounded up the three steps, keys in hand, opened the door, almost fell inside, slammed the door shut, locked it, and pushed the metal desk squarely against it just as a bullet ripped along the door jamb.

Nine-one-one. She grabbed her phone from her purse, slumped to the floor, and dialed. Another shot, then another, both glancing off the metal door. Lucky for her, he didn't seem to have sufficient fire power. But even luckier, her cubicle was made of insulated sheet metal with two-by-four studs.

The operator picked up immediately. Mo's teeth were chattering but she gave her name, the address, and what was happening. She was even able to give Geoff's number before she slipped down to a prone position behind the desk to wait. But she knew they were gone. Probably with gunny sack in hand. She wasn't going to move the desk to make certain, but the quiet seemed to seep under the door.

Two squad cars were there in under five minutes. And so was Dr. Mitchell. She remembered he rented a seaside condo—maybe three minutes away. The next thing she knew, he was banging on the office door.

"Mo? Are you all right? Open the door. They're gone." He sounded frantic. That gave her a tiny thrill.

She moved the desk to one side and opened the door about a foot.

"Oh, God, Mo … I was so worried." He pushed the door open the rest of the way and she had to admit he looked scared to death. He grasped her arms above the elbows, but she gave a tiny shake of her head and pulled away. She stepped out the door. No matter how upset he was, it was suicide to let anyone see a show of affection—even under the circumstances. She might not like what they had to do, but she was rational.

"This is all my fault. I know the value of what we have here. I should have hired guards. All the publicity we've gotten has made us sitting ducks for theft." He seemed absolutely distraught as he followed her out onto the five-by six-foot metal mesh balcony. "Jesus. Look at this."

Mo leaned against the railing and surveyed the damage. A mess. Rows of seedlings knocked to the gravel, gaping holes where various plants had been staged high above the greenhouse floor. She was devastated.

He stood beside her, "As much as these plants are my life, the only thing that matters is that you're safe. You could have been killed, and I would never have forgiven myself."

He leaned on the railing next to her, his arm touching hers. She wanted to turn into him, bury her head in his chest, feel his warmth and know his safety, and hang on. Of course, she didn't. She couldn't.

Instead, she was simply businesslike, "They were taking orchids from that corner." Mo pointed to the ladder still leaning against a cork wall, and was secretly proud that her voice was strong, no shakes, no weak knees. "I won't be certain until I get a closer look but I think ten Guatemalan miniatures were taken. I'd just finished photographing that area."

"Are you okay?"

She turned. Tim Foley was addressing her but his eyes were taking in the roughed up doorjamb.

"I think you can be relieved that they were shooting .22s. Twenty-two longs to be exact." He had a shell casing in the palm of his hand. "Must have had some sort of Saturday night special. You're lucky. It's nice to find you in one piece." That boyish grin and more than just a hint of familiarity—which wasn't lost on her boss, she noticed. Geoff's smile was a little forced as he turned and held out his hand.

"I'd like you to meet my boss, Dr. Geoff Mitchell. Detective Foley has been handling my case from school."

"Is there someplace where we can talk?" Foley asked. "I need to get started on a report. I'd also like your input, Dr. Mitchell. Can you make a rough assessment of what's missing?"

"Rough, but close. Because of the grant status, most of the rare plants have been evaluated recently. We can meet in my office—through there."

Geoff's private office was not only comfortable, but spacious—big enough to contain a full sized conference table and ten chairs. Two high-backed leather occasional chairs faced each other in front of a large oak desk with a coffee table in between. Wood paneling in a muted gray ash was a nice professional touch—along with the two Persian rugs in navy and cream. Opulent. But he would have to have a place to meet with the dowagers. Still, she'd had no idea. He was on loan but it looked like he thought his would also become a permanent position.

Geoff pulled out a chair for her at the conference table. She was facing a wall map some ten feet in length, a map of the world with different colored pins and tiny flags— probably with the names of species from that area. There was a cluster of pins in Costa Rica and twenty in the state of Florida. Geoff sat at the end and Tim across from her. The detective had taken out a notebook and was reading a page of text before turning to her.

"Let's start with Mo. Do you usually work Saturdays?"

She shook her head and reiterated how she'd had her order of new checks sent to her office and stopped by to pick them up on the way to run errands.

"Did you notice anything unusual when you pulled up?"

"There was a black pickup in the parking lot. I'd seen it here before and I assumed it belonged to a worker."

"Did you get a plate?"

"Frontera—Chihuahua. The truck's a newish model Ford 150 with lots of chrome and wide mud flaps. The kind with the outline of a nude in repose."

"Mexico. This mean anything to you?" He'd turned to Geoff.

"Yeah, unfortunately it does. The truck belongs to Trini—Trinidad Garza. He'd worked here for maybe six months, had signed on as foreman over the entire operation. Unfortunately, I had to fire him last week."

"Because?"

"Not dependable. I couldn't count on him to get things done. He was in charge of deliveries and he headed up the construction crew working on the fourth greenhouse. We're way behind schedule."

"Was he upset?"

"Yeah, there was a lot of yelling and finger-pointing. Deliveries were behind because of a lack of drivers, and he'd been having trouble finding reliable framers. Maybe that was the truth—but it wasn't an answer I could share with the directors. They just want to see results. The money was allocated months ago." Geoff pushed back the lock of dark blond hair that fell over his left eye. "I had no idea that he would come back—"

"Did he have keys?"

"I'd collected what he had, but I'm sure he'd had dupes made. There doesn't seem to be sign of a break-in. I feel like this is my fault. But I had no reason to think he'd be violent or steal from the foundation, for that matter."

"Would he know what to take?"

"Looks like he did."

"Any idea of worth?"

"Not without doing an inventory. It's not going to be less than 25K and could run as high as 300K. I'm assuming he was stopped before they'd had a chance to pick up any endangered species. But I'll have to check. That could put the tab way up there."

A low whistle. "I had no idea. Are orchid plants something he could easily fence?"

"Yes, with the right connections. There are a few, what we call, world-buyers. If he has access to them, the plants are gone within twenty-four hours. There's quite a network."

Tim turned to Mo, "I'm glad you're getting a gun. You've ended up in a dangerous business."

"A gun?" Geoff was looking at her with disbelief and disapproval.

"Yes, I started classes this morning."

"I think that's an insane idea. Don't you know how many people get killed with their own gun? You're inviting trouble. If you don't know how to use it—"

"I think that's the purpose of classes—I'll know how to use it."

"But could you kill someone?"

"Yes, if threatened."

"I don't believe you. There's nothing I've seen in your behavior that even suggests that capability."

They were skating on thin ice here. One, Mo felt herself getting angry—how dare he tell her what she could and could not do; and two, he was beginning to suggest that he 'knew' her, perhaps, more than being just an employee could account for.

"I think it's a great idea. I have faith in Mo." Tim not only put an end to the bickering but managed to tick Geoff off with what must seem like one-upmanship. Mo wanted to smile, but couldn't.

"Well, she won't bring it in here." Geoff crossed his arms and leaned forward on the desk.

"If she has a permit to carry, she will." Detective Foley countered.

"Hey, that's a couple months off. If I don't feel comfortable carrying a gun, I won't. But I think classes are going to be invaluable. Today made a believer out of me." Time to defuse the discussion, move on *and* stand up for her rights.

Tim looked back at his notes. "I'd like to see if your descriptions of this Garza match."

"I know it's the person Dr. Mitchell fired. I overheard the shouting that day—not what was being said but how—lots of anger and door-banging." She couldn't help but notice Geoff's raised eyebrows—a look of complete surprise. "I heard him say, 'just do it', before this Garza took off in his truck."

"I thought I was being a little more circumspect than that. But I have to admit, the guy got to me. Nothing but excuses."

"I still need a description."

"Five-eleven, beer gut, dark hair cut short, florid complexion, black mustache, one gold tooth in the front, always wears a straw cowboy hat with a broken brim—"

"It was a solid brown felt one today." Mo interrupted. She only remembered because it had fallen off—caught on an edge of a seedling rack—and he'd paused to scoop it up.

"He's in his forties. I believe has a family in Chihuahua. My guess is that's where he's headed."

"Identifying marks?"

"Tattoo of an anchor and chain on his right forearm."

"Anything else? Mo?" She shook her head.

"I have an application on him somewhere. If I remember correctly, there's a local address and phone—possibly not legit, though, or maybe it's a relative. He was recommended; I admit to not checking credentials. We've needed to get this project off the ground in record time. A few corners have been cut. He had a green card—that was my main concern."

Geoff went to the credenza behind his desk and pulled out a cardboard folding file. "If it's not here, it's online. My secretary is only part-time but she just about has us totally electronic." The first file didn't have what he wanted, but he found it on his desk computer. He quickly made a copy and handed it to Tim.

"This is enough to get him in the system. Thanks to both of you. I'll make sure you and the foundation get a copy of my report."

Mo and Geoff gave Detective Foley the grand tour on the way to the front door of Greenhouse One, Geoff pointing out some of the more expensive inhabitants. Tim seemed truly impressed.

"If you're ready to leave, I'll walk you to your car." Tim turned to Mo.

"Thanks, Let me get my purse. I'll be just a minute." She turned to go back to her office, and didn't even glance at Geoff Mitchell.

"Got time for coffee?" Tim opened the door to the Volvo for her. Who said chivalry was dead? He closed the door and leaned down, palms of both hands balanced against the car's roof as the window whirred down. She found herself hoping Geoff was watching.

"Sure." The afternoon was pretty much a loss, but she could go to the drycleaner later. "Starbucks? It's close."

Ten minutes later, they had a table by the window, and now the west-facing glass's warmth felt good.

"Ever think of finding another job?" he asked.

"I hear teaching elementary school is nice and safe."

Tim laughed. "Okay. Stupid question. I suppose there's nowhere safe. I think I should know that." He stirred his coffee and dumped in a second packet of sugar. "By the way, I'm not buying the construction-worker-as-thief theory. Doesn't it seem odd that someone who hired on to build a greenhouse and oversee crews of workers would know what to steal? Seems like pretty specialized knowledge, what's rare and what's not, no?"

"Yes, very specialized. Maybe he's working for someone."

"Or maybe we'll find a gunnysack full of plants in the alley and can chalk it up to malicious retribution for being fired, like your boss seems to think."

"I'd rather see the plants in the hands of a black market collector than just tossed."

"I'd say the fact that you were shot at says it was more than just getting even. The stakes are usually higher if you have to get rid of a witness—a carjacker kills, someone just keying your car doesn't."

She was quiet for a moment. "He definitely knew what he was after. The guy on the ladder was following orders— at least, I remember it seemed like that. This Garza would point and the other guy would take down a plant and put it in the bag. I saw that much. And the fact that they were in the corner by the miniatures says they knew value and where to look."

"Do you know which ones were taken?"

"I'd bet the Kegeliella kupperi is gone. It's very rare. An endangered Costa Rican specimen."

"Any idea of its worth?"

"No, not really, but several thousand—over a hundred thousand probably. It was a specimen plant—fully mature, blooming in exceptionally rich color—deep maroon and cream. In that corner of the greenhouse, there were probably half a million in plants."

"Wow. I wasn't certain whether your boss was telling the truth or just blowing things up a bit to make us act." He paused. "Doesn't it strike you as odd that this treasure trove wasn't protected?"

"In retrospect, yes. But I know of lots of private collections that make do with nothing more than a burglar alarm."

"Your greenhouses don't even have that. Aren't there any safeguards built in?"

"There's no good way to secure a greenhouse—tough to lock up glass or polycarbonate see-through panes. Safe-keeping would have meant a guard."

"Was there money in the grant to cover protection?"

"I haven't seen the books but I haven't heard we're short. The group continues to fundraise. This has been such a popular project for the County, and with University backing—throw in the Government's emphasis on the centennial and I can't imagine a request would have been turned down. In addition, the project has the full support of the American Orchid Society. They recently launched a fundraiser to collect money to safeguard endangered species. I would think that's another source to draw from."

"The amount, and the fact that federally protected merchandise was stolen, takes the case out of my hands. I expect you'll be contacted to reiterate what you've told me today." He studied her for a moment. "Can I say something?"

"Sure."

"I'm really impressed with how well you're doing. A couple weeks ago, you'd be ordering pizzas in every night."

"How'd you know about that?"

"I put your house on the patrol route. Either I or a fellow officer would cruise the neighborhood a few times during the evenings." He was grinning. "You've come a long way. I can only imagine how terrified you must have been this afternoon."

Mo nodded. "Yes, but it wasn't my house. It wasn't one of my students. Frankly, it wasn't personal. I wasn't really the target. Just a matter of wrong place at the wrong time. That can happen to anyone. I think it's the rule of three. When something bad happens, usually there will be two more incidents before that particular phase of bad luck passes. This was the third incident and I'm still alive—and I'm not going to be a victim. I interrupted a robbery—Dr.

Mitchell will add guards, and I'll carry a gun. Simple."

"Great. I didn't want there to be some delayed reaction to what happened this afternoon."

"There won't be. I promise. I love this job; I think it's going to turn into something permanent. I don't want anything to mess that up."

"It seems like a terrific opportunity."

"I couldn't have designed a job better suited."

"Before I forget, can you tell me any more about the fight? The one you overheard when your boss was firing this guy?"

"Probably not. There was just a lot of yelling—more on Dr. Mitchell's part. He even followed the guy to the parking lot. The man left and Dr. Mitchell came back inside. The only thing I overheard was Dr. Mitchell yelling 'just do it'. Apparently, there was a problem concerning workers— finding licensed ones to both unload a transport of orchids and continue with the framing. Dr. Mitchell gave him the okay to hire undocumented people—said he'd overlook University policy in favor of meeting deadlines."

"That could get people in trouble."

"I know. But the pressure's on to complete everything in time to kick off the centennial."

"Does your boss have a violent temper?"

"Not that I know of. I'd never seen him upset before."

"But you definitely feel he was angry?"

"I'd swear to it. It sounded accusatory. Which makes sense if the guy was behind on his contract."

"Maybe. I'm not a proponent of letting anger get in the way of a message. I hope there won't be other firings."

"I may not have anything to worry about in another six months. I'll be working outside the Whitney location after the first of the year. Only off and on."

She filled him in on doing field work in the Everglades with maybe a first trip this summer. Dr. Mitchell had made it official. Hit a home run with getting the lab and greenhouses off the ground here, and there would be future off-campus assignments.

"What will you be doing?"

"Classifying plants, photographing them—documenting their capture, so to speak. An in-state census of endangered species hasn't been taken in almost twenty years."

"Sounds like fun."

"More like hard work. The laboratory and greenhouses that are being set up are an extremely valuable tool—more than just a tourist attraction. I think we can save some lives."

"Excited?"

"I think it will feel good to get away for awhile. I'm pretty sure I have a house sitter set up here. So, no worries; I'll be able to concentrate on the job."

Chapter Twenty-one

So, what do we have? A white van, picture of an Indian on the side, driven by a man, for a woman in a bear costume who might be married, and who gave a gun to a kid and used a brand new bike as bait to get him to shoot someone." Tim Foley just shook his head. "And everyone seems to have just disappeared or pointedly isn't talking."

"Any businesses in the area drive white vans with Indian graphics?" Ben had stopped by the detective's office to see if he had any new information.

"Thought of that. Locally, we have Arrow Heating and Air—no Native insignia on their van. Dreamweaver Mattresses with a dream-catcher as their logo but only on letterhead, nothing in their motor pool. Only group that comes close would be the Seminoles—"

"Florida State University?" Ben interrupted but that seemed way too farfetched.

"Yeah. Think about it. The graphic is usually prominently displayed—the head of a warrior. And while I'm thinking about it, doesn't the tribe find that offensive? Like the Redskins logo?"

"Actually, no. The Seminole have accepted the use of their name by the state school as something flattering—a recognition of sorts—reminds people of their place in this state's history."

"Tough to keep up with what's correct anymore. But I don't know what a college vehicle would be doing two hundred miles away from the Tallahassee campus."

"Sounds like another dead-end. No ransom request?"

"None that I know of. Of course, I'm not sure the parents would tell me if there were. Even taking into consideration his running for office, they're very private people."

"Have you run any background checks on the councilor?"

A slow smile. "Wouldn't be doing my job if I hadn't. And I'm sure I don't have to remind you that this is privileged information "

Ben nodded. "Not a problem."

"Well, I'm going to file this under a 'need to know,' seeing as how you were hired by the councilor."

"Thanks."

"On the surface, everything looks good—tribal leader, philanthropist, well-educated with trusts set up for Native boys to attend local schools …" Tim paused.

"But?"

"Nothing recent but about ten years ago, a younger,

brasher Councilman Wolff got involved in some kind of payoff scheme. Apparently he was approached by outsiders with the big bucks to pave the way for a casino to be placed on Creek land in Alabama. I don't know the details, tribal sovereignty and all that. But there was a rumor that the Wolffs—the old man and his son—had lined their own pockets at the expense of the tribe. Probably one of the reasons you have the son living here, in Florida."

"Could be a reason to go after his family."

"Only thing I'm coming up with. I'm not good at sitting and waiting, but damned if I know anything else that even remotely could be a possibility."

Chapter Twenty-two

Is that something to eat?" Toby eyed the bulging gunnysack tied at the top with twine. The captain had tossed it into a corner of the boat's cabin. Captain. Toby wasn't sure you could be a captain if your boat was really small and smelled bad. Ships had captains, not boats. His dad owned a yacht and nobody called him captain.

"No, kid. This here is money. A whole bag of money. The green stuff." Then he laughed as if he'd just told a joke. "And this here is a whole sack of Whataburgers. Hungry?"

Toby nodded. "Can I have a Coke?"

"Sure. Take one of these." He handed Toby a six-pack of bright red cans dripping with condensation. "Don't throw nothing overboard. Even the little pull-tabs. If you take care of the fish, they'll take care of you. You can't go throwing shit in their house."

Toby had no idea how fish could take care of him but he didn't ask questions. And he wasn't going to throw anything into the water because he couldn't get close to the water. He had to stay in the cabin. He was tired of Whataburger. He wanted to go home. The captain said he had to stay in jail because he'd been bad. Why didn't his parents come to see him? Or the Indian doctor? Dr. Pecos helped him feed the ducks.

When he cried or begged to go home, the captain threatened to feed him to the sharks. He'd throw him in the water and the sharks would circle and eat his arms and legs one at a time. Toby thought maybe that was a fib but didn't want to find out.

So today, when he heard the sound of an outboard motor coming toward them, he was excited.

"Don't go getting any ideas. These men are coming for that sack there. You stay put. In fact, let's put you under this desk here. Yeah, that's right, crawl to the back so I can push this here chair under. Now, stay put. Don't yell, don't come on deck, don't do nothing. Understand?"

Toby poked his head out, nodded and pulled back under the desk against the wall.

"That's good. You be quiet, and I've got a treat in mind for later." With that the captain grabbed the gunnysack and hurried on deck.

Toby huddled against the wall and listened to the men but he couldn't understand anything. They talked funny. Sort of the way his grandfather spoke his Indian language when there was a ceremony. It didn't take long before he heard the boat start up and move away from the trawler. When the captain came back he didn't have the gunnysack. But he looked really happy.

Chapter Twenty-three

It took a week to inventory what was missing and then Mo wasn't certain she hadn't overlooked a plant, or ten. It was easy to just check gaps where plants had been—on the walls, wired to improvised tree trunks or rocks—against the master drawing. But she knew the plan was two years old—drawn up long before many plants were introduced and, more recently, plants taken down for propagation or treatment might not have found their way back to their original spots.

So, a lot was guesswork. She'd look at the list and then comb the greenhouses. Slow going, at best. Species that started out in Greenhouse Three had migrated to the species' specialty house once it opened. A number of these switches weren't noted. Now, that notation was part of her duties. One thing was certain, so far she'd uncovered the loss of fifty-three rare and endangered orchids. Ones that were protected by their countries of origin, and permits to gather had been released only to the laboratory for propagation. The loss had far-reaching consequences, including certain extinction for some if the plants fell into the wrong hands—cloning and preservation if they went to someone with expert knowledge.

The furor over the theft culminated in the hiring of three guards. Two shared a day-shift and one spent the night. At least they were armed. No impotent playground cop-pretenders—these were the real thing. There was a collective sigh of relief. Geoff seemed more at ease and, after the initial shock, the governing board blamed themselves and jumped at a chance to protect the rest of their charges. Mo had become somewhat of a hero for thwarting the thieves when she did. Consensus of opinion said it could have been far worse.

All seemed calm—if a beehive suggested calmness. The construction crews put in twelve and fifteen-hour days—and the third greenhouse neared completion with shelving in place and water piped in. Two more semi-truckloads of plants arrived—this time containing a nice array of bromeliads. Mo's part time job became full time. Paid full time—and in a short three weeks, memories of Jefferson Elementary had all but completely faded.

She was enjoying the self-protection class; they had finally graduated to the field, and every Saturday was taken up with firing away at paper 'men.' Next week they had to bring their own weapons. Tim Foley had been as good as his word, and an afternoon in a gun shop had given her a snub-nosed thirty-eight with oversized grips. There was a more feminine Smith &Wesson, "Lady Smith" for Julie.

Mo carried the .38 in the car, in her pocket while she did housework, in a side holster at work, and stuck it under the pillow next to her at night. Overkill? Probably, but she felt safe. Well, safer, at least. Her boss didn't approve but kept quiet. She was legal and felt comfortable and was going to stay that way.

Avoidance. That summed up her interaction with her boss. And that seemed to be the safest, too. But it broke her heart. He'd open his office door, see her coming in the opposite direction and step back inside. It felt as if someone had slapped her.

But Mo was persistent in helping set up his presentation; she doggedly continued with the slides, staging, photographing, downloading, adding definitions where needed, building the Power Point presentation. *His* Power Point presentation. When she had to be out in the greenhouses, she made certain that he wasn't. She worked on the slide show in the mornings, spent her afternoons checking plants for pests or disease, and leaving notes for the maintenance people to spray. She never gave these 'orders' directly to the crew but left the typed directive in his mailbox to do with as he pleased. It gave her some bit of satisfaction to note that he followed her every suggestion.

She also made time for work in the library, the new addition of a floor to ceiling collection of plant books in an alcove off the main exhibit entrance. The University of Florida had contributed several thousand volumes and all donations needed to be catalogued as well as on-line listings updated. She put several interns to work and it gave her time to read, catch up on orchid lore, and be knowledgeable when questioned about the contents of the greenhouses.

There was so much work at the project that she'd only had two days off in the last twenty. Her main reason for being hired, photography, was being neglected. Mo needed to change her routine. She started by setting aside two days a week to photograph plants in the morning, catch up on her notes, and then help the maintenance crews with repotting or even watering in the afternoons—if she wasn't, of course, working on the PowerPoint presentation. They were down to the last afternoon before the Casa Monica soiree and tour of the greenhouses and lab.

Geoff had been absent a lot the last couple weeks and was now sitting at her computer trying to proofread and rearrange slides. She didn't dare let on that procrastination drove her crazy. He hadn't had the luxury of time to spend on it, she kept reminding herself. But now he was vaguely out of sorts, facing the deadline, no doubt, and peevishly expecting her to make changes, help load the van, and get ready to go.

"I want the annotated slide of *Lepanthes felis* followed by a slide of *Lepanthes heptapus*. It makes sense to point out their differences."

He moved his chair to the left, and Mo scooted hers forward to position herself in front of the screen. The presentation would begin at eight tonight. The social hour was between seven and eight. Drinks, hors d'oeuvres and working the room. Something she'd love to get out of. But they needed to put on a charming, united front—and keep their hands out—palms up.

It was already two-thirty; it would take a half hour to get there, an hour to set up, and she still needed time to dress. They had to leave by five at the latest.

Five interns had been chosen to conduct the five

o'clock on-site tours of greenhouses and labs—three of them doing post-doc studies in botany. They would do well and could answer any question. Mo had drilled the group on which plants should be spotlighted. But she was getting antsy. He only had five more slides to check but she wished they could move faster.

Because they were taking plants, Geoff had checked out a university van from Gainesville and driven it over earlier in the week. A big part of the evening would be show and tell. Nothing made the rich reach into their pockets like meeting their wards in person. Mo helped him pack plants, then filled her car with handouts, her computer and projector, microphones and miscellaneous audio-visual equipment. Geoff would drive the van and she'd follow in her car.

Mo checked her watch. They'd gone ten minutes without Geoff finding anything that needed changing. "I really need to finish loading the van and then get dressed."

They were being civil with one another. A little difficult to continue the avoidance tactic. She now admitted her job was more important than risking it all on some romantic encounter that was probably doomed from the start anyway. He dismissed her with a nod, eyes glued to the computer screen. She had another half hour of hauling plants out to the van.

Mo had brought the necessary equipment for the formal evening, even make-up. It was still in a bag in her car. But she wanted to shower first. At least there was indoor plumbing. Something called the GS, gardener's safeguard, had been installed in the back of the nursery building. Originally designed as a wash area for tools and boots—sort of a disinfect before visiting the babies in the nursery—some original sort had rigged a shower head on an extended pipe above the cement slab with a drain in the center, then added a twenty-five gallon hot water tank to one side. Not luxury, but a workable shower when you needed one. She pushed her chair under the desk and turned to go.

"You look beautiful. It won't take an hour to slip a dress on."

It was the first time in almost three weeks he'd made a personal comment. She was caught off guard and knew she was blushing.

"Thanks, but I'd hate to embarrass you tonight."

"That could never happen, Mo." Soft brown eyes searched hers. She could feel her breathing quicken. She needed to break the spell.

"Is there anything else you want me to do to the slides?"

"No. They're great. I really appreciate all the work you've put in. It'll pay off, believe me. The biddies will be duly impressed and literally come running forward brandishing checkbooks."

"I hope you're right." She smiled her thanks, "If you find anything else, I'll be in number three or in the van."

"Think I'm fine here. I need to run through the slides a couple times—firm up what I want to say." He looked up and slipped off his reading glasses. "Do you think I should take some of the crosses? *Sophronitis* adds such color to the miniatures."

Mo could imagine how a diminutive scarlet Brazilian *Sophronitis coccinea* would send patrons racing to the front of the room. Or, at least, she hoped so.

"I saw a nice *'Lady in Red'* on the back bench. I'll throw it in." Figuratively speaking, of course, she added to herself.

"And a Ghost Orchid—I won't forget that one." It was important to show off Florida's endangered species, too.

Mo left the office and moved to retrieve the Lady in Red, whose blooms had opened yesterday morning, three perfectly formed flowers nestled against a half dozen stubby green pseudo-bulbs, each flower almost three inches across, in shades of deep blue-red with a bright yellow splash at the throat. Wonderful color contrast, sure to be a real crowd pleaser. And the flowers were shaped like smaller versions of the easily recognizable *Cattleya*, the old corsage orchid. This would be a great plant for display and could withstand the pawing of eager contributors.

She separated the *Sophronitis* from its friends on the back bench and whispered a little pep talk. "This is your chance, kid. Wow 'em. Free up the old checkbooks." Mo sort of tweaked the closest thick, rubbery green leaf. She'd like to think the plant would have winked if it could have. There was no doubt that it was up to the task. She misted the bark compost that filled the red-brown clay container and took a full minute to just enjoy the perfect form of the three flowers. Then she wrapped the pot in corrugated cardboard for extra insulation and adjusted an inverted paper cone around the plant itself. Lastly, she stabilized the three flowers by fastening each short stem to a matchstick. There. Guaranteed to make the trip in good form.

She looked over her shoulder a couple times—somehow it would be embarrassing caught talking to plants or simply patting them. Geoff was a little too cut and dried for the froufrou stuff. Most lab-types were. Yet, Mo talked to her plants a lot. Nothing too challenging, but some of her Phals had silently endured their sounding board status through two divorces and then this last debacle. The talk of murderous third-graders was almost too much for them. She frankly didn't think as many were putting out flower spikes for summer blooming as usual. She hoped it was just her imagination.

She checked her watch and chided herself for wasting time—it was so easy to lose track when working with the flowers. But she'd better get a move on. Tonight was one of the most important events of the year—she needed to remember that. State dignitaries, a few people from Washington—department of Interior, Ben Pecos representing the BIA—lots of important folks including some well-known, local, moneyed supporters of noble causes.

Even her darling sister and orthodontist husband were coming. No wonder Geoff wanted everything to be perfect. God knows Claire had instilled in her that private donations were needed to keep the doors open. And some of the state's deepest pockets would be gathered this evening. It was rumored that the governor would attend.

She carried the Lady in Red out the door and placed it in the van. Propping it behind the covering over the wheel well, then securing the pot with masking tape guaranteed it would remain upright. Tucked in right beside it, wrapped loosely in green florist's tissue paper but anchored to the Lady in Red's pot with more masking tape, was the Ghost Orchid. What a contrast—one so festive and bright, the other a mass of roots that only the educated would recognize as a plant.

She did a quick visual inventory and thought everything they had planned to take was in place and secured. Transporting fragile flowering plants had its own set of challenges. Parked in the sun, the van was warm bordering on hot. But the plants wouldn't mind. She cracked two windows and quickly misted, then closed the back door.

Mo had parked beside the van. The late afternoon was unseasonably warm. Especially for late May. There was a promise of an early summer—heat and humidity descending with a bang. Days of sticky warmth that would force her indoors in another couple weeks. Now, the weather just seemed unsure of itself, warming to the mid-eighties one day, then ten degrees lower the next. She gathered dress bag, overnight case, towel and hairdryer from her car—had she forgotten anything? She guessed not and headed back to the first greenhouse.

"Plant 10-22 mm long, epiphytic, caespitose, roots fine … leaf erect, coriaceous, elliptical, obtuse to subacute …"

Lepanthes microscopica, Mo said under her breath and was secretly pleased that she knew the plant. If she were facing a test, she'd feel pretty confident. Geoff was practicing his talk, and she continued past him and headed toward the nursery.

Geoff had the look of a fund-raiser about him. Polished, articulate, handsome—Mo just knew his tux would fit him perfectly. He probably owned his own. Now, *that* impressed her. She hadn't thought of it before, but unless you got married in rapid succession a man really wouldn't need his own. And there's only one senior prom. No, Geoff struck her as a banquet-pro, one accustomed to the circuit. Wine and dine with the best, and leave with more money than you had when you came in. Yes, that would require his own tux.

She walked to the back of the GS and opened the door to the adjoining tool room. Benches lined both walls beneath green metal lockers, some with combination locks, a few standing open. There was even a utility sink and a mirror. Not luxury, but very doable. She slipped the dress from its bag and, twisting the hanger's hook, hung it on a locker door. Steam from the shower would pull out every wrinkle. Towel and hairdryer she placed next to her overnight bag beside the sink.

The shower itself was a phone booth sized acrylic semi-circle with green tiled back and floor. She reached in, adjusted the nozzle, and turned on both hot and cold faucets. She'd test the temperature before she committed but give it a minute to warm first. Rummaging in the overnight case, she brought out shampoo, shower gel, perfume and body lotion—same scent—and toothbrush and toothpaste. She stepped out of her clogs, pulled the five-button Henley over her head, unbelted and dropped the chinos, then added bra, panties and socks to the pile.

She'd be a lot less encumbered later. The dress she'd chosen was a pale lilac, silk "slip" sheath, higher in front and lower in back, with the slimmest of cord straps. The dress barely brushed mid-thigh but clung to every curve perfectly, moving with each step, but only to hint at what it concealed. Jewelry was cabochon amethyst stones in plain silver settings at her ears and a large cabochon amethyst on a sterling collar at her throat. Strappy silver sandals with four-inch heels completed the look. Simple, not too expensive but head turning—what more could she ask?

She gathered up gel and shampoo, found a sponge in the bottom of her bag, tested the water and stepped into the shower. Water—running, standing still, salty or clear— had always been a weakness. Result of being born by the ocean? She thought so. Walks on the beach, as well as, long, steamy showers were a passion. But not tonight. She quickly scrubbed, rinsed, a second shampoo, rinsed, shut off the water and stepped out.

The steam layered in the room. And that's why she didn't see him until she leaned over to pick up her towel. Standing in front of her about three feet away.

"What are you doing here?"

She was absolutely cool and didn't wrap the towel around her until after he'd gotten a good look. Then she tucked in a corner and simply stood silently in her terrycloth sarong. But could he see, maybe sense, the beating of her heart?

"Mo, I've been wrong."

She waited. He seemed to be choosing his words.

"I'm falling in love with you. Yes, I mean it. And I can't take this." And then his arms were around her. She closed her eyes and let herself be pulled close. The smell of him, woodsy and crisp, surrounded her, and her arms went up to circle his neck.

"Nothing's changed. This is still dangerous," she murmured against his chest. "I don't want to take chances with scandal … with our jobs." She didn't add how it would be difficult to face Claire if she botched this opportunity. Big sis would not be understanding—that she knew.

"We'll figure something out. We'll be able to travel together. You'll be on your way in a few weeks. I'm scheduled to work in the lab this next week and the one after that and then join the project in the Everglades." He put a finger under her chin and tipped her head back to look into her eyes. "It's ready-made camouflage. I want you so much. I don't want to wait."

He pulled out the tucked end of the towel and let it slide to the floor. Then he stepped back, cupped both breasts with his hands and lightly stroked her nipples with his thumbs before bending down to run his tongue over each.

She wanted to scream, claw at his clothing, pull him down on top of her but instead caught her breath and jumped back at the sound of a knock.

"Anybody in there?"

"That you, Daniel? I'm just getting ready to jump in the shower." Geoff pulled off his shirt, undid his slacks, grabbed her towel and motioned her back inside the stall before opening the door. "Got a presentation in town tonight. I'll be out of here within the hour. Want me to take care of locking up?"

"Yeah, if you don't mind. I need to get away a little early, but Pete should be here by seven. We'll be unprotected for a half hour. You cool with that, Doc?"

"Shouldn't be a problem. We've got the tours coming through. I think we're covered but thanks for letting me know."

Geoff waited until retreating footsteps led to a distant, muffled clang of metal, then opened the shower door.

"Close." She reached for her towel.

"Mo, I'm staying over at the Casa Monica tonight. I have a meeting with the Governor at eight tomorrow over breakfast at the hotel … seemed stupid to load up the van and drive out here, unload, then go home when tonight will probably be a late one. I'll keep most of the plants in my room." He took her arm and drew her to him. "Stay with me."

"Do you—?"

"Think it will be safe? Probably as safe as we'll ever be until we can get out of here and do a little traveling."

"I'll meet you there."

"Now, I won't be able to think of anything else. Hope I don't flub my lines." A wry smile which somehow made his hazel brown eyes more vibrant. Then he leaned down as her hands met behind his head pulling him into a kiss. Lips parted, breathlessly pressing into him, she realized how much she wanted this … wanted him.

"No, I'm sorry. Not here. Someone might still be on the grounds." She pulled back. "Tonight, later."

"The voice of reason. I hate that voice." But he was smiling as he kissed the tip of her nose. "I love you, Mo. I mean it. I want to give this a chance. I didn't think I could feel this way—so quickly. I don't want us to ever be apart."

Chapter Twenty-four

It was ten 'til five when they finally headed out. He in the university's white van with the two side windows and Mo in her trusty, if nothing else, five-year-old Volvo station wagon. Going north on A1A, two convertibles, tops down, passed her doing well over the fifty-five mile per hour limit.

Spring fever was a real disease. It was easy to lust after summer—and push its arrival—even when you lived in a land of almost perpetual warmth. She'd probably come back as a lizard on a rock herself. Still, even a little taste of winter and spring was refreshing. Northern Florida had it all over Ft. Lauderdale and Miami. She wasn't heartbroken when she had to dig out a sweater on a January morning. There was a lot to be said about flip-flops and shorts nine months of the year; she could endure those other three.

She always liked to think that come what may, she was prepared—be it weather, a new job, a crisis—she could endure anything. That was her maddening practical side—and with a dash of doggedness, she was perfect for this project. Without her, would this project be ready for show time now? Probably not. She had become invaluable. In more ways than one, it seemed. To find Geoff, work at what she loved, travel … it was almost too good to be true. But then wasn't it just meant to be? Oh God, echoes of her mother. She needed to listen to herself more—make sure those mom-isms weren't sneaking into her thought patterns.

But it was difficult not to dwell on the promise of the evening. A night at the Casa Monica. Eight hours with the man of her dreams. Did she feel the same? Would she be able to say, 'I love you'? She knew she would. She felt exactly the same way—she never wanted them to be apart. It was going to be a really long and wonderful night.

She kept the van in sight. Easy to do because traffic was light. The ocean on her right, a light breeze with the windows down. She switched on an oldies station and "Miss American Pie" blared out. Everyone knew disc jockeys played it when they needed a bathroom break. Wasn't it four or five minutes long? But then she swallowed hard. "… drove my Chevy to the levy, but the levy was dry … this will be the day that I die." She punched the scan button on the radio and settled for something more upbeat.

But not quick enough to keep the refrain from replaying in her head … "this will be the day that I die." It was the song she listened to on her way to school that morning, almost a month ago. The day was receding but thanks to this trigger came crashing back. She didn't even know there were leftover triggers—ones she hadn't already exorcised.

She felt her palms become moist against the steering wheel. No. No. No. That was all behind her. She admonished herself to get a grip. It was in the past and was going to stay that way. But hadn't Dr. Pecos warned her that there would be flashbacks? Just when she thought there wouldn't be, and she'd just have to take them one at a time? There didn't seem to be a one-size-fits-all cure.

Mo felt she owed much of her sanity to Dr. Pecos. She really had to give Claire credit—it had been the right thing at the right time to insist that she see someone, take her to her first appointment just to make sure she followed through.

The doctor had been a life-saver. Like when Mo decided that the only reason she didn't die was because nobody would care one way or the other. She was suddenly, and possibly irrationally, convinced that no one would come to her funeral. So Dr. Pecos suggested that she talk with her friends and family, share her worries and then call him. Homework designed to help her seek and receive the support Dr. Pecos thought she needed. Except Mo made the mistake of starting with her mother. She could laugh now but at the time, Marjorie was a little unnerving. Her first comment? "I won't even think of cremation. I want a sense of closure. I want to see you in that box."

"Mom, you can gather around and stare at an urn and get the same feeling when you dump me on the garden."

"Don't be morbid. I want to see you laid out in all your finery."

"What finery?"

"Your first wedding dress, silly. I'll be buried in my wedding dress. I don't care if you have to slit the back from neck to hem to make it fit. I'll go on a bed of pale ivory satin, wearing a gown to match, with seed pearls and lace. I just can't make up my mind about the veil. Sometimes I think it might be just that little bit too much. But the overall effect would be nice. I think it's fitting to be laid beside your father looking like his bride."

"Mom, we haven't heard from Daddy in over fifteen years."

"He'll come to his senses. I'm his wife. There will always be a space beside me for his final rest. And I want you to leave the pearls on me. They're my mother's. I'll take them with me. Of course, if you go first I'll let you borrow them but just until they close the casket."

"Gee, thanks. You don't think people will wonder when they see you snatching jewelry off the corpse?"

"Of course not. It will be perfectly obvious what I'm doing. Oh Maureen, isn't it good to be talking like this? You and Claire both need to know my wishes."

As often as Mo replayed the conversation, she could never see how she could have regained control. As always, she'd lost center stage—probably before she'd even taken it. But Mom hung up happy—convinced she'd been heard. So, who was supporting whom? But her wedding dress? Mo honestly didn't think she'd be able to dress Marjorie in something so inappropriate. And Mom was only going to be sixty in June—she had to keep reminding herself of that.

Still, the exercise had cured Mo of the nightmare of waking up in a chapel alone. Somehow it didn't make so much difference anymore. She really didn't want to think of her mother even being there, reaching in to remove a string of family pearls. Now, *that* was a reason to stay alive.

Mo vowed, then and there, to make Claire swear to have her cremated. No viewing, tasteful urn only. And if she knew Claire, she'd do it to spite their mother.

But that didn't mean the thought of death didn't make her swallow hard and will her hands to stop rattling against the steering wheel now. She applied extra pressure and nixed the idea of pulling over. She just needed to collect herself. Not give in. The good doc had said it was all right to stop everything, take a few deep breaths and get oriented. A little adult time-out. But Geoff was racing away from her, becoming swallowed up by traffic, and she wasn't sure where they were supposed to park. The Casa Monica was a block from the plaza, facing King Street in the busiest part of town.

She was already breathing easily. Quite frankly, the near-attack of panic surprised her. She'd been doing so well. But then hindsight reared its ugly head—it was the song that had brought everything back. Certainly when she heard it a month ago, it had foreshadowed dire events. Should she view it as a warning now? A premonition of things to come? Some unforeseen, but equally as disastrous an event just waiting to happen? No, that was just too woo-woo, even for her. Mo smiled. Far less than this would bring on Claire's 'you have to be grounded in reality' lecture. Had they really been born of the same mother and father?

Perspiration brought on by the vivid recollection of Toby Wolff provided evaporative cooling. Not something that was comfortable once the sun set. She reached to turn off the Volvo's air-conditioning. By the outskirts of St. Augustine, she was enjoying the evening again— the anticipation of a night with Geoff. Life was back to registering an eight on the ol' one-to-ten scale.

She liked driving along the ocean in the late afternoon. The dunes speckled with wild sea oats and an occasional century plant. When she was a child, she tried to imagine the families dwelling inside the million dollar homes that now blocked her view of the water. Were they happy? Was there a mother and a father just sitting down at the table with their 2.5 children? Smiling, asking the children to share what had happened that day? Then taking the bowls and platters of food handed off by uniformed attendants who moved quietly in the candlelight, hovering just out of sight near the sideboard.

Wow. She was sure Dr. Pecos could do something with that. Longings vs reality. What could have been instead of what was—a mother who thought they could eat chicken pot pies seven days a week—a father who traveled. The same old tired euphemism.

But Mo had made it to high school before she realized it was a euphemism. Quite simply, her father really did travel—a lot. She'd never thought to examine it. He sent a check and called. He never forgot birthdays. He was home most Christmases. It was only when he stopped coming home altogether, even then it took her six months to realize that good ol' Dad had finally just kept on going. He didn't even pause long enough to get a divorce. And his memory immediately failed him when it came to family events. Gifts became a thing of the past.

Marjorie was devastated, wore black for a year and didn't even change to something more becoming when she had to find a job. When questioned, she'd always say he was dead to her and, apparently, no one could prove that he wasn't really underground. Black seemed to be tolerated in the dentist's office. So, Marjorie quickly adapted to two-piece polyester pants suits—two in her closet, wash one, wear one—and dyed her hair black to complete the look.

Claire was gone by then. In college on a full scholarship making the most of her 145 IQ. Claire at four years older, escaped early. Mo had four years of high school to keep Marjorie on the straight and narrow, before she bolted. And then to the local state university so that she could live at home and help out. Escape for Mo meant getting married the first time.

She snapped herself back to the present and followed the taillights of the van up and over the Bridge of Lions. A few short blocks later, she maneuvered the Volvo into a parking spot on the right-hand side of the building and watched Geoff back the van up to the door opposite the loading zone sign. He was one of those brainy types who also seemed adept with machinery, unlike husband two who hadn't learned to drive until his twenties. Mo had done all the driving—or most of it. When she thought he'd kill himself on the highway sometime, she bought the Volvo. Indestructible, or so *Consumer Report* had led her to believe. Actually, she'd lost patience before any accident, and she'd sent him home to live with his mother. Cute, and sweet, yet ambition wasn't even a word in his vocabulary.

Mo gathered an armful of electronics from the back of her station wagon, waved to Geoff and hoped there was nothing to leak onto her dress. How messy was a computer anyway? She looped an extra extension cord around her left wrist and started for the door. A chivalrous sort ran toward her with exclamations of "Why didn't you tell us you were here?" as he motioned two obvious flunkies to take the equipment.

Mo didn't mind passing on the task of packhorse.

She held the doors for them and ran interference down the long hall that finally emptied into roughly a thousand square foot ballroom. Geoff had referred to it as having an "intimate seating arrangement, but Mo saw nothing "intimate" about a room that could seat several hundred people, eight apiece, at circular tables.

But the first thing she noticed about the room was the amount of fur—no longer on four legs. It looked like a game preserve. Fox, Lynx, mink, sable—she was astounded. Where were the people with the ketchup? And not that far from the animal shelter that probably held an errant ferret or two, or baby porcupine—the latest wild-animal-as-pet craze gone wrong. Wasn't this some kind of effrontery? And what did it say about her own faux fur shrug? She'd like to think it said she was on the right side.

"Hey, how about some help? Anything I can do?"

"Dr. Pecos, good to see you. Is Julie with you?"

"Somewhere around here. I left her taking pictures."

"I'll catch up with her later. I've been meaning to call—is there any word on Toby? Are you any closer to finding him? A ransom demand, maybe?"

"No, I wish there had been. It would have at least assured us that he's alive. His disappearance has everyone baffled."

Two dowagers approached her, asking about setting up the head table. She said good-bye to Ben and turned to address the elderly women. Both murmured appropriately when she mentioned being Dr. Mitchell's assistant. It seemed the one might be faintly jealous. Another victim of Geoff's charm? Of course, maddening as it was, there was no way that she could indicate "assistant" was hardly the word for her own relationship with the man and that she considered herself possibly very much a part of Dr. Mitchell's future. For the ten-hundredth time she wished they could be open about their feelings.

"We so want this evening to be successful. It was so kind of Dr. Mitchell to take the time to be with us. I'm Lilian Ainsworth, Chairman of Floridians for Green Space and Event Chair for the Centennial kick-off." Her hand was slightly damp but her eyes were earnest and her royal purple, cut-out velvet jacket and long skirt looked expensive. "That's Lilian with one 'L'."

As if Mo cared. But the Lilian Ainsworths of the world expected you to. Mo nodded politely. She was here to separate the hosts from their purses. Not to pass judgment.

"Is there anything else that you need?" The second woman, somewhat younger called Nancy, pointed to a lectern and two tables down front.

"That will be fine." Mo smiled.

Nancy's smile just twinkled. She was such a petite little thing; it wasn't a surprise when she whispered that she raised miniatures and specialized in South American species. Mo thought she could like her.

Geoff gave Lilian a buss on the cheek, and Mo watched her simply ooze gratitude at being singled out for attention. Was that a whiff of old hormones waking up? Lilian had to be seventy-something. Mo made a silent vow to not make a fool of herself past the age of fifty-five.

She hurried past Geoff, who was now caught up in a throng of well-wishers, and continued to the front of the room. The least the assistant could do would be to set up the room. She eyed the mike and then moved the lectern to the far side of the table. She set things up the way she'd want them if it were her presentation. There'd be time to change if Geoff didn't agree.

An usher delivered a box of plants then stepped aside as two other ushers placed boxes on the table. She didn't see the "Lady in Red" but suspected it must be in another group. Perhaps, Geoff would show it off after break. She began to arrange plants on the table. The Styrofoam carriers had kept their charges safe. Some of the taller blooming plants that stuck up above the cases had cones of plastic bubble-pack around their flower stalks and arrived in perfect condition—thanks to *perfect* insulation. Mo stood back and surveyed the table. She didn't see one plant that wasn't exquisite.

Mo began dismantling the plants' protective covering, folded and tucked everything and placed it beneath the skirted tables alongside the Styrofoam carrying cases. Everything out of sight.

Then she tested the lectern mic, plugged in the laptop after finding an electrical outlet under the table, connected it with the overhead projector and finally pulled down an oversized viewing screen. What else? She was running through a mental checklist. She brought up the PowerPoint program he was going to use and left the introductory slide on the screen. Geoff Mitchell could do a lot worse than have her as an assistant. Geoff winked his approval as he walked toward the lectern. Mo checked the time. A huge round wall clock above a side door said it was just 7:30. Still plenty of time before he'd begin.

"Mo, this looks great." Geoff stopped by the table of orchids. "Thanks. I can't imagine doing this without you."

"That's the idea. I'm going for the Miss Indispensable title."

"It's yours." He grinned and then just continued to

smile, looking into her eyes. An intimate moment in a crowd of two hundred. The intimacy and danger sent a shiver through her. She could get used to his attention.

He started to say something but was pulled away by an overeager senior who had a plant in her hand. One that apparently needed immediate attention. People could be so rude and not even know it.

Someone handed Mo a flute of champagne as she made her way back to the audience. She had marked a chair at a table in the front row on the aisle by leaving her purse in it. No one was crass enough to move the flap of purple suede with a rhinestone clasp. She'd never tell anyone but it had cost more than the dress. But less than her shoes.

She'd read once that you should put all your money in accessories. They were the only things that count. Good clean designer lines and lots of accessories. And her closet proved she'd taken the advice to heart. It was bursting at the seams with scarves and purses and jewelry, all crying out to be mixed or matched. But somewhere along the line she'd realized third graders couldn't care less and her dress became the sturdy uniform of elementary teachers—slacks, camp shirt, maybe a decorative vest—but nothing easily ruined by anyone's upchucking or bleeding.

Small groups chatting over glasses of champagne were slowly breaking up, moving behind her to fill the good, up-front tables. Little trills of laughter floated above the crowd. This was a friendly group, all on a first-name basis, gathered for yet another *cause* célèbre. Mo wondered if the purse was richer if you caught them earlier in the year—would the February gatherings be more lucrative than the August ones? And just how did a philanthropist divide his gifts? She envisioned little bags of silver tagged and waiting to be meted out, drawn up with the help of a trusty servant each January first. But, then, maybe she'd read a little too much Dickens.

She scanned the audience for Claire, then reminded herself that the ever-beautiful Dr. Roth was away, attending some convention in San Francisco with the dweeb orthodontist. An email that morning had offered advance congratulations and an admonishment to 'break a leg'. Claire was once again being nice but wasn't Mo's even being there another feather in her cap? Wasn't this just more of Claire taking credit—even long distance?

The Doctors Roth … they truly were the original odd couple. Or was it just a case of beauty and the beast? No, that was way too harsh. Marty might be twenty years older than Claire, but he was generous—if short and a little paunchy. And he was a collector—orchids being his specialty. That had to be the attraction—what a plum to land a beautiful botanist, known in her own right for the culture of the plants he loved. And he'd given dear old Mom a job all those years ago—was that also part of the bargain? In order to capture the hand of Claire Beltzer, he had to gainfully employ the mother first? That sounded like Claire. Mo could fault her for a lot of things but she did take care of her own. More recently, even her sister— look at the job she'd helped Mo get.

Mo turned in her chair to look at the audience. It was a shame that the Doctors Roth couldn't be there. The gathering was just Claire's sort of thing. She had never seen Marty Roth in a tux but with the right corset, he might cut a somewhat dashing figure. Roly-poly Roth was not her favorite person but she kept her opinion to herself, seeing how Marjorie and Claire were his biggest fans. Both were counting on him for a well-heeled retirement.

She wasn't jealous. She simply couldn't imagine relying on someone else to take care of her. Maybe that was part of her problem with men—she didn't even pretend to need them. At least not monetarily, that is. She could earn her own way, and being rich was never a motivator. All she wanted was someone who respected her mind—thought of her as an individual and supported her capabilities. Was she looking at that man at this very moment?

As if on cue, Geoff cleared his throat, gave her a quick half-smile, took a moment to arrange his notes, clicked the remote slide changer and watched the laptop screen change to a photo of the Everglades. Someone dimmed the front bank of lights from a panel on the sidewall. The show was about to begin.

Mo wasn't sure what struck her first. The really professional level of the slides—including those she had made—or the nonchalant, yet purposeful posturing of the presenter. He was a natural at it. Relaxed, good-looking … she was half tempted to pass a plate and see how much loose change she could collect. He certainly seemed the Elmer Gantry of greenhouse growers. But instead she settled into the padded-back, folding chair and watched a master-act unfold.

"It's estimated that there are fewer than five hundred of this particular species available in the wild, and a scant fifty can be traced world-wide under cultivation." Geoff clicked a slide forward and, picking up the pointer, called attention to a tiny pinprick of vibrant purple that peeped out from the crotch of a twisted-root tree. It wouldn't have covered the nail on her little finger.

"The University of Florida's new botanical gardens at

the Whitney Labs has been granted a collector's certificate and will add this rare find to its permanent collection." There was the sound of collected ah's and a smattering of enthusiastic applause.

Geoff ran through a series of recent acquisitions, plants from the swamps of Florida, then donations of plants that had outgrown modest greenhouses. Big *Vandas* that required ten square feet of room to hang. And vanilla orchids, *Vanilla planifolia*, whose name came from the Spanish *vaina* or 'sheath" which came from the Latin for vagina. Orchids were so earthy, Mo thought, regular sex-pots on stems. Several slides showed the sprawl of one plant well over twenty feet crying out for room to move.

Next, he clicked through several collections—*epiphytes, masdevallias*—orchids with pseudo-bulbs, those without. Some growing in air, some in soil. There must have been fifty slides—the brilliant color and shape of the flowers was mesmerizing. Other than the intermittent oh's, and ah's, Mo could have heard a pin drop.

At last, Geoff paused, "Of course, you know what comes next. This can't be done without your help." He continued to list current, as well as anticipated, costs as four slides in a row supported what he was saying.

Mo stole a look sideways. Nancy had plopped down beside her with Lilian on her left. Neither batted an eye. Mo guessed that if you bothered to show up at these things, you knew what was expected.

"I hope my fifty thousand will encourage others to be generous." This from a man in the back.

There was a slight nod of agreement from Lilian then she chimed in to add fifty thousand. Mo felt like she was on the floor of a Sotheby's auction house. They could have been talking about Van Goghs or signed porcelains. Geoff beamed his thanks. Mo had no idea how much he'd hoped to raise that night. And she was losing track of promises being shouted out from the audience. Would they walk away with five hundred thousand? One million? Maybe lots more? If there were two hundred people present and each chipped in a paltry ten thousand … she suddenly had a very clear picture of how lucrative this business was. And how very important it was to have Geoff Mitchell at the helm.

There was a short question and answer period before Geoff suggested a thirty-minute break. He announced the program for the remainder of the evening: a lecture on Florida's Super Berry by Dr. Benson Pecos, an overview of what was being highlighted around the state in various state parks for the Centennial, and an auction of the orchid plants on the table in front of him.

A lame joke about the champagne getting warm brought people to their feet and moving toward the back. Mo needed to find a restroom and headed to the hall. She thought she'd passed one on the way in. She waved at Ben and Julie who were setting up for Ben's talk. Julie's off-the-shoulder midnight blue mid-calf sheath played up the perfect rosy paleness of her skin—freckles and all.

Geoff was surrounded by well-wishers including Lilian. There would be no prying him loose from that group. Of course, later she would have him to herself. She gave a little shiver of anticipation. Falling in love was her favorite pastime. Or illness, because wasn't it always a feverish, all-consuming passion that overrode everything else in her life including caution? But would she trade this feeling? No—a resounding no.

Several patrons, mostly older men who seemed to be without a spouse or date, tried to rope her into joining them in a small discussion group at the back. She was polite but, besides needing to find a bathroom, she had better things to think about, such as a room upstairs in this very hotel. She only hoped the night wouldn't turn so cool that they'd have to bring the collection of plants up to the room. She hoped they could mist them and just shut the van up tight. But if they had to cart them in, the plants would offer a familiar backdrop.

She pushed open the door marked "W" and instantly felt the coolness of the tiled walls. There was a waiting line and, wouldn't you know it, there was Nancy.

"Isn't he wonderful? You know, I was on the committee that brought him here."

"Really?" Mo wasn't that interested but there were ten women in front of her. "Who did you steal him away from?"

"University of California, Santa Barbara, and more recently, of course, University of Florida. But he wasn't always just a college professor."

Just a college professor? What did that make Claire? Chopped liver? Mo knew she shouldn't get her feathers ruffled but she wasn't good with snobbery. And, God forbid, she should ever mention teaching third grade to this crowd.

"I think we were interested in his family. Father a diplomat ... mother, an heiress. Of course, the money was unfortunately lost but breeding can never be taken away. Don't you agree? And the connections, they've already paid off."

Mo nodded. She was curious but didn't ask how. So

Geoff was a blue-blood. Sans money, it would seem. Not exactly a trust baby. It really made no difference to her whatsoever. She'd just taken a lipstick out of her bag and moved to a vacant spot at the mirrors when Lilian pushed the door open.

"I thought I might find you here. Dr. Mitchell has been looking everywhere for you."

Accusatory tone, no less. Was there some hint that she didn't have the right to go to the bathroom until the master's wishes had been met? Mo gave Nancy a look that hopefully conveyed she expected her to hold her spot in line, then added, "I'll be right back" before she went out the door.

The hall was almost deserted but muted laughter floated in from the ballroom. The champagne must be flowing freely. And slouching in the doorway with an arm casually thrown around the shoulders of a man whose picture she'd seen in the papers was the handsome Dr. Mitchell.

It was hard to keep her knees from knocking; expectation alone was giving her the jitters. She couldn't remember anticipation affecting her this way. Mo only knew she simply beamed when he looked at her and smiled in that "I only have eyes for you" way. Could a person's heart really stop? She took a deep breath as he motioned her to join him.

"Have you met Senator Nelson? Bill, this is Maureen Beltzer, my assistant. You have her to thank for the quality of the show tonight."

Mo shook hands amid the Senator's congratulatory remarks, then he excused himself and told Geoff not to forget that luncheon date. And they were alone.

"I'm missing the *Sophronitis*. You did bring it?"

"Yes, but it would be easy to overlook. I had help unloading. I'm sure it's still in the van. Are we missing anything else?'"

"A couple *Vandas*. Big guys. I put them up front so they could hang behind the seat. Oh yeah, the Ghost Orchid. Give me a hand bringing them in?"

He smiled down on her, and she could feel the heat. Their bodies simply responded to one another, clothed, unclothed, alone or in a crowd.

"Sure. I'll meet you at the van. Let me grab my purse. I left it in the john."

"Get it on the way back." He formed a kiss with his lips and had that sloppy in-love look that cut to the core of her. His meaning wasn't lost; if they left now the alley was probably dark enough and deserted enough for a quick kiss. Still, her purse, credit cards, driver's license … phone … nothing she'd want to lose.

"I'll just be a sec." She almost reconsidered when she caught his crestfallen reaction. "Girl thing. Gotta have my stuff." She winked and returned the airborne kiss before turning to push back through the restroom door.

Later she thought of how easy it would have been to trust luck and the good intentions of those present in the bathroom. Maybe Nancy would have kept her purse safe. She had been so tempted to just go outside with Geoff. But as fate would have it, she pushed back through the swinging door and had just picked up her bag when the bomb went off.

Chapter Twenty-five

The explosion was barely muffled by the bathroom walls. There was a nanosecond *whoosh* of sound, so deafening as to be un-registerable on her brain. In that same instant, all the oxygen seemed to be sucked up into a vacuum, out of the room, held in an infinitesimal moment of stillness before bursting around her in dust and debris. She was rocked off her feet and ended up under the row of four sinks that hung from the south wall.

Mo didn't know how she'd gotten there, but suddenly she was on all fours, pressed against cracked blue-green tile and curved drain pipes. She narrowly missed the shattering burst of the mirrors that ran the full length of the wall above the sinks. Only their sound reached her in a musical tinkling of sparkling slivers that bounced against the floor and skipped outward.

The shrieking was deafening. Women who had been in the stalls seemed to have fared well—better than those who had been leaning against the wall that had collapsed. And then she realized that she was looking up at the stars. A chunk of the west side wall of the building was gone. A large round hole had been blasted through layers of mortar and brick—a portion of the outside wall was simply rubble.

The van. Oh God. What had happened to the van? She struggled to stand but couldn't get her feet under her. Geoff. She was barely seconds behind him. They were going to meet at the van. He'd been headed toward the loading dock—right at the source of the explosion.

She heard a sound leave her lips, something a wounded animal would make. This time she made it upright, dislodging her right foot caught under half of a sink, only to immediately lose her balance and pitch forward onto chunks of concrete. The palms of her hands stung with the impact. She tried again and managed to stay upright.

Her view of the alley and side street was unobstructed and the sight was daunting. This wasn't Iraq or Afghanistan, some war-torn country that lived with car bombs and devastation. But that's what it looked like.

Eerily, under the full mulberry moon, the stark outline of the van's frame was all but obscured by black smoke with intermittent bursts of flame. Charred crisps of pieces—what was left of the van presumably littered the parking lot. Along with pieces of the Volvo. Oh no, her ever-trusty car was gone, decimated. Parked next to the van, it had no chance. All its glass was gone and the tires were smoldering.

She didn't see Geoff. She heard a siren in the distance

and knew it was coming her way. Suddenly people were everywhere. Yet, she couldn't move, couldn't call out— even form the words to ask if Geoff was all right. She closed her eyes, deep breath, opened them and inched forward.

She had to find him. Had to know he was all right, but had to be prepared for the worst. Could she handle it if she found a speck of human flesh, complete with hair from chest or scalp or underarm? She didn't think so.

She was oblivious to her own injuries and absently wiped aside a trickle of blood that seemed determined to slide into her left eye. Her right ankle didn't work properly. Every step forward almost brought her to her knees. Gritting her teeth, she forced her body to move.

Geoff. What if he was hurt? What if he was trying to find her? Or worse, caught under something, calling out, but no one listening. She simply had to believe that he was all right. Surely, he was out there in the crowd somewhere, looking for her. She pushed her body to respond. She was hobbled, pulling her right leg, gingerly putting a moment's weight on it before hopping on her left. Too slow. She had to get to the alley. She dropped to her knees clawing at a pile of rubble to get over it.

"You can't get any closer. It's too dangerous."

Ben Pecos caught her around the waist and didn't seem in a mood to let go. She was anchored firmly, a safe twenty feet from her destination, the smoldering pile of destruction.

"Please, I have to—"

"Mo, we need to get you fixed up."

Ben lifted her over the last of the rubble and didn't put her down until they were in the back of the ballroom and then he gently eased her into a chair. She tried to question him but realized that her voice wasn't working. Ben waved over another man; Mo gathered he was a doctor from the expert way he went over her body.

"Nothing's broken. There's some bruising and you took a hell of a thump to the left hip and leg. Even the cut above your eye won't need stitches. Lots of *owies* but you'll mend. An icepack to that ankle would be a help. Do that and keep it elevated, and it'll be as good as new in a week."

"What about … the others?" Mo croaked. Paramedics were rushing around behind her and she could see people being carried out on stretchers.

"Not to worry. There are probably more docs here than there'll be in any emergency room." He patted her on the shoulder. "And don't worry about your throat. It's going to be sore for a few days—you swallowed some dust out there."

"But did anyone die?" She was looking up at him from the plush coziness of the chair, her leg stuck out in front of her, balanced on a box that had appeared from somewhere, the ankle bruised and turning purple. She suddenly felt small, her voice an echo from some distance. "Please, I need to know."

"You need to rest here until we can come up with a ride for you."

Quickly, Ben knelt beside her. He patted her arm. "Hang in there, Mo. You're one of the lucky ones. What can be done is being done."

It sounded profound. She nodded solemnly. Someone handed Ben a blanket and he cocooned it around her. Was he worried that she would go into shock? Because that was the strange part. She felt remarkably in control. Calm, rational, maybe on the edge of an abyss but certainly not piling over the side … just yet.

She drew in several deep breaths and made eye contact. Ben was gentle; Julie was lucky. He tucked the edge of the blanket behind her. "Think you'll be okay if I leave? I'll get Julie to check on you but I'm needed back out there."

Mo just nodded. Be okay? Would she ever be okay again?

"I mean it. I want you to stay here and not move. I need to make sure you don't need a trip to the hospital and then we'll give you a ride home. I don't want you driving."

She nodded. Not that she could drive anywhere. She pictured the smoldering remains of her car.

"Good. I need to see if I can be of use elsewhere—You'll be fine, Mo, trust me. Please, don't worry about anything until we have answers."

Ben would be good with children, Mo thought, with his ready smile, comforting touch.

She watched him walk toward the back, stopping to help an elderly man to stand.

"Mo, oh my God, you're hurt. Ben didn't warn me, he just asked me to keep you company." Julie stepped around Mo's elevated leg and dragged a chair to sit beside her.

"I think I'm going to live." If I don't think, look around, or ask to see anyone who might be in a body bag …

"Oh, I meant to tell you earlier. I loved your dress."

Past tense. Not good. Mo hadn't been thinking about clothing. Without opening the blanket to inspect she knew the lilac silk had bought it.

"A Georgianne?"

Mo shook her head. It was an "off-a-the-rack-o" but nice to think Julie assumed Mo could afford the expensive designer.

"Do you know what happened?" Mo asked.

"Some kind of explosion. I overheard someone say a car bomb."

"In the university van?"

Julie shrugged. "I can't say where, exactly." But her expression said Mo's guess was right on.

The van. The one Mo had helped load, and then followed, had been wired to blow up … it was almost unbelievable. Incredible that maybe terrorists had found some reason to do this in St. Augustine. It wasn't as if Casa Monica was a mosque or a black church or a gay bar … but the governor, Senator Nelson, local dignitaries—it could have been meant for anyone.

"How many people were killed?" It was time to ask this question. Mo needed to know.

"I think they've found two bodies and, of course, your—"

Mo knew she was going to say boss but stopped abruptly with an intake of air.

"I'm sorry. I wasn't sure you knew it was Geoff Mitchell."

"Oh God." Maybe earlier had been just a premonition, but she knew. She felt herself go cold as she swallowed hard.

"It's such a shock. So pointless." Julie's chin quivered and her eyes had turned luminous with tears. "I was sitting next to a Nancy Kildere. One minute we were talking and the next she was killed in the restroom."

Julie's tears almost sent her over the edge. Mo took a shaky breath, reached out and took her hand, "All of this is so truly awful. And impossible to make sense of it." There was no sense to be made of it, she could only stay strong.

Julie fumbled in a stylish shoulder bag and came up with a Kleenex and blew her nose. "Look, I'm supposed to be helping you pack up, not blubber away. Someone from the university is coming to retrieve you and the plants—get everything safely back to the Lab. Should be here in thirty minutes. If you show me what to do, I'll get the plants lined up and in their traveling containers. You can just rest here." She smiled, a forced, perky parting of the lips, but not very heartfelt.

Mo knew her own smile was forced. Tragedy and how you handled it said a lot for character. She'd probably have to remind herself of that because right now the only thing she wanted to do—needed to do—was be alone to cry. She was forcing pictures of Geoff from her mind, willing herself not to dwell on what might have been. Instead of walking into a suite upstairs about now, she would be hobbling out to a van or truck, driving back out to the greenhouses, unloading, and placing some hundred plants back where they'd come from. Maybe by midnight, she'd be home.

From where Mo was sitting, she could tell the tables and lectern hadn't been touched. A few dozen orchids sat beautifully oblivious to the destruction nearby. Mo marveled at her own control but knew it would be helpful to do something that would keep her mind occupied. Keep her from thinking ...

"I forgot to ask, do you feel you should go to the hospital? I'm not being a very good nurse, am I?"

"No hospital needed—leg up, ice pack—that sort of thing is what the doctor said. That can be done at home." Mo didn't want to sit in an ER for half the night. Besides, she was responsible for the valuable plants spread out across the front of the room. "Let's see if I can stand."

With Julie on one side and the back of the seat in front of her, she wobbled upright, paused for a moment, then slipped out of the blanket and started down front. The doc was right about the hip and the ankle. She had a goose-egg knot on her quads four inches above the knee. Julie caught Mo's elbow and provided balance.

"Are you sure this is okay? I mean should you be moving around at all?"

Mo nodded and surveyed the table. And then it hit her. The *Sophronitis coccinea* hadn't made it in from the van. Mo had been on her way out to get it. The adorable Lady in Red was blown to smithereens, minute particles of red petals and green foliage blasted into oblivion.

Along with Dr. Geoff Mitchell.

Mo had no warning as her knees buckled, sending her sprawling to the floor.

Chapter Twenty-six

Funny how cheating death—bullets and car bomb—three times in the space of one month could give one a sense of bravery—invincibility, actually. False though it probably was. Or did it have something to do with Geoff's death? He had lost his life, and she was no longer afraid to do the same.

There was some sort of weird logic to it. Even though she didn't believe for a minute that she'd meet him on the other side … the other side of what? Whenever she heard that phrase as a child she'd always equated life with climbing a really big fence and then one day simply plopping over the top. Into nothingness. She'd upset her mother's ingrained Baptist upbringing with that theory.

So, she healed. Alone in a house she no longer kept

locked. One tiny step at a time. Forcing her numbed self to go to work every day, then come home, fix a sandwich, watch the news, wash her underwear—do the hundreds of little things that kept her from staying in bed all day. She survived random visits from Marjorie and Claire and Detective Foley and Ben and Julie. Even the FBI. Lots of tsking and hand-holding and questioning.

A group who called themselves Defenders of the Americas took credit for the bombing. No one had ever heard of them. And the FBI seemed skeptical but resigned to give the group credence as no other leads seemed promising. Their on-line presence seemed to indicate they existed to preserve green space—stop people from raping the fragile habitat. Stop the stealing from nature. Somehow blowing up people trained to save nature didn't make sense.

The bruises disappeared long before the numbness. And she couldn't even discuss the numbness—the *real* numbness—and its cause with anyone. Least of all dear ol' Claire. A widow would receive compassionate time off work, would get cards and letters, condolences and shoulders to cry on. But Mo couldn't even talk with her family because even in death, it was best to keep her liaison with Geoff a secret. But liaison? Was that the right word? Certainly what was about to happen had been squelched before it blossomed. But he had said he loved her. Didn't that count for something? She finally stopped reliving that moment in the shower. It was just too painful.

She'd gone on crutches to Nancy's funeral and to Geoff's memorial. There had been a quick cremation for Geoff. Of course, why not? There wasn't even a decent amount of him found to bury and, if you wanted to be brutally honest, he'd already been cremated. The candlelight tribute was held in the evening along the Intracoastal behind the Whitney lab and the new greenhouses, Geoff's work, Geoff's love. It was beautiful and fitting. Everyone was given a small paper 'boat' with votive candle to float on the water. Some two hundred small vessels twinkled as they dipped and bobbed along the shoreline. The *Recorder* reported two hundred and twenty people in attendance. She couldn't tell. She only knew it was a crush of humanity—the curious, the slightly acquainted, and those who really cared. A number of fellow professors and students came from as far away as California.

She would have even welcomed Claire's company, but big sis was still on the West Coast, off on another trip. This time to meet with architects of yet another planned observatory and tour several structures already in existence—one in Balboa Park, San Diego and the other in Portland—gathering ideas from the one just completed in Florida.

Mo knew, to honor Geoff's memory, the most important thing was the work would go on. Orchids and other endangered plants would be saved, cloned once the laboratory was finished and returned to their native habitat if at all possible. Of course, the habitat of so many species was fast disappearing itself. Could Geoff have chosen a better epitaph? She thought not.

Even in death he would continue to save the living. When the lighted candles were placed in the small paper boats, she tucked a small orchid bloom in hers and said a silent and personal good-bye. And resignation, if not a sense of closure, set in.

She'd met with the University of Florida's Board of Regents and St. Augustine's Parks and Recreation council, with a representative from the Department of the Interior sitting in, and was surprised when, to a man, they begged her to continue with the project—as its Director.

They were behind on their international pledge of manpower—that is, one photographer and lab manager for the new sister facility in Costa Rica—so it made sense to replace Geoff here with someone who knew the ropes already and could support projects currently underway. Once past the Centennial year, the project would take on global stature. Thanks to interest in Climate Change and Global Warming, funding was not perceived as a problem. She would become a full-time employee at twice her current salary.

Of course, there would be extra compensation, as well as overtime and travel. And the university thought it had two interns lined up for the remainder of the summer, perhaps, keeping them on for the Fall semester. Mo agreed to their offer.

That put off the trip to the Everglades by another couple weeks, probably longer, but that was okay, too. She could be gone up to three months, and she needed to find a house-sitter unless she talked Marjorie into it. Two or three weeks to get things in order would be fine.

Life seemed destined to slip into humdrum. She went to work every day and found it therapeutic. The interns were bright and eager and made the job of training easy. There were three of them—girls—geeky, sweet, and dedicated. Two post-docs in botany and a BS-level fine arts photographer. And by waiting a few weeks before taking off, Mo would be able to help with the local Garden Guild's spring show.

Had that been part of the plan? She would swear that

no one had mentioned it when she was hired. Mo didn't really care; the new pay scale more than covered "additional duties as assigned."

She sat in on the design stage and pledged her help in setting up the show, if needed. Formerly it had always been held at the Armory in town. They had requested use of the greenhouses, but the show conflicted with a Department of Interior tour. So, the Armory it was, with Mo supplying many, if not all, of the orchids used to decorate the entryway.

The Botanical Garden patrons seemed to be bogged down in politics and in-fighting. But what was new? Volunteer groups could be nasty and impossible to organize—hadn't someone equated it to herding cats? Mo suggested she bring twenty-five plants, all in bloom, mostly showy Phalacnopsis because of their long sprays of pendulous blooms.

Not everyone agreed—there were some holdouts for Cattleyas even though apparently, two years in a row a spectacular—six inch across—white flowering Moth Orchid had taken best in show. But her reminder fell on deaf ears. A small contingent of dowagers was holding out to totally revamp the show—entryway and all. They wanted something "catchy and modern". A theme— maybe something from a Broadway musical. Whatever that would be. Maybe dozens of *Oncidiums*—the dancing lady orchid—swaying to tunes from West Side Story? She admonished herself not to get sarcastic. They would come to her when there was a plan; she could only hope there would be time to get everything in order.

So, for a couple of weeks, Mo had actually forgotten about the show—other than making plans to go to the

Friday night reception. But at ten on Thursday morning, the phone rang. One of the prickliest of the volunteers, a woman who'd thrown every roadblock in her way earlier.

Sorry to be so late in requesting, but under the circumstances, wouldn't she like to contribute? Wasn't it really *the* opportune time to show the public the pride of U of F's botany department and the new additions out at the Lab? Wouldn't Dr. Mitchell have wanted this? They were counting on her. *Would* she be good enough to bring over twenty-five plants? Yes, yes, of course, anything showy in full bloom—the bigger, the better. And wouldn't she like to show them? Enter them for prizes? The armory would be open at seven-thirty in the morning.

The chirpy voice just dripped conciliatory honey, but Chirpy was used to getting her way. The dowager expected Mo to drop everything and hop to. Because, oh, by the way, the plants needed to be in place before three that afternoon—especially if she planned to show. It was exactly what she had been afraid of—they had waited until the absolute very last minute to let her know what they wanted.

"Damn." Why couldn't these people get it together? Surely, they'd been planning the show since last year. Hadn't anyone heard her when she reminded them of what she could do if given a reasonable heads-up? Once again, the inventory and training were put aside. First of all, transportation needed to be arranged. Little really would fit in her BMW sedan, a rather neat replacement for the Volvo and a congratulatory gift to herself on obtaining full-time employment.

Under the circumstances, maybe an intern could bring a van over from Gainesville this afternoon. Mo called their motor pool and ordered a van. They would *try* to get one to her by eleven-thirty today. Fine. Try. She was finding she had little patience for step 'n fetch it.

But the van was there on time and she had rounded up eight of the promised twenty-five show-stoppers—at the top of the list was a purple *dendrobium, Andre Miller,* with over one hundred quarter-sized blooms, a green and wine-red *Cymbidium chawalongense,* a new discovery from Tibet with five loaded flower stalks, and an *Oncidium, Gower Ramsey,* an oldie, but goody, with fifteen pendulous sprays of bright yellow fluttering 'skirts' on its dancing girls—just in case that Broadway musical theme had come to fruition.

The others were, perhaps, less attention-demanding in color or form, but top notch in their own way. Maybe an overly large flower like the superb *Paphiopedilum,* a *Rothschildian* cross, deep red maroon with a gigantic hairy pouch, or the *Vanda,* again a cross, *V.Karaulea x V. Gordon Dillon,* with long arching spikes of blue flowers would win the attention of the judges. In any show it was tough to second-guess personal preferences.

Mo liked her choices—a nice variety. How could the dowagers not be impressed? Fingers crossed they would pass muster. But now for the hard work.

Transporting orchids was always the challenge— hadn't it taken her an hour to load the van for a twenty-five mile trip into town last month? Again, some plants would have to hang on the back of the van's front seat. Others would be covered in plastic 'peanuts' in deep boxes. And still others, she would wind cardboard cones around their fragile flowers, gently cushioning buds with strips and blocks of Styrofoam. Lunch would have to wait. She wanted everything in place by mid-afternoon and noon was coming up quickly.

The day wasn't unseasonably hot but the bright sun made it feel warmer than it was. Purely psychological. Hot was hot, but this was typical Florida. The winter had been mild and the spring milder. Now the second week in June, and the day was pleasant this close to the ocean. Humidity was below eighty percent according to the hygrometer in the lab. Perfect for her but the orchids would have liked a little more.

She lined up the twenty-five plants in their various types of packing material along the back wall of Greenhouse Three. She'd load them one by one, taking the ten steps to the open back of the van as quickly as possible and not leaving the doors open longer than necessary. She'd started the van and it was idling smoothly, cool air blasting to the max. She grabbed the Vanda by its wire hanger and headed out the door.

She leaned in to set the plant halfway back from the door and then crawled in beside it. She'd hang it from the bar behind the front seats and tape the hanger to the bar to keep the plant from shifting. She'd considered covering it with light sheeting but was afraid even that might be too heavy for the pendulous, delicate flower spikes.

Five minutes later she was ready for plant number two. She eased backwards on hands and knees, stretching her foot out to gage the edge of the van's floor.

And that's when she saw it. To her left behind the wheel well in back of the driver's side seat was a plant—but not just any plant. *Sophronitis Coccinea*, the superb little *Lady in Red*, lay neglected, partially concealed, as it drooped against the van's metal wheel wall. Dangling next to it, taped to its pot, was a tangle of roots that could only be the *Ghost Orchid*.

Mo quickly sat back on her legs, carefully peeled the tape away from the wheel covering and gathered the plants to her. She carefully unwrapped the *Lady in Red* and slipped the small Styrofoam cone which held the three perfect blooms, now wilted and spent, away from the foliage. Was its host still alive? Mo knew the vans were kept on the bottom floor of a parking tower at the University— shaded, so not all that hot but safe from exposure to the elements and direct sun.

Thank God the outside temps had been reasonable. And it still had its protective cover. It could probably be saved. Orchids could be resilient. She felt as though she was trying to reassure herself.

But the question, the one struggling to push to the surface of her brain—if the van that had carried all the plants for show and tell—all the props for the fundraiser— had been obliterated by a bomb, and she hadn't had time to retrieve it, how had the *Sophronitis Coccinea* gotten here alongside the twisted 'body' of the Ghost Orchid? Exactly as she had wrapped them both *and* exactly where she had placed them?

Chapter Twenty-seven

She couldn't suppress the trembling that ran through her body. This was the van she'd helped to load two weeks ago. The van Geoff drove to the Casa Monica. The tiny orchids gave it away. Because she'd tried to keep them from getting squashed by placing them behind the wheel well, it would have been easy to overlook the plants. She was on her way back out to this very van when the bomb went off. Or she thought it was this van.

A van had been obliterated; no one questioned that. But vans had been exchanged, another one with this one, before detonation. That was the only explanation. But why? By whom? And when and where had it been traded?

There had certainly been plenty of time during Geoff's presentation, over an hour and a half to be exact. But someone had to have keys and access and know where to find it. She walked back to her office, hanging the Lady in Red on the edge of a five gallon bucket of nutrients and water, making a mental note to retrieve it before she left for the day. It wouldn't hurt the roots to soak up some jump-start fertilizer. It could be saved but a couple weeks in the van hadn't done it any favors. And the Ghost Orchid she dropped in a cheesecloth bag and dangled it from the edge of the same bucket.

She sat behind her desk a few moments before reaching for her phone, opening the camera app and walking back out to the van. Before she did anything else, she wanted pictures. She opened the van and took several shots of exactly where the orchids were found with remnants of masking tape still adhered to the wheel well cover, then one of the back, the side, the license tag, and a shot from the front before locking the van and walking back inside.

Should the van be dusted for prints? Probably, but she doubted there would be any other than University personnel—but then, maybe she was overlooking school involvement. Still … Sense. Logic. It wasn't making any.

She brushed a strand of hair out of her eyes, scooted the chair up to her desk, checked the contacts list on her phone, and tapped in the number.

"University of Florida, Motor Pool, Larry speaking."

"Larry, this is Maureen Beltzer over at the greenhouses, Whitney Labs. I wonder if you could give me a little history on van number …" She pulled the key ring closer in order to read the identifying tag. "H as in happy, Z as in zebra, I as in icicle, 4982."

"That the van I delivered earlier? Don't tell me it's acting up again."

"Yes, er, no, it's fine." She hesitated a brief second

before pushing on. She didn't want to explain anything she didn't have to. "Wasn't this the van we checked out for the presentation in St. Augustine the last week in May?"

"Yeah, one of them. But it had some engine problems—barely made it into town. Kept cutting out. Your boss ordered another van after he got to the hotel and we drove up and made the exchange—towed that one back. I don't have to tell you what happened to the one we delivered. The big boom …" Silence, then, "Um, sorry, didn't mean to sound flip. I'm sorry about your boss. Dr. Mitchell was well liked."

She hung up quickly after assuring Larry that that was all she needed. And then she just sat there. Engine problems? Barely made it up the road and across town? She'd followed Geoff. The van was fine. She would bet it wasn't cutting out. And Geoff called to get another? It made no sense. First of all, he would have asked her to make that call—at the very least, tell her what was going on. He certainly had his mind on other things. But he'd asked her about the *Sophronitis*—whether she had brought it in. And the Vandas—she thought it was Vandas that had also been left in the van. He was going out to get them. They were both going to meet at the van.

Not a new, just delivered van but the original van—the one she had packed about an hour earlier … good ol' HZI4982. Obviously, Geoff didn't know the vans had already been exchanged. But how could he? She knew … *knew* that he hadn't ordered the second van. So, who did? Too many questions.

She hit redial. "Larry? Mo Beltzer again. I meant to ask earlier, did you find a couple big plants secured to the bar behind the driver's seat? Sort of hanging behind the seat?"

"Yeah, somebody from maintenance gave 'em to one of the interns working over your way."

"I've been out for a couple weeks. I'm sure I've just overlooked them. Thanks again."

She put the phone down. Well, at least the Vandas were safe. But why would the vans be switched? Give someone more time to plant a bomb? An involuntary shiver. That had to be it. And if someone needed time to plant a bomb, where had the van been that replaced the first one? Who had had it that afternoon?

She hit redial. "Larry, look I'm really sorry … I'm just not thinking straight, but I meant to ask you, who was the last person to check out the van that was blown up?"

"No problem. Gimme a minute."

Mo wasn't even sure why this was so important but it might be.

"Here it is. Looks like you did. Your signature a big M and a big O with some squiggles in between?"

"I suppose that's an apt description." Except I didn't check out that van or any other van, Mo thought. "My memory's a little foggy … when did I check it out?"

"That afternoon. You sent an intern over with the paperwork. Thought you might need two vans for transport and you just wanted to make sure you were covered."

"Oh, right." *As in, wrong.* "I hit my head in the bombing and—"

"Hey, no need to apologize. Glad I can help."

"When did I cancel?"

"You didn't, exactly. You told us to leave it in the parking lot at Marineland—You chose that parking lot because of the upcoming bus tours. My notes say you wanted to make sure there was plenty of room for the tour buses over behind Whitney. Looks like we delivered it at one-thirty. When your boss called that night, he requested we pick up that one and bring it up as the replacement. It saved time on the paperwork seeing as you'd already checked it out."

"Yes, of course." Her mind was spinning. She did not check out a van; she did not leave it in the parking lot on A1A. Her boss did not call and request it …

"Do you need anything else?"

"No." This time after thanking him, she pressed the disconnect but continued to hold the phone in her hand. Should she call someone? Detective Foley? Did the cops already know? Maybe they had questioned the guys at the car pool. Found out the vans had been exchanged. But no one had said anything to her.

But sometime the afternoon of the presentation, someone had that van long enough to wire it with explosives and return it to the Marineland parking lot—after she and Geoff had left. This suggested a lot more premeditation than had been originally thought.

Had Geoff been targeted? Or maybe she was the target … she sat up straight both hands gripping the desk's edge. An attempt on her life? Another attempt, that is. Another involuntary shiver made her draw her arms closer to her sides.

Then she grabbed her phone, pushed away from the desk and walked back through the greenhouses and outside. Sunshine, fresh air … normalcy. A couple deep breaths were soothing. But she needed to call someone. Detective Foley. She hadn't talked to him since being debriefed after the bombing. She brought up the contacts on her phone and pressed his number.

"Sorry, Foley is no longer at this station. May I direct

your call to another detective?"

"No. I've been working with Detective Foley. Is there some way I can reach him? Maybe just leave a message?"

"Let me transfer you to his former supervisor. Hold, please."

How strange. Mo listened to the bad Muzak while she waited. He hadn't said he was leaving.

"Lt. Polaski."

Mo jerked back to the present. The man sounded harried.

"Hi, sorry to bother you but my name is Maureen Beltzer. I've been working with Detective Foley and would like to reach him."

"Not with us any more."

Mo waited but nothing seemed to be forthcoming. "I know he was working on the bombing of the biopark van a month ago."

"Took a transfer. He's unavailable. I've assigned Detective Nolan—"

"That's all right. Thank you for your time." Mo hung up.

Why wouldn't Tim have told her if he was transferring? She was sure of it. Wait.

Over a month ago after the first scare, he'd given her his private cell number. At the time she'd thought it was really sweet and thoughtful. She went back to her office, opened the middle drawer of her desk, moved a few paper clips, a cord to something electronic—she remembered keeping his card with the number on the back. Thank God she took after Marjorie and never threw anything away. There it was.

She still hesitated to dial. Would he think it an

imposition? Whatever he was doing now, Lt. Polaski made it sound like he was in a completely new job, maybe even undercover. But she'd never know unless she tried. She tapped in the number and sat back as it rang. At least it hadn't been disconnected.

"Yeah."

The curtness made her stutter. "I, uh, this is Mo—"

"I'll call you back."

The click was still ringing in her ears when her phone rang.

"Whitney Labs and BioPark, Maureen Beltzer."

"Mo, I can't talk now but let's meet. How 'bout meatloaf at seven?"

"Perfect."

Again an abrupt click.

It was difficult to concentrate the rest of the afternoon, once she'd sent the orchids off to the flower show. She'd start a project then absently put it down. Curiosity was killing the cat in slow increments.

Chapter Twenty-eight

Every time Ben saw Councilman Wolff's number come up on his phone, his chest tightened. Utter frustration didn't even begin to describe his feelings of helplessness. Ben simply had no new information. Fingers crossed there had been a ransom note.

"Councilman."

"Let me run a couple ideas past you. Do you have a minute?"

"Yes, of course."

"I'm tired of dead ends. I know the detectives don't want me to do this but I'm offering a reward. Do you think $100,000 would catch attention? I'm willing to pay for information—anything that might shake loose some greedy SOB who knows something. If it leads to an arrest and the return of my son, it's little to pay. But is it enough?"

"Attention-getting and generous, I would say. Could I make a suggestion?"

"What's that?"

"Print notices to be posted around town—everywhere—bars, restaurants, churches, the soup kitchen on Ribeiro. Don't just rely on newspaper or TV coverage. Get the word out in the old fashioned way. And, print the notices in both English and Spanish."

"Good suggestions but why two languages?"

Ben filled him in on the earlier theft of plants from the greenhouses by suspected workers from Mexico, and noted that there were still several green-card workers on the Whitney Lab site. "Sometimes word of mouth spreads information within close-knit groups."

"Good point. I'll get my office personnel on it."

Ben was glad to have been of help, even more glad when the call ended. He was on his way out, to pick up Julie and head for a special meeting.

+ + +

Mo almost didn't recognize Tim Foley in jeans and denim shirt. But the table in the far corner by the window and the steaming plate of meatloaf, mashed, no veggies, side of salad gave him away. And Ben and Julie Pecos were sitting opposite him with their own plates of meatloaf.

"There's another one of these on its way the minute you sit down." Tim grinned down at her after standing for a quick hug.

"Thanks." A nod to Ben, a hug for Julie, and Mo pulled a chair out hoping no one had heard her stomach growl. A

Pavlov reaction to meatloaf for sure, and one of the signs that she was back to normal—or almost there. "Smells wonderful."

"It comes highly recommended," Julie added, pointing at Tim.

"Mo's the one who got me hooked. Beats a chicken pot pie anytime, and what'd I tell you?" The waiter put a duplicate steaming plate in front of Mo and picked up the flag that had led him to the right table. Tim continued to watch as she took a couple bites.

She looked up sheepishly, "I didn't realize how hungry I was." Everyone seemed relaxed and since the others were well into their meals, Mo decided to hold the questions that had nagged at her all afternoon.

"I fully plan on being here through dessert—did you see that apple pie on the counter?" Ben pointed over his shoulder. "Looks lo-cal."

Julie gave him a withering look, "Sure."

Conversation was put on hold, other than comments on the food, until they had finished, then Tim went for a couple lattes before motioning for a waiter to bus the table and ordered a beer for himself. Ben offered to share his pie but didn't have any takers.

Tim took a swallow of beer then leaned forward, both elbows on the Formica table top. "Now, what's going on?"

"First of all, I was afraid I'd lost you," Mo said. "Lt. Polaski made it sound like you'd dropped off the edge of the earth."

"Mike can be a little melodramatic but truth is I've taken another job—a promotion, sort of. Better money and better opportunities heading toward retirement."

"But you're still a cop?"

"With the Feds, no less. I'm a Federal Marshal—or will be soon."

"Wow. Sounds important. You probably won't have to look under beds in that job." Mo smiled and got the laugh she anticipated.

"I'm gonna miss that."

"And how about you? Aren't congratulations in order? Don't we have the pleasure of having dinner with the new Director of Operations at the Whitney Botanical Gardens?" Julie asked.

"Well, yes, thanks. I'm still trying to get my mind around all that's happened."

"You seem to be doing well," Ben said. "But if you'd like to talk, I'm still at Flagler College. Just give me a call."

"Thanks. So far, so good but odd things keep happening." Mo told them about the van, actually the two vans that had been switched.

"We knew about that. It sounded plausible when we checked the records. Van acts up and project director orders a back-up, nothing suspicious there."

"But I didn't order a van and I'd bet my life Dr. Mitchell didn't order one either."

Foley looked a little embarrassed. "I believe you. It was my oversight not to follow up, ask questions. I'm sorry." Tim sat staring down at the table, his fingertips lightly tapping his coffee cup. "It looks as though someone bought a few hours in order to wire the replacement van. The bomb was sophisticated—used remote control. Whoever detonated the bomb controlled the timing. Doesn't rule out that eco group but no one found anyone bright enough for that kind of job among the members we interviewed. And seldom do environmentalists intentionally kill."

"So, who do you think—"

"Someone who wanted to kill your boss or—" He paused and made eye contact.

"Me … it's okay. I'm resigned to it." But she knew the feeble smile wasn't convincing. Tim seemed about to say something else and she waited.

"There's been increased activity internationally in contraband species of plants—orchids in particular. Several multi-million dollar deals are being reported out of Interpol. You know the robbery at the biopark last month—how we said a fired worker wouldn't know what to take?" She nodded. "Well, we have reason to believe that he was shopping for someone—went in with a list. Knew exactly where to go to get the good stuff, so to speak—as you know."

"But who would have that information?"

"For starters, we were going to ask your boss."

"I can't imagine Geoff would have any idea who would have set the robbery up."

"Unless he did it himself. School records show he'd had several business interactions with Mr. Garza over the last six to eight months involving the transport of plants. It would appear that Mr. Garza would have had some idea as to what was valuable."

Mo stared at him, shaking her head too shocked to speak. "No. That doesn't mean Geoff set up that robbery. There's no way. And where did the orchids go?"

"Good question. They just disappeared. We'd get a lead—we have agents in the international markets—but the orchids never showed up. INTERPOL reported big money was being transferred to off-shore holdings, but putting names or faces to any of it has been a dead end.

But maybe that's why Geoff Mitchell was killed—dabbling in something pretty big and he got in over his head. And then if he knew too much, someone had to get rid of him."

"But why? Why would he protect plants—spend his life saving the threatened ones only to steal them?"

"Money. Doesn't greed drive the world these days?"

"I don't think he was interested in money. I never saw any indications—living beyond his means, driving too expensive of a car—"

"He was pretty heavily in debt."

"How?" She slumped against the booth's high back. But didn't Lilian indicate he'd lost his inheritance?

"A business deal gone bad. Seems a former partner stole a patentable idea before it was registered. Some kind of tempered polycarbonate building material for large greenhouses. He was incorporating BPA—stands for Bisphenol A—into large sheets of the plastic that added unheard-of strength. He began producing the material in his own manufacturing plant but was beat to the finish line by a cheaper, easier to produce product from China. Dr. Mitchell's life savings were invested. He lost everything."

"So you think he set up the robbery?" Tim nodded. "But the night he was killed ... do you believe he had the van wired?"

"We know he reported his van malfunctioning and asked that it be exchanged with the one ordered earlier in the day."

"How could you know that?"

"Voice patterns. Luckily he left a message before calling back to confirm. The maintenance department seldom erases anything incoming. We compared that message with several of his taped lectures. Perfect match, Dr. Mitchell ordered that van."

"It would seem obvious that he wasn't planning to kill himself."

"I'd say that he was double-crossed … again. Guy sure had shit for luck with friends."

Mo felt like the air had been kicked out of her. What she wasn't saying was that Geoff had asked her to help him carry in the overlooked plants, the *Lady in Red*, the *Vandas*, the *Ghost Orchid* … meet him in the alley, he'd said … could he possibly have been setting *her* up? She couldn't even go there. Geoff, possibly a thief? Having the van wired? Maybe a murderer? Planning on killing her? But by some accident was killed himself? No. They were going to spend the night together. It was just too preposterous. She wiped sweaty palms on her jeans. Hadn't he said that he loved her?

Chapter Twenty-nine

Foley seemed ready to drop the subject, but Mo couldn't let it go. "Look, I'm still stuck on that van. Are you sure the one that was blown up was a university van? Here's a picture of the one Geoff originally drove to the Casa Monica. They are all alike. It would have looked like this." Mo pulled out her phone and brought up the side view of the Ram cargo van.

Tim leaned forward, "Ben, look at this." Tim handed him the phone.

"I'll be damned. The one graphic we didn't think of—the state seal complete with a Seminole woman scattering flowers. This is what Toby saw. The graphic of an Indian on the door of the Van's cab. Buckley Bear, the driver, and probably whoever abducted him drove a University of Florida state vehicle."

"Convinces me it's all tied in together. Maybe Toby was abducted because someone was afraid that *he* knew too much," Ben offered.

"That's crossed my mind. Without a ransom demand, it makes the most sense. I only hope the kid's all right because that's been another dead end. Local cops are on it and so are the Feds. The kid has simply vanished. We haven't had one reasonable clue—lots of phone-ins wanting a reward."

"Councilman Wolff is offering $100,000 for information," Ben told them. "That should shake something loose. I hope he gets the result he's hoping for."

"Do you think Toby's—?" Mo couldn't bring herself to say 'dead'. Who would kill a child? The meatloaf was beginning to feel like a lump in her stomach.

Tim was watching her. "Listen, we've probably said too much. It's all conjecture and absolutely horrible conversation when food's involved. Are you okay?"

"I'm fine." A little lie but he wouldn't know. "Everything helps me make sense out of it all. Or at least gives me something to think about."

"I haven't just been sitting on my hands …" Everyone turned to look at Julie. "For the fun of it, I decided to run down the elusive Buckley suit. It just seemed odd that it would have been so easy to steal. The poor man who usually plays Buckley on weekends, has been charged a hundred-fifty dollars for losing the suit. Seems like someone from the restaurant dropped the suit at the cleaners. When the Buckley guy went to pick it up; it had already been claimed—by a woman. But between dark glasses, a long coat, and a scarf, no one at the cleaners could give me a good description. And the head that was found at Mo's was returned to the restaurant then sent back to the cleaners before anyone thought to check for DNA. The suit itself never turned up. Sorry, I'm afraid that's just more info that doesn't lead anywhere."

"Maybe, but more proof that a woman was involved in confronting Toby. I have to admit I'd been a little skeptical. Actually, that's a pretty good piece of sleuthing. If you ever decide to give up that newspaper gig, look me up." Marshal Foley got the laugh he wanted.

"Mo, I meant to ask when you leave? I take it you're still on board to do that swamp time in the Everglades?"

Mo smiled. "It's coming up. Believe me, I'm looking forward to it. Would you believe it if I said I needed a change of scenery?"

"I'm going to be traveling in your neck of the woods. If anything—and I mean anything—catches your attention, either now before you go or while travelling, I want to be the first to know. It can be anything—maybe something seems out of place, call me. You know, someone approaches you to buy plants or wants you to identify plants … lead a forest or swamp expedition …" He looked at her intently. "I mean it. Don't put yourself in danger. You know better than anyone these guys play for keeps. Use my cell number. I'm in training for the next few weeks but I'll get there or send someone."

"I can't believe that there would be anything. But, thanks."

"You never know."

Chapter Thirty

Today's treat had been an ice cream shake. When he was good, the captain got him something special. Usually, Oreos and cream, his favorite. He used to get those with his dad. He didn't know how long he'd been on the boat but school was out. There was a calendar on the cabin wall and the captain had turned the page up and it said June.

When the captain was there he'd take him out on the deck and they'd toss a baseball back and forth, or sometimes they'd play this shuffleboard game with brooms and flat, round cans of tuna. And no applesauce or apple juice. He had fries all the time now and he drank cokes. In fact, his burgers were always regular size, too. No kid's stuff.

The captain seemed real proud of him for following orders, like when those men had come for the sack. Today along with the shake, he'd brought him fries and a burger in a black and white bag from someplace new. There had been slices of brown things on the burger and Toby took those off and left them on the paper plate that the captain handed him.

Otherwise, it was lots better than a Whataburger.

"You don't like mushrooms?"

"No."

"Okay, then, no more mushrooms."

The captain seemed really happy about something. He kept looking at his watch and humming some song.

"Can we go somewhere?"

"Not right now, little man, but maybe later. We're supposed to be getting some company. And if you're real quiet, and hide under that desk again, we'll take this old tub for a ride. I'm thinking we just might want to talk to your dad. What do you say to that?"

"Okay. I mean, yeah, I want to talk to my dad. That's cool. Are you going to take me home?" It had been a really long time and he knew his mom would be really upset. He had to go home. "Please?"

"Well, we'll have to see. The better you follow directions, the better your chances will be. You understand?"

"Yeah. But I want to go home real bad." Toby couldn't contain his excitement and bounced around doing some kind of crazy dance bumping into the furniture in the close quarters.

"Okay, okay, slow down." But the captain was laughing. "Be careful, now, can't afford any damaged goods." Then he held up his hand and put a finger to his lips. "Hear that? Sounds like there's our company. Right on time." The captain checked his watch.

The motor didn't sound very large but it was coming their way. Finally, the motor cut off and something bumped against the side of the trawler. The captain warned him once again to stay out of sight, then rolled the heavy desk chair in place before he opened the cabin door and walked out on deck.

"Hey, the doc come through with my money?" There were sounds of someone climbing on board—one set of footsteps on the deck, followed by another.

"It's all here."

"Well, hand it over."

Toby almost cried out at the gunshot.

Close, big, it made the window above him rattle … and he knew the captain was dead even before he heard the drag of something big bump across the wooden slat decking to end with a splash. Then hurried steps, the thumping of the ladder against the side and the roar into action of the outboard finally retreating into the distance. Toby huddled under the desk for a long time.

He couldn't stop shivering. Sharks. Was the captain already eaten? Toby waited until he couldn't hear the motor any longer, then strained to hear any sound on deck. He was alone. Finally, he pushed the chair away from the opening and crawled out. The captain had unlocked the cabin door when he went out on deck so Toby could walk outside by himself.

He walked along the railing all around the trawler's edges ducking the long arms that held nets wrapped around them. It was a weird boat. When they played shuffleboard even the captain would sometimes hit his head. It wasn't like his dad's boat. He looked in the water and then in the distance away from the boat and didn't see the captain or any land. Just water. Everywhere, just water. Would sharks eat a man really fast? Toby guessed they would or pull the body under and maybe keep him for a snack. Toby was scared but he knew one thing—he didn't want to be a shark snack. So, what to do? Would those people come back?

The captain's outboard that he took back and forth to town was tied in back. The captain had left it in the water when he brought the burgers. It was tied next to a rope ladder. Sometimes the captain put it into a kind of sling and pulled it up out of the water.

Toby didn't want to be there if anyone came back. He climbed over the side, turned and felt for the ladder. His rubber-soled sneakers slipped on the rungs but he grabbed the hand-holds and carefully backed down. Once in the boat he untied it and pushed away. The current caught the lightweight skiff and rocked it silently away from the trawler, listlessly tugging it toward the open sea.

Chapter Thirty-one

The eerie opening bars of the *Twilight Zone* theme song pushed into his consciousness. Ben sat up in bed and fumbled for his phone. He'd taken it off vibrate, but this ringtone was just way too spooky to wake up to. Six a.m. and barely light but caller ID identified Tim Foley. He pushed answer.

"We've got a body."

"What? Where—?"

"Meet me at the County Morgue—4501 Ave A." Call terminated.

"Who—?" Julie turned toward him.

"Tim. Apparently a body's been found."

"Oh no—Toby?"

"He didn't say. But maybe that's why he called me. He

knows Toby's father asked me to work on the case." Julie had voiced the dread he was beginning to feel.

"Guess I'll find out."

Julie feigned sleep but watched Ben pull on a pair of jeans and a sweatshirt through half-closed eyes. Her husband. Still a concept that was taking some getting used to. And not that she really wanted to go look at a dead body, but still she was feeling left out. But Toby? What if it was Toby? That would be hard to take.

"Hey, I almost forgot. Hate to leave you with something I should take care of but not sure how much free time I'll have."

"What do you need? I'm free today." And every day, she added to herself. She had given into feelings of 'poor me' the last couple days. The word 'abandonment' had been on her mind. But maybe she could help …

"Ginny, Mo's aide at Jefferson Elementary, texted that she'd like to talk. I honestly don't think local law enforcement really followed up with her like I suggested. I interviewed her but I've always thought she had more to tell. Mind giving her a call?"

+ + +

St. Johns County Medical Examiner's or Coroner's Office was a newish building located at the edge of town that served three surrounding counties—St Johns, Putnam and Flagler—an indication that the place was probably never overcrowded but could easily serve three communities. This was definitely rural Florida.

Ben pulled his pickup into a space on the building's north side. His was one of three cars in the lot and he thought the newish white BMW belonged to Mo Beltzer. Not a bad set of wheels and a nice replacement for the obliterated Volvo. And it seemed to indicate she was back in the real world despite all the setbacks.

He walked to the front of the building. Locked. Like any place of business they probably had set office hours. Though it was odd to think of a morgue that way—of it being a business. Fluorescent lights glowed dully through the narrow glass pane in the metal front door. A press of the button on the side brought Tim Foley.

"Hey, sorry to drag you out so early but I've got a couple things I want to bounce off you."

"Is it Toby?" Ben didn't realize he was holding his breath until the air in his lungs sort of whooshed out.

"No, no. Wow, I'm sorry, man. I should have said. The body of that Garza guy washed up just north of here— Vilano Beach. Got the call about four-thirty. Mo is the only one I know who could identify the body as the Garza who worked for Dr. Mitchell. She's waiting for us in the coroner's office. I called you because I have an idea about Toby."

"Which is?"

"First, let me fill you both in and then get Mo to take a look at the body." Tim indicated the first door on his right marked appropriately, Office. Ben shook hands with Mo and commented about maybe trading her his Ford 150 for the Beemer. The laugh probably meant a "no."

Tim leaned against the desk. "I'll tell you what I know. We probably have more questions here than answers though. I know Mo hasn't had a chance to take a look but Mr. Garza was shot in the head at close range. He was found in the water. Now we have a choice—either he was killed somewhere in town and his body dumped in the ocean, or he and his killer were already in a boat somewhere on the water and the killing happened offshore.

"And that's my guess. I asked the shore patrol to check logs of any craft leaving the area or any stationary boats—like fishing trawlers—especially ones that may have been in position for more than a day or two or seemed to return to the same spot. If we don't come up with anything, we'll check boat rentals once businesses open."

The office door opened and the coroner stuck his head in. "I'm ready for a viewing."

"Maureen Beltzer, Dr. Pecos, this is George Andrews." Introductions completed, Mo followed the man back out to the hall.

Waiting until they left, Tim motioned Ben over to the desk. "Here's what I wanted you to see. Actually the reason I called you. I need your feedback."

He slipped on latex gloves and opened a waterproof packet containing a billfold and several papers. "We're lucky he kept his papers safe. This is called a Dry Pak. Always a good idea if you're near the water. First, look at this. A receipt for a T.E.D.—A Turtle Excluder Device. I think Garza owned or operated some kind of trawler, probably a shrimper. These devices fit into a net to guarantee that any turtles caught can escape and make it to the surface for air."

Ben nodded, "Also makes sense that he would have some kind of boat if hiding or fencing stolen goods. A moving target just makes detection that much more difficult. And it would make trips to Mexico and Central America more convenient."

"Now this might stretch your imagination but I want

to know what you think."

Tim spread a handful of receipts in front of Ben. "Whataburger, McDonald's and Steak 'N Shake. See anything interesting? Read the food orders and the dates they were placed."

Ben leaned forward. "Looks like he had company. Apple juice, apple sauce … a Happy Meal. Kid's meals." Ben looked up, "I don't think we're talking adult companionship here." Ben couldn't keep the excitement out of his voice. "And this McDonald's receipt is dated the morning after Toby disappeared. And this one from Steak' n Shake from day before yesterday. But this … this folded up flyer asking for information about Toby's abduction and offering $100,000—this seals it."

"Exactly. You're thinking what I'm thinking."

"The guy had Toby."

"Yeah. I think it's probably more than a pretty safe assumption. The question is, where's the kid now? If Garza was killed on some kind of boat and thrown overboard, did his killers do the same to Toby or take him with them?"

"Could be $100,000 has kept him alive. But I think there's a certain urgency here—"

"Couldn't agree more so let me get your feedback on this idea. My hands are tied when it comes to appropriating funds for a search. I'm in limbo until I go on payroll with the Feds. I can go through regular local legal channels provided by the state and get the shore patrol out there, but that wouldn't include hiring a helicopter to sweep the area."

"But Toby's father would jump at the idea." Ben interrupted and pulled his phone out of his pocket.

"Exactly. I have a friend who owns Old City Helicopters.

We're probably talking four-fifty an hour but it's the only fast way to do a thorough job of checking miles of off-shore area. The thousands it may cost could turn out to be cheap if we're successful. And we're still probably twelve hours behind."

Ben walked out into the hall, dialing his phone on the way. He got Councilman Wolff on the first ring, explained what they knew so far and got the resounding "Okay" to rent a helicopter. He'd meet Ben at the Northeast Florida Regional Airport, north of town on Highway 1 in twenty minutes. Tim called his friend and it was a go.

As the plan went into action, Ben just felt guilty. This was not a guaranteed win-win situation. There was a high probability of loss, finding Toby dead, or just coming up empty-handed. He couldn't help but replay the excitement and relief in the father's voice. Should he have waited to get the councilman involved? He could only imagine what the family was going through. But sometimes action trumped inaction and it wasn't wrong to offer hope. Still, dread blocked his previous euphoria. He had liked the kid. And for whatever reason, right place-wrong time, Toby had ended up in a life-threatening situation set up by thugs.

Chapter Thirty-two

Over the phone, Ginny Allen did a 'maybe what I have to say isn't important' attempt to downplay her reason for contacting Ben, or maybe she was just upset to find out he was married. Whatever the reason for a change of mind, she made Julie work for an interview.

Finally, coffee at the Casa Monica at ten was decided upon and Julie was left wondering what could be so important that Ginny had insisted on meeting where they could sit outside—away from any crowd. It was a warm June but the umbrella-topped tables at the corner of the building would catch the breeze. Still Julie wouldn't have minded a little air-conditioning. The hotel had been quickly repaired after the bombing and the outside patio expanded. They wouldn't be close to anyone. Under the circumstances, it was probably a good choice.

"Hi, I'm Julie." She'd immediately stood when she saw the dark-haired woman walk up the steps from the street. "I haven't ordered yet. Latte? Regular coffee? My treat. I'll let you hold onto our table."

Julie returned with one plain and one hazelnut flavored Latte and sat opposite Ginny. She had to be around her age, early thirties or late twenties, but lines were already etched at the corners of her eyes and around her mouth. Dark brown hair was slicked back into a pony tail and her jeans had honest-to-God worn spots across the knees—distressed by real wear and tear, not ordered that way from Nordstrom's.

"Listen, I hope I'm not wasting your time."

"I'm sure you won't be. It's difficult to know, but anything could be helpful."

"It's just that Toby … I can't believe he's still missing. And I'd never forgive myself if I kept quiet when I might have helped. I mean if something happened to him."

"I know. I appreciate your willingness to get involved."

Ginny still seemed to stall, folding her napkin in half, then in quarters, then rolling it between her fingers before taking a swallow of coffee.

"I'm just going to start at the beginning." A sheepish grin, then a deep breath, "I've been doing on-line dating. There's a free site called Kettle of Fish. It's, like, not the best but there haven't been many scammers and I've met a couple interesting guys." Another sip of coffee. "Sometime in May this guy writes me. I almost don't answer because he hasn't posted a picture. Believe me, you want to see a picture. One time I met a guy before I saw a picture and he was in the process of having all his teeth pulled, you know, for dentures. And, well anyway, I think he lived on the street. He didn't have a car."

Julie nodded. She made herself not interrupt but she was beginning to realize that this could take awhile.

"Anyway, I wrote back asking for a picture but he had a really good reason for not posting. Said he worked for the government and wasn't allowed to 'advertise' himself. Indicated he worked on secret projects and couldn't say anymore. I was still skeptical but he kept kidding me about not taking chances. Said he wouldn't disappoint, that he would blow me away. Well, a cup of coffee was worth finding out if it was ego talking or if he really was a looker. I could always walk away if he wasn't what he said he was. But I'm really a sucker for good-looking guys."

"And was he—what he said he was?"

"Oh my God … was he ever! Drop dead gorgeous. I'm not kidding. I could have just sat and looked at him all day. I loved his hair—and a butt, he had this perfectly adorable tush, and his jeans were really tight—"

"What was his name?"

"Ron … Ron Stiles."

"He was your age?"

"A little older, maybe forty or forty-two."

"Did he talk about his work? I mean, did you believe him about why he couldn't post a picture?"

"Oh yeah, he was really smart. Said he'd worked for the government for fifteen years. But he couldn't really talk about his job other than to say he travelled a lot. But that wasn't the weird part. You know how hindsight kinda puts things into perspective?"

Julie nodded.

"Well, speaking of jobs, he was really interested in

what I do. Seems like he was starting a community soccer league—one for kids, boys, actually, eight to ten years of age. He wanted to know about every boy in Mo's class—his size, agility, whether he could follow directions, who was most popular—that kind of stuff."

"Odd, don't you think?"

"I didn't at the time. I could see how following directions would make a difference to a coach, for example. But it was later after what had happened that I began to suspect Toby had been singled out—set up, maybe because of what I told this Ron. Toby fit the bill—he was perfect. He had the swagger, the know-it-all attitude. The other boys in class followed him."

"But if this man was putting together a team, why the interest in just one boy?"

"Exactly. You see, later, I called the city's recreational department. There had never been any Ron Stiles hired to recruit and coach a soccer team. That was all a lie."

"Why didn't you tell anyone this before now?"

"I was afraid. Someone gave Toby a gun and told him to kill Mo."

"Not just frighten her? I thought you told Ben that you didn't see anything."

"I know. I'm really sorry but, at the time, I thought someone might kill me, too. I have little children … The truth? I saw Toby put the gun against her head and pull the trigger. But you know what? I think she knew the first chamber was empty—that she wouldn't die."

Julie took a breath. Wow. This was news. "Why do you say that?"

"Little stuff. Okay, mostly it's just a feeling but she made a big point of 'I'm the teacher here, you better do as I say.' You know, bravado that I know she'd never have shown if the gun had been fully loaded. I like Mo but she isn't someone I'd run around with. She's pretty much a know-it-all, if you know what I mean. Spouts off, but doesn't back it up."

"Why didn't you share this with Detective Foley? I think you need to go to the police about this Ron Stiles."

"Frankly, I was afraid to, and now it wouldn't make any difference."

"Why are circumstances different now? Aren't you still afraid?"

"No. 'Cause Mo quit and Ron Stiles is dead."

"Dead?" Julie sat forward, what was Ginny talking about? "The guy you had a date with is dead?"

"Here. Look at this." Ginny reached in her purse and then unfolded a newspaper article and pointed her finger at the photo attached to the obituary of Dr. Geoffrey Mitchell.

"That's the man who called himself Ron Stiles?"
Ginny nodded.

"Did you see this man again? After the first date?"

"His profile was deleted and I didn't have any way to contact him. And he didn't get back in touch with me, which made me suspicious. I mean we had made plans. He thought I was sexy." A self-conscious shrug. "We were going to spend the weekend in Key West. He was a fantastic kisser."

Julie's mind was racing. He lied about his name, his work and wanting to start a soccer team. And he'd been interested in Toby. Way too interested in Toby. But why? Why would Geoffrey Mitchell want to kill Mo Beltzer? Because not for one minute did she believe that Mo knew the first chamber of the gun was empty.

He'd hired her to help with a very important, high profile job. And he'd been the one killed. Had he outlived his usefulness? Had someone or some group needed to get rid of him? And how was Mo involved? She couldn't have been. That was preposterous. Ben had been really concerned about Mo. There's no way he could have been fooled. Mo had struggled with the aftermath of that gun incident—to the point of having psychotic episodes.

"We may never have answers," she told Ginny. "I'm not sure where it all fits in but thanks for sharing."

+ + +

Julie walked back to the apartment. Did she believe Ginny about Ron Stiles being Geoffrey Mitchell? Maybe. That was more believable than Mo being in on Toby's threat. Knowing there was no bullet coming her way when he pulled the trigger.

That part of Ginny's story smacked of sensational school gossip—the kind of thing that kept a titillating story alive and circulating. There was probably more than a little envy at work in their relationship; the aide wishing she were the one in charge. Too transparent and too fabricated.

But there was something she could research and now it was her turn. She needed to put her investigative reporter skills to work. Who was Ron Stiles? Or maybe better yet, who was Geoffrey Mitchell?

She made a ham and Swiss sandwich, mayo and sweet mustard on twenty-one grain bread, got a glass of milk, and sat down in front of her computer. How many times had she done background checks—chased a name across the screen from LinkedIn to paying $19.95 to access criminal records? Lots.

Within fifteen minutes, she'd hit pay dirt: *Ronald Waltham Stiles, born 1947, died 2008. Married 1970 to Margaret Hurst-Becker, divorced 1990. One child, Geoffrey Alden, born 1978, Sacramento, California. Occupation: Founder and Chairman of the Board for Fossil Fuel Research Institute.*

So far, so good. Now for a check of Ms. Hurst-Becker Stiles. And bingo. *Remarried, 2002, Conner Mitchell, corporate attorney.* Geoffrey would have been a little old to adopt, but he certainly had started to use his step-father's name. Research into Conner Mitchell may have produced an answer—money.

The elder Mitchell seemed to bring a good old-fashioned fortune to the marriage. According to the article on Wikipedia, he saved the faltering Fossil Fuel Research Institute, in addition to having funded several other Silicon Valley research efforts. An unfortunate car accident in 2014 claiming the lives of both Mr. and Mrs. Mitchell made Geoffrey very wealthy—even if only for a short period of time.

One more interview probably needed to be made—Mo herself. Julie reached for her phone.

+ + +

"I didn't realize you lived so close to me." Mo had walked the few short blocks to Julie and Ben's rental.

"It's a great area of town." And it was. Julie had taken the time to explore George Street, the fort, several historic homes, the cemetery … and Ben was promising her a day on the water. "I hope I didn't interrupt your day."

"After getting up at the crack of dawn to identify a body? This is a treat."

"Good news that it wasn't Toby."

"Hopefully we're closer to finding him. But the bullet-hole to the poor guy's head only underscores what kind of people we're dealing with. This Garza guy was in beyond his depth apparently. Maybe just knew too much. I'm really afraid for Toby … for the outcome."

"Me, too." Julie paused. "This is as good a segue as any. I had coffee with Ginny Allen this morning and she identified someone who might have set up Toby—encouraged him to take a gun into the classroom. Actually, probably gave him the gun."

"You're kidding? Why didn't she tell the cops before?"

"Fear. She might not have ever come forward if the suspect hadn't died."

"Another body we didn't even know about? Now I am curious."

"Well, this one I think we did—we just didn't know the extent of his involvement."

Julie briefly filled Mo in on how Ginny had met this man, Ron Stiles, online and how he'd shown interest in Toby as a potential soccer player, and added, "Ginny identified a picture of Geoffrey Mitchell as the person in question."

"Oh come on. That is absolutely the most ridiculous thing I've ever heard. I thought you said the man's name was Stiles."

"I was on your side until I did some research. Look at this." Julie slid a typed sheet across the table. "Ronald Stiles was Geoffrey Mitchell's father. When his mother remarried, Conner Mitchell, it appears that Geoffrey took his stepfather's last name."

"I can't believe this."

"I don't think Ginny was lying. She was quite taken with Ron Stiles, your Dr. Mitchell. It seems there was the start of some sort of romantic liaison—at least a steamy weekend planned in the Keys. Remember, she'd met him on a dating service. He was obviously putting himself out there. And she said he was a terrific kisser."

"It's lies." Visibly shaken, Mo pushed back from the table.

"She identified him."

"This is just not something Geoffrey Mitchell would do. I do not believe that he gave a gun to Toby. He was not online. And I'd bet my life that he never came on to Ginny Allen."

"Look, I'm sorry. I honestly didn't mean to upset you. I just thought you should know."

"Okay, you've done your job, passed on bogus information. Nothing like maligning the dead. How can she strike out at someone who can't defend himself? I just wonder what Ginny is getting from all this 'cause, believe me, she doesn't do anything without getting something in return. She could have looked all this up just like you did."

"Mo, I'm sorry. Don't kill the messenger."

A pause, a couple deep breaths on Mo's part, then, "If I'm to believe what you're saying, Dr. Mitchell set up Toby to kill me. Only, less than a week later, he handed me a fantastic job ... I can't see a reason for going from kill to hire—does that make sense to you?"

"No, Mo, it doesn't. But I wanted you to be the first to know what Ginny was saying. I agree, we don't know if her story about the online meeting is even truthful. Guess we'd have to have her computer to prove it even though she's said Ron Stiles' contact information had been deleted. True, or just convenient? I also agree that she could have done a little research like I did and come up with names. Of course. But why? Why point a finger at Geoffrey Mitchell? There's a lot that doesn't make sense here. I only want you to know what's going on—behind your back."

"Sorry. I just have a lot on my mind. I'll be in Savannah for a conference first of the week. The prep isn't going that smoothly. And now this. I hate to think of people whispering in the halls … It's just, I'm a private person; I covet my privacy. This is really upsetting, disappointing. I've always liked Ginny."

"I didn't mean to hurt you."

"I know you didn't. No hard feelings … really. Thank you for letting me know." There was a quick hug before Mo picked up her purse and walked to the door. "I don't blame you. I mean that. I'd rather know than not know what was being said."

Julie waved to Mo from the balcony and watched her walk up the street. Had she done the right thing? Or had she caused more hurt? But she'd had no way of knowing what Mo's reaction would be. Of course, loyalty to the man who hired her, gave her a real plum of a job … she could understand that, but it seemed a little over the top. Julie hadn't anticipated the anger.

In hindsight, Julie was glad she hadn't brought up Ginny's idea about Mo knowing Toby would be pulling the trigger on an empty chamber—knowing she couldn't die. Wasn't that the most farfetched of all? Maybe Ben would have some ideas because at the moment she was completely stumped.

Chapter Thirty-three

It was laughable. He had not wanted her dead—nor set up a child to do it. He had said he loved her. And she believed him. No, they hadn't known each other for long but things sometimes happened that way. Wasn't 'love at first sight' a real, tangible possibility?

For one thing, the chemistry was real. There was no explaining that and no faking it. They had been almost intimate on two occasions. They were going to spend the night together. He fought with his emotions, afraid of exposing the two of them to possibly being fired. He was careful and caring. She *knew* this man. There was simply no way he'd made promises to her aide, and why would he? Lie about his intentions, single out Toby, set her up to get killed ...

What was more likely was that someone wanted *him* dead—the bomb meant to kill him because of some double-cross concerning money. Maybe take her, too? Thinking she knew something just because she was with him? That made more sense than some trumped up story about singling out a third grader and giving him a gun. There was no way Geoff Mitchell had done that. No way, none.

But who was behind it? And why … why had a third grader pointed a gun at her head in the first place? And why was Ginny Allen telling lies?

It would be good to get away. She needed time to just be alone. No talk of guns, no casting aspersions. If it hadn't meant extra work, the trip came at a good time. She needed distance.

Mo was glad she was flexible, but a little irked that no one had told her about the upcoming symposium in Savannah—until it was too late to find someone else to represent the program. But, of course, she was the director; she would have to be present. And she would be one of the speakers. Her fear of public speaking kicked into high gear. Why couldn't she just spend the night in a room full of spiders?

She wasn't Dr. Geoff Mitchell and would never be able to handle the presentation the way he could have. But she could add some new photos of current progress to the old slide presentation—actually, she'd be fine. She'd go to Savannah a couple days early. The conference started at noon on Monday. If she left Friday afternoon, she'd have one long, relaxing weekend in one of her favorite Old South cities. A dinner at The Olde Pink House off the square, maybe breakfast at that French deli—perfect. A mini vacation.

Besides, she looked forward to a little road trip in the new BMW. She could stop in Gainesville on the way home and visit Mom and Claire. Out of her way either direction, but she knew a visit would win points—prove to her family that she was doing just fine, standing on her own two feet, no more jumping out of her skin at a loud noise. She was a professional, director of a lauded, well-recognized program with national clout. This admirable plan went south the minute she called Claire.

"Oh, Maureen, this is too perfect. Mom and I will be in Chicago that weekend. Marty has an orthodontist convention and he's taking us along for a treat. Actually, Mom has put together an absolutely fabulous booth. But I need someone to babysit the greenhouse for three days. Pretty please? You always do such a good job. I wouldn't be so worried but the automatic timers are out. I need someone to water and mist by hand."

Mo hoped the sound of grinding teeth didn't carry over the phone. Typical of her sister to completely re-plan Mo's schedule without a thought. This wasn't at all what she'd envisioned. She took a deep breath—wasn't she looking forward to a little downtime anyway, needing this time away? The where wasn't as important as the when.

A respite before her debut as presenter and on-stage director of the prestigious Botany Labs at the Whitney institute could be taken anywhere. She could kick-back at Claire's and practice her presentation as easily as at some beach bungalow, and maybe she could stay an extra day in Savannah after the conference. But more than anything, didn't she owe her sister one? More than one, actually. She loved her job and knew she wouldn't have been hired had it not been for Claire.

"Sure, count on me." A grimace but Mo reminded herself again to suck it up.

"I'll leave watering instructions." Encyclopedic in size, Mo mused. "And the key will be in the usual place. The code at the gate hasn't changed."

Claire went on about food and not to touch the closed half crate of wine in the cellar—it was for a doc friend of theirs. And don't touch the thermostat ... Marty was so particular about inside temps. Mo tuned her out. It would all be written down somewhere anyway.

Chapter Thirty-four

The salt water made him itch. The boat wasn't very deep and it was impossible to keep the waves from spraying him as they rocked him up and down, back and forth. He slept a lot. And he was thirsty and hungry. But he didn't cry. He had to be brave or the *Stikini*, the owl-beings would come.

When he was bad, his father would tell him stories about them. How they looked like members of his tribe during the day but would come at night and change into monsters. They could vomit their insides and their souls and then would feed on the hearts of men. Zombie owls, the undead that stalked their prey. To mention their name out loud could turn you to stone.

Toby hated the night. The sun would fall into the ocean

probably sucked under the water by Trickster Rabbit. And then the moon turned the sea into a shiny path. It looked just like he could step right out of the boat and run on it. But it didn't go anywhere—not to land, anyway. He couldn't see any land. And he couldn't see the shrimp boat any longer. He thought he saw a shark and hoped he wouldn't eat the boat. In Sunday school there was a story about a man who was swallowed by a whale. He wondered if there were sharks in the Bible, too.

At night he dreamt of the white wolf. Only it was a puppy that snuggled next to him and licked his ear. The puppy whispered to him that he was waiting. Toby only had to come and find him. Did he mean walk across the moon's path? Was the puppy waiting there? He named the puppy, Lobo, after the wolf in Dr. Pecos's storybook from New Mexico.

Chapter Thirty-five

Ben pulled up beside the tarmac at the old airport on Highway 1 fifteen minutes before the helicopter was due; Councilman Wolff had already beaten him there. This was the first solid lead they'd had; Ben could understand his excitement.

Still, Ben was dreading possible disappointment—not finding Toby, or worse. They checked in at Atlantic Aviation which housed Old City Helicopters and were told Mike, their pilot, would be ready to take off from the pad directly in back in ten minutes. The councilman took care of the arrangements and there was still time to get a bottle of water from the machine.

"You know, it will be great if we end up giving Toby a ride in a 'copter. He's crazy about planes—any kind. Remember the models hanging from the ceiling in his room? His mother and I take him on a flying trip somewhere every summer."

"Fingers crossed we give him a 'copter ride home," Ben agreed.

"You know, his birthday's next week. Hard to imagine he's going to be nine. His mother and I always thought we'd have a large family but it wasn't meant to be. I'm afraid we've doted on Toby. Hopefully made his life special." He put a hand on Ben's arm, "Dr. Pecos, he's a good kid. I have a hard time trying to understand what happened—how he could have been bribed to do such a thing to his teacher … scare her like that. He always spoke highly of her. And sometimes I think I'm being punished for making him lie. I was just trying to protect him."

"I like Toby. I'm not a parent—I hope to be someday—but I can only imagine how important it would be to protect our children." Ben smiled. "Don't beat yourself up. Our task at hand is finding Toby and then working out the best way forward. I was just getting to know him and was looking forward to more visits this summer."

"I'm having a disagreement with his mother over his birthday present. My brother, who lives in Alaska, raises Malamutes. He's sending Toby a puppy, a little all-white guy. Toby's been begging for a dog. I think he's old enough to learn about caring for one, but his mother disagrees. Do you have any thoughts?"

"Nine can be a good age to teach responsibility with a pet. A puppy must have structure and routine. And kids, too, thrive on order. By watching a puppy grow he'll see the result of his attention to the puppy's needs. Of course, I know he'll have your supervision and support as he learns.

I think it's a great idea. I wish you the best." Ben added to himself, please dear God make this wish come true.

The 'copter was right on time. Ben watched it land, wishing he didn't have to get in. He didn't like fixed-wing, single engine planes and didn't like helicopters much either. Not that he'd had any real experience. Only one other time to be exact. A scout trip to the Grand Canyon, and ten boys were shown the beauty of nature and he'd thrown up. But then, he didn't ride on rollercoasters either for the same reason. At thirty-six he was pretty certain he wouldn't upchuck and if he did, no one here would tease him. Mercilessly, and forever. Still, old memories were tough to put aside.

The 'copter was bright yellow, and the bulging, overly large front Plexiglas windshields and glazing gave it a bug look. It was small, only holding two passengers plus the pilot—and rules dictated no passenger could weigh three hundred pounds. That made sense. He and the councilman would probably only make three hundred seventy-five combined. But Ben was glad there were rules. Takeoff was smooth, if noisy, and he felt safe buckled in, even with the top of the door panel open to allow easy viewing below.

Tim Foley must have sent the report on currents, location of where Garza's body was recovered, and estimated time of immersion. That combination would narrow the search. They would be looking for a trawler first. Mike adjusted his headset and pulled the mic closer to his mouth. It was too loud for normal conversation, but Mike pointed to areas of interest before they followed the coastline and then headed out over open water.

Ben looked at the vast nothingness of endless ocean. Needle in a haystack didn't even begin to cover what they were about to do—search for a child, maybe already in the water on a flotation device, maybe in a boat. But out there somewhere, alone for two and a half days. A not quite nine-year-old. If Toby wasn't found on the trawler, chances of ever finding him in the open sea were slim to none.

The grim set of the councilman's mouth told Ben he was thinking the same thing. The best case scenario—maybe the only one with a happy ending—depended on finding Toby onboard a stationary boat where Trini Garza had held him captive.

But it wasn't meant to be. With exact directions from the Coast Guard, their helicopter located the RB-M, a Coast Guard Rescue Boat-Medium, within thirty minutes. It was idling alongside a weathered shrimp boat that had definitely seen better days. Ben wasn't even certain it could still function as a money-maker; one net was in tatters, another missing. As they neared to hover some thirty feet overhead, a man emerged from the cabin waving a baseball cap and pointing at it.

"That's Toby's." The councilman grabbed Ben's arm. "He got that during the Marlin's spring training—an exhibition game last year. He's there! I knew he would be." He pulled against his restraint harness to get closer to the window. Then the man on the deck below shook his head.

Mike half-turned pointing at his headphones. "They're saying no one has been found. Evidence of Toby having been on board, but he's not there now." Mike slipped the headphones off to rest around his neck. "Look, I'm sorry. We've got about twenty minutes before we get some high winds while a squall blows through. I'm going to make a few circles to the north."

Toby's father slumped against the back of his seat

murmuring, "I thought he'd be there."

Mike banked the 'copter sharply to the right. "They're saying that the trawler's skiff is gone. There's evidence that until recently it had been secured on board or tied alongside. Your boy could have taken off when his captor got shot. Kids are smart nowadays—they watch enough TV to know what to do. You'll find binoculars in a box under your seat. Take opposite sides and scan for anything moving, or not moving for that matter. A bit of debris might tell us more than we know."

Ben saw Toby's father sit a little straighter, give a wan smile, and cross his fingers. "Here's hoping." He pulled out a pair of binoculars and adjusted the sight.

"Gonna have to get this little lady back to town." Mike swung his arm in a half circle pointing at a bank of clouds to his left. "Storm's coming up fast. The Guard's going to ride it out and continue their sea-search. That's probably our best bet for recovery. Sonar will pick up any vessels or flotsam on the surface as well as submerged. I think we're leaving the rescue in good hands." He flew the 'copter in ever-widening circles out from the trawler for fifteen more minutes before straightening his flight pattern to head for St. Augustine.

+ + +

Ben walked Toby's father to his car and saw a wire dog crate in the back of the SUV. "Getting ready for the newest member of the Wolff family?"

"I'm on my way to JAX to pick up the puppy I mentioned earlier. He's coming in at 2 pm. I hope there's good news by the time I get home."

"Me, too." Ben watched him pull out, drive through the parking lot, and wave before continuing north on Highway 1. Keeping busy and hanging onto hope. Ben wasn't sure he could handle such a situation as well.

"Hey, Pecos, you got a minute." Mike had walked back out of the office and was motioning to him.

"What's up?"

"You got kids?"

"Just got married a few months back, so, not yet."

"Well, I do. A ten year old boy—guess I'm gonna say this is all hitting just too close to home. I can only imagine what that kid went through. And I'm not ready to give up. Now that we know we have a missing person, the Coast Guard can send up one of their aircraft—one better equipped for a sea rescue than the tourist cutie we rent. You in?"

"You mean go back out now?"

"Yeah. I've already called and gotten the okay. We're just waiting on a pick up. I've got a cert in rescue swimming and I suggested you because you're the boy's doc."

"Sure. I'm with you." Ben wasn't certain Mike understood that he was a psychologist and not a medical doctor but he wasn't up to explaining now.

"The Guard has all the rigging for an air-to-sea rescue. There'll be a pilot, a tech and the two of us. The tech is also an EMT. I'm betting the kid's dehydrated and that might be the least of it."

"You talk like we're going to find him."

"Yeah, I know that's crazy but I think we will. I'm not promising a happy outcome, but I think we'll get some answers."

By the time the Coast Guard copter set down it was

after one o'clock and the rain had moved inland. Just another coastal shower, don't blink or you'll miss it, Ben thought, then smiled. It hadn't taken long for him to start sounding like a native. From the desert to the ocean—still a jolt to his system.

"Ah, the HH-60J Jayhawk. Perfect. That baby can carry four and rescue up to four, maybe six, and remain on the scene for forty-five minutes with enough reserve fuel to return to base. That is one smooth operator. Think of an 18-wheeler transport in the skies."

Ben marveled at the awe, no, actual reverence, Mike had for the piece of equipment. Did his wife get the same level of respect? Gear-heads, a challenge at any age. Ben climbed onboard and let the tech adjust his harness. This time he was sitting by a door that opened all the way. Unsettling, but he didn't really feel unsafe. Mike looked like a kid who had just gotten locked in a candy store.

"You know why we have a good chance of finding Toby?"

Ben shook his head but knew he was about to find out.

"For one thing, we're not flying blind—literally or figuratively. The trip out today already represents a few hours work—calculations provided by SAROPS—fantastic software—that's short for Search and Rescue Optimal Planning System. The program simulates the drift trajectory for whatever they're trying to find—person, boat, cargo— different stuff drifts in different ways. They'll probably calculate for a skiff as well as a raft or kayak. The program can honestly figure thousands of guesses as to what might have happened in the water—where something might be headed. In addition, wind and other environmental data is included. We're talking the complete picture."

"I assume the St. John's River and the Intracoastal would play a part?"

"Absolutely. These are variables that can change the surface current. I'm not kidding; this program is fantastic and expensive. But without it we might waste days looking in all the wrong directions. Let's hope he's in a boat or hanging onto something large. If he were just floating by himself, seeing his head in the water would be like locating a soccer ball in an area half the size of Texas."

Wow, that's graphic, Ben thought. But still, for the first time in a long time, he felt they might find Toby. And if not, his conscience would be clear. He would feel that everything humanly possible had been done—they hadn't stopped after some haphazard fly-over. No, this was in-depth, state-of-the-art technology. It was their chance ... probably their only chance.

An hour later Ben was beginning to wonder. Sensing his growing disappointment, Mike leaned over to reassure him.

"Hey, man, why the long face? We're just getting started."

Ben could do without the pep talk. Time was important and it was getting away. He had a right to be worried.

"On your left." The yell from the Tech barely superseded the 'copter's quick descent. Ben braced himself against the side of the door opening and looked down. There, some forty feet beneath them was a skiff, aimlessly bobbing up and down. As the 'copter hovered, Ben could make out a bundle of material behind the front plank seat—that's what it looked like, until Ben saw an arm and a hand stretched out above Toby's head.

"Rescue swimmer, prepare to be lowered."

Ben moved as far as his harness would allow as Mike was hooked to a winch and cable that would lower first him and then a basket. It would be his job to secure the skiff's occupant in the basket, send it up and then follow. Ben watched breathlessly and shouted in joy as Toby moved his arm and stood with Mike's help. Mike didn't give the sign to bring him up until Toby was belted in and the straps pulled tight.

Ben helped bring the basket inside, then steadied Toby until he was unhooked and out of the container. The child fell against him, and wrapped his arms around Ben's neck. With the Tech's help, the two of them gently lowered Toby to a cot in the aisle.

"Thirsty?" Toby was sunburned and gaunt, obviously dehydrated, but had the energy to lift his head. The Tech took a bottle of water from a cooler, tore the covering off of a straw, and added it; he continued to hold the bottle.

"Think you can handle this by yourself?" Ben had situated a seat cushion behind Toby, propping him up. Mike got a nod and handed the bottle over.

When he finally spoke, Toby's first words were, "This is cool." He looked around at the 'copter's interior. Ben couldn't help but smile. The kid was going to be fine—already he was interested in his surroundings instead of any possible aches or pains. A sea rescue would be worth some bonus points in the re-telling. Ben had taken a pretty good video via his cell phone. He'd bet somebody's friends were going to be jealous.

"I'm going to follow protocol and have an ambulance meet us at the airfield," the Jayhawk's pilot said. "I'm not in the mood to take chances. We'll get Toby checked out at Flagler Hospital. I'll leave calling the family up to you, but let's have them join up in the Emergency room."

Happy endings were worth their weight in gold or diamonds or platinum—whatever was the most expensive. And this one was priceless. The Wolffs pulled up just as the ambulance doors opened and, with the help of aides, Toby stepped out. But just as Toby's mother opened her door, a white bundle of fur with two startlingly blue eyes tumbled over its own four puppy paws to rush toward Toby.

"Lobo, Lobo!" Toby sank to the ground gathering the excited puppy into a hug. "I knew you'd find me."

"Wasn't this a birthday surprise?" Ben was taken by how boy and puppy seemed to know each other.

"Supposed to be. But looks like he has a name already." The elder Wolff moved forward and, taking his wife by the hand, extended his other hand to draw Toby into an embrace. Mike exchanged a smile with Ben, nodded, and gave a thumbs up.

Ben pulled out his phone to call Julie.

"Oh, Ben, that's the best news yet. I'll try to catch up with Mo. She may already be on her way to Savannah for the conference, but she'll be thrilled. I know how worried she was. And I've got a surprise, too."

"Something I'll like?"

"Well, I think you'll be happy for me. The *Herald* has asked me to fly to Miami for a follow-up interview—their nickel. They're considering me for a department director's position. I leave Friday but will be back Sunday."

Chapter Thirty-six

Another trip to the airport and Ben was beginning to see a pattern to having a two-career relationship. But he wouldn't say anything to dampen Julie's enthusiasm—this was a job she really wanted. A part of who she was, and what he loved about her was her dedication and creativity. He could survive for another three days, and he would plan a just-for-two type getaway for when she got back.

He stole a look at his freckled wife. Job or no job, he couldn't imagine being without her. He pressed cruise-control and reached out with his right hand.

"I'm missing a little skin-to-skin contact. We need to remedy that Sunday night."

"I think that could be arranged."

"I keep forgetting to ask—did you ever talk to Ginny Allen?"

"Oh, my gosh, I didn't tell you what I found out. I don't even know what to make of it." Julie started with the Stiles/Mitchell connection and ended with Ginny saying Toby had held a gun to Mo's head and pulled the trigger, with Mo knowing the first chamber was empty.

"That last bit doesn't make sense. I basically treated a pretty straightforward case of PTSS. Mo wasn't acting. The incident terrified her."

"Unless Ginny has some reason for setting Mo up. There's no love lost between them, and when I mentioned how Geoff Mitchell had come onto Ginny, Mo was downright defensive."

"That just doesn't sound like the head of a prestigious department at a major university. Using another name to find out information about students in Mo's class? Sounds like Toby was singled out, but why?"

"I know. And I can't think of what Ginny might have to gain—why would someone pay her for spreading false information? Incriminating information."

By the time they reached the airport in Jacksonville, they weren't any closer to answers. Once again Ben found himself kissing his wife good-bye and heading back to St. Augustine by himself.

Chapter Thirty-seven

Friday morning. Toby was safe and Mo's world was beginning to lose its tilt and right itself. It was sweet and thoughtful of Julie to call her. She hadn't realized how worried she'd been about Toby. There was nothing those thugs who killed Trini Garza couldn't have done. A bullet in the head, a drowning—it's possible that they didn't know Toby was on the trawler, but still, a very brave little boy managed to beat the odds. Floating around in the ocean for three days? He must have been terrified.

And, speaking of terror, she was actually looking forward to taking off this afternoon, see new surroundings, put some distance between her and the scene of the crime—several crimes, really. A quick trip to Gainesville to babysit Claire's greenhouse of orchids and finish writing her speech, then on to a conference and some sightseeing plus fabulous food. It was amazing how things were working out. She could pretty much shelve the old bogeymen and breathe easy.

She got in a little after four, driving to the outskirts of a college town preparing to come alive on a Friday night. The Roth's gated community was remote, hidden by woods and barely concealed lakes. She pressed in the code—the last four digits of her own Social Security number so it wasn't likely she'd forget it—and the wrought iron double gate swung open.

The first left took her through the pretty, wooded community of very expensive houses and manicured grounds until she got to the house on the end of a secluded street. Even then, she decided to put her car in the garage— easier to unpack the few orchids she'd brought from the project. Show and tell—always a winner and actually spoke volumes of how successful the Whitney Labs' program had become. She was so proud of the summer bloomers— silently proving they were doing something right.

She brought her overnight case in through the kitchen and, yes, there on the dining room table was what looked to be four or five pages of 'instructions.' Mo just rolled her eyes and continued emptying the car. The lanai that ran the full length along the south side of the house contained an Olympic-sized swimming pool, a Jacuzzi, steam cabana, a bar, and tables and easy chairs that would accommodate at least fifty. Money must be nice, Mo decided for the umpteenth time. But right now she could only think of going for a swim.

When hunger finally took over, she opened the fridge and found it stocked. That was a first. But it certainly meant she wouldn't have to leave the house for anything. She could hunker-down and 'rough' it for two and a half days. Maybe she should check to make certain there were no notes to 'not touch'. No, she was hungry; she'd take her chances. There was a bagged salmon entre on a shelf in front complete with veggies that just required thirty minutes at 375 degrees and someone had penciled on the bag to try the good Chardonnay in the cooler section of the walk-in. Yes, a walk-in wine cooler. Marty Roth's hobby on full display.

Further sleuthing in the fridge uncovered more meals and accompanying wine suggestions—enough for three meals a day for the next two days. How thoughtful. The pecan and cream cheese stuffed French toast really had her name on it—not literally, but she had plans for it to disappear in the morning.

A swim, dinner on the lanai, then a couple of episodes of *Game of Thrones* streamed on the sixty-four inch TV screen—life was good. Staying in on a Friday night had its perks. She even had a fantastic idea as to how to bring her talk into the present, hoping to capture the interest of the laymen in the audience as well as the scientists. And she had two whole days to make hers the best presentation of the conference.

Saturday morning presented its own set of challenges. Hand misting Claire's eight hundred square foot greenhouse with twenty foot ceilings was a chore—time consuming by demanding careful attention to detail. In this case, a wall of miniatures that couldn't tolerate dripping wet conditions. They preferred a light once-over, provided more than twice a day. Mo really did understand why Claire couldn't trust just anyone with her collection. And sprinklers were life-enhancing additions to any greenhouse. They had to be kept in good working order.

In fact, she may have discovered the problem with Claire's sprinklers. It was tough to see exactly, but it appeared that one of the security cameras which plugged into the back of the timer had come loose. It was dangling against the unit, keeping it from operating, let alone rendering the security camera inoperable.

Thank God she wasn't afraid of heights. The ceiling was twenty-five feet high and the timer and sensors were situated at the top to monitor temperature changes. The camera oscillated from a small platform. Oh well, she would drag the collapsible ladder in from the garage and have everything working in short order. Living alone, she'd learned how to do lots of things. Not that she expected it, but Claire should be ecstatic.

Thirty minutes later, she dragged the ladder back to the garage, but not before checking the room of monitors next to the walk-in pantry. Everything was in working order. She watched as the camera haltingly turned to survey every corner of the greenhouse, recording its jerky circular motion to a hard drive. Mission accomplished. Now to get back to her presentation. She needed to come up with a theme—some all-encompassing idea that would be thought provoking and memorable.

And bingo! There it was right in front of her. A *Brassia*, the showy spider orchid spilling over the top of an individually lighted growing shelf, gave her an idea. It was a mature plant with more than a hundred flowers zigzagging from one side of a flower spike to the other—and there must be six to ten spikes. She'd have to check the tag for the origin of this one, but most came from Australia with a few from Indonesia. She'd love to take the entire plant to the conference but too risky—this one would be a bear to pack and have it arrive unscathed.

Camera-capture was the only answer and she could turn it into a screen-saver—the image that would be in front of the audience before and after the slide show. Maybe a video showing a three-hundred-sixty degree continuous shot of its opulence. Yes, that idea had merit.

And its importance? This one plant could be her signature offering at the conference. It would leave people with a story and image that wouldn't fade soon. She was absolutely gleeful. And it all had to do with global warming. Talk about a hot topic. The plant was having its moment in the spotlight because it proved, in a relatively unintentional way, that the hemisphere's warming was real and could have far-reaching consequences.

The flower's tendril-like "legs" mimicked an actual spider—the prey of spider wasps—right down to the release of a copycat pheromone. Male wasps emerging from hibernation and looking for female wasps to mate with instead copulated with a flower, pollinating the plant and assuring the continuation of that variety. However, global warming was bringing the orchid into bloom two to three weeks before the wasps emerged, so pollination was sketchy to none and threatened several *Brassia* with extinction. It was perfect for a slate of presentations that contained such topics as, Coral Reef Rejuvenation, Plastics—Man and Our Waterways, and even Sub-Zero Catastrophe—Artic Animal Annihilation.

Mo's leisurely Saturday turned into one of frenzied photo-taking. A number of Claire's plants were summer bloomers and truly in their glory—as her mother would say. She made a quick call to Claire to get some background on the *Brassia*—how long she'd had the plant, country of origin, the sort of thing an audience might ask, but Claire's phone immediately went to voicemail. Just as well. This really wasn't the time to bother her. Mo hung up without leaving a message.

The difficult part of finishing her speech was editing—choosing the best photos and reworking the slide presentation. More pre-packaged meals with accompanying glasses of wine, six hours on the computer, and she was finished. A two-hour lecture, including a thirty-minute Q and A, backed up smartly on a thumb drive, just in case. She was ready and more importantly, no jitters. She was looking forward to this. Maybe she wasn't a Geoffrey Mitchell, but she knew she'd be good.

Geoff. She realized with a start that she'd tried not to think of him. But denial was as dangerous and detrimental to getting well as remembering. So, if she were to 'fess up—she missed him. Achingly so. She wanted him there to hear her lecture, compliment her on her brilliant choice of topic. Well, maybe not *brilliant*, but she knew it was going to be a hit. And he could have helped her with a title. Life could have been so good, shared work, mutual attraction … it was as if it had been almost too good to be true. She took a deep breath. Enough. She had moved on.

What she didn't allow herself to dwell on was Ginny's supposed ranting to Julie about soccer teams, and kisses, and trips to Key West … why would she make that up? What was she covering up—trying to throw authorities off target, to gain what? There was nothing she said to Julie that couldn't have been discovered with a little Google search. But why malign the dead? Other than he remained a convenient, and mute scapegoat.

But again, it came back to what? She knew she could never work with Ginny again. Another good reason she had moved on.

The evening meant more TV, a prepared dinner, wine and early bedtime. Sunday was a catch-up day—laundry for a few small items, clean kitchen, check the misters, a couple last minute shots of buds that were just opening up, and a long leisurely swim in the afternoon.

She needed to allow three hours to get to Savannah and wanted to be on the road by five a.m. She packed as much in the car as she could, leaving out clothes and make-up bag—only the things that she'd need in the morning. Registration started at eight-thirty so that timing would be perfect.

She turned off her phone and even muted the landline in the kitchen. She didn't need to be disturbed and she certainly wasn't expecting any calls. Bed by eight was a little early but she knew four a.m. would seem like the dead of night. She was glad this wasn't something she did very often.

So in hindsight, when she would replay that night, loop it through an already bruised brain, she knew that moment in time was the beginning of the end—the end of sanity, of friendships, of any normalcy. And it all started when four Federal Marshals kicked in the front door at three-thirty Monday morning.

Chapter Thirty-eight

The passenger pickup area at the JAX terminal was busy for a Sunday evening. Ben deftly maneuvered his truck to the curb just as Julie came through the revolving doors—timed perfectly. They were beginning to have pickup and drop-off at major airports down to a science. He jumped out of the cab and grabbed Julie around the waist.

"How can three days seem like three years?"

She laughed but stood on tiptoe for another kiss—this one longer—before murmuring into his shoulder, "How long is it going to take us to get home?"

"Too long." He placed her bags in the bed of the truck, anchored to the back with bungee cords. "Should I assume you don't want to stop anywhere for dinner?"

The withering look was exactly what he'd hoped for. "Well, guess we better get a move on."

Julie was just turning to climb into the cab when she saw Mo—about fifty feet away in the parking lot shuttle loading zone. She was waiting in line to get into the van that, according to signage on its side, was heading to level one or the short term parking area.

"Mo!" When yelling out her name didn't catch Mo's attention, Julie tossed her purse on the seat of the truck and turned to walk toward the shuttle, only to see its accordion doors snap shut after the last person boarded, and the lumbering vehicle lurch into traffic.

"I know she heard me. She sort of half turned around."

"I thought so, too. Pretty tough to mistake that white-blond hair even if it was covered by a cap."

"But sunglasses? At this time of day? It was as if she didn't want to be recognized." Julie paused. "She had luggage; she had obviously just landed, but she never mentioned flying anywhere when I called to tell her about Toby. I even said I had an interview in Miami. She told me she'll be attending the conference in Savannah tomorrow—*driving* up—after babysitting her sister's greenhouse in Gainesville over the weekend. This makes no sense."

"Maybe it wasn't Mo." Ben was intent on trying to maneuver through two lanes of parked cars to reach the exit, but no one was moving very quickly. At this rate, it was going to add fifteen minutes onto the trip home. Airports and big cities. Not his favorite.

"You saw her. You thought it was Mo."

"True." Ben finally caught a break from a motorist who let him cut in front, only to wait in line at the exit. Finally, after a twenty-minute delay he hadn't counted on, they were up to speed and heading toward I-95. "Quick, look to your right. The white BMW sedan—isn't that Mo merging into traffic?"

"You're right." This time Julie watched the driver—the cap was off and the white-blond bob was easy to make out, even two lanes over. And no sunglasses. But there was no getting closer—traffic was just too heavy. "I don't think it's Mo."

"That hair and driving a new white BMW? What are the odds?"

"I know but something just isn't right."

Ben knew better than to question Julie but who would impersonate Mo? And why?

Chapter Thirty-nine

Sweetheart. We came the minute we were notified." A uniformed officer held the steel door open, first yelling out that Mo had company.

"Mom, Claire. How did you get here?" Mo was sitting in a holding cell in an orange jumpsuit in the Alachua County jail, but at least she was by herself. "Who told you I was here?"

"We took the red-eye when that nice Officer Foley called. I can't believe it's only ten-forty-five. Of course, I look a fright. The older I get the more beauty sleep I require."

"*Marshal* Foley. He works for the feds now."

"Well, whatever, he was very concerned and felt we should be involved."

Mo glanced at Claire. "Sorry this had to interrupt your conference."

"We were due to come home today anyway. I left Marty to pack and ship the booth. Now, what's all this about?"

"Honestly? I may know as much as you do. I have to wait until they receive some kind of info from Central America."

"Central America?" Marjorie repeated.

"Something about endangered species—recent poaching. Apparently this proof of my involvement is being sent electronically, and they're a couple hours earlier than we are."

"I can't believe they can just hold you—incarcerate you on some flimsy assumption."

"Now, Marjorie, I'm sure Mo is on top of this. Who's your lawyer?"

"Lawyer? I don't need a lawyer. It's some error. I'm only worried about the conference in Savannah—I don't present until tomorrow but I hate to be missing out on today's lectures."

"I'm not pointing a finger, but Federal Marshals don't just arrest the innocent."

"Claire." Marjorie turned, arms akimbo, "I don't want to hear another stupidity come out of your mouth. This is your sister we're discussing."

"I'm just saying, after the robbery at the greenhouse, even Dr. Mitchell shared his concerns with me."

"Concerns?" All Mo's instincts were on alert. What was Claire getting at?

"Well, it was odd that these men took the most expensive specimens—did someone help them do that? Point out these plants? And then shoot up the place to confuse law enforcement."

"Dr. Mitchell was not concerned about my being in on any theft. He was scared to death that I'd been injured. He, well, we … were in love—"

"What?" Claire whirled to face Mo.

"I know what you're going to say. Thirty days isn't long enough to experience that sort of feeling, but it's the truth."

"Slut. And some other words that I won't use in front of my mother. You jeopardized that job and Dr. Mitchell's position by what? Chasing after him in your sad little puppy dog way, and when he wouldn't even look at you, you fabricate some lie? Poor Mo, but look world, someone loves her. What did you do? Offer to fuck him?"

"Actually, it was the other way around. Do you want the particulars?" Mo's anger was barely concealed.

"More lies? I can do without that. Marjorie, I hope you're listening to all this. And don't try to tell me this is Miss Innocence here. Come on, we have better things to do. She's on her own."

"I need to see about bail."

"Don't you dare. Being her mother not withstanding, you are not compounding this family's shame by aiding and abetting a possible criminal."

Mo watched as Claire actually forcibly took Marjorie's arm and propelled her toward the door. Even for Claire, this was below the belt. Mo was so stunned she couldn't even cry as the door slammed behind them.

"Hey, just tell yourself we don't get to choose our families."

'Thanks." Mo smiled at the guard. She'd forgotten he was in the room.

Chapter Forty

With all due respect, Sir, you've got it all wrong."

Gas station coffee was the pits, but colored water at this hour was acceptable if it had caffeine. Tim choked down another lukewarm swallow before placing his cup on the table in front of him. A makeshift interrogation room, uncomfortable in its starkness, folding metal chairs, scruffy table—what the hell was he doing there? But he knew. His new boss was prepping him before the two of them were slated to rake Maureen Beltzer over the coals.

"Foley, listen to me. You're new here. I understand being a newbie, but look at the evidence. What are your instincts telling you?"

"That there's no way Maureen Beltzer is guilty."

"I'm gonna go through the evidence real slow. You tell

me what doesn't work for you. And we're gonna have a problem if personal feelings are involved here—we clear on that?"

Tim Foley nodded. Monday morning, start of his second week as a marshal and now some kind of trial by fire. Only, he was close enough to this one to get singed. But he better take notes and try to refute whatever case his boss thought he had against Mo. Talk about shit for luck, the kid couldn't catch a break. Now they were trying to pin a charge on her of transporting endangered plant species out of their countries of origin—in this case Costa Rica—for profit. Big profit.

"We have surveillance tape from the gated community where she was staying—coming and going—and the timeframe fits perfectly. Plus that fifty-thousand cash found in her car—what more do you want? Ms. Beltzer flew from JAX to San Jose, Costa Rica, and back—total air time a little over eleven hours, easily doable in a forty-eight hour timeframe—between Friday night and Sunday evening."

"I'd like to take another look at the tape of her car leaving the compound in Gainesville—leaving her sister's house."

"Here you go. Gate security tape from Mrs. Roth's compound." He turned the monitor toward Tim. "Leaving at one-thirty a. m. Saturday morning. New BMW 3-Series, white, Florida license plate: BNR-35T. That's a clear picture of the plate."

Federal Marshal Garrison Thomas paused the tape. "Yes, the plate is issued to Maureen Beltzer, St Augustine, Florida. You can catch a glimpse of the driver in this next shot. That signature white-blond hair is a give-away. Second shot is her return, Sunday, now wearing a cap, but her hair still recognizable from the sides and back. Again, license plate clearly visible. Got an explanation?"

"Not off the top of my head."

"Well, it gets better." Marshal Garrison turned off the tape machine and reached for his laptop. "I've been waiting for corroborating evidence from San Jose customs. They couldn't release the entire entry-exit tapes but I just received a series of stills taken from those tapes. Fairly clear picture of Ms. Beltzer from the side, and a clearer one of her passport and papers as the agent checks them and clears her to enter the country. Yes, she was legitimately booked on a six a. m. flight to SJO, returning to JAX Sunday evening."

He forwarded through several more photos until ones of what appeared to be Mo attempting to leave the country. "Here she's just been taken into custody. She was released pending notification of US authorities. Because her passport had been confiscated, it was assumed she was not a flight risk. Their customs notified our authorities but somehow, in the meantime, Ms. Beltzer returned to the States."

"Without a passport, she was able to get back into this country, land at JAX and elude law enforcement?" Tim knew he sounded skeptical but it was difficult to put any truth to this.

"Some details we're still working on. But that's what Ms. Beltzer is going to tell us. She's the one who can fill in the gaps." There was a quick staccato knock on the door. "Ready to find out? Let me take the lead on this. I'll let you know if I need you to chime in."

"Give me a couple minutes. I need to make a call." Tim

left the room and pulled out his phone, dialed, and waited. Connecting with Ben Pecos could be crucial to proving Mo's case.

"Ben, Tim here. Listen, no time for small talk. Sorry to call so early on a Monday, but I need you in Gainesville as quickly as you can get here. I think Mo's being framed—I can't prove it, but I'm betting her shrink could provide some background info that would help her out—at the very least, give her a character reference and make a case for her not being a flight risk. Gotta go. See you at the county jail."

+ + +

The room at the jail, which also housed local law enforcement in Gainesville, suddenly got smaller as two guards escorted a handcuffed and very disheveled Mo into the room. One pulled out a chair on the side of the table opposite her interrogators and not too gently forced her to sit. The other guard flipped the on-switch to a video camera and recorder bolted to a tripod in the corner. So much for state-of-the-art, built-in, digital recording equipment, Tim thought.

"Looks like we're ready. Let's start by you telling us why you're here." Marshal Garrison dragged his chair around to squarely face Mo.

"I'll leave that up to you because I don't know."

It wasn't said with any snotty, I-dare-you overtones … more honest-to-God, I don't know. Tim made a note on the yellow pad in front of him. She looked tired. He idly wondered if having family visit had helped at all.

In short order Marshal Garrison ran through the

highlights of the case: intercepted on trip to Central America to accept and pass on priceless plants—estimated value 1.5 million. What was probably her cut—fifty thousand dollars—was found in the trunk of her car.

"Impossible. I was babysitting my sister's greenhouse over the weekend. I never left the house."

"Proof? Visitors? Eat out? Order in?"

A wan smile for Tim, "I don't order in anymore."

"Then you'll be able to explain this." The marshal cued the security gate tape and slid the monitor closer to Mo.

If Mo looked pale and drawn before, Tim now thought she might faint. A hand flew to her mouth and she mumbled something about, "I gave that shirt to Goodwill six months ago." But she couldn't stop staring, watching the tape every second. "That looks like my car." She leaned closer. "That's my tag." She continued to stare at the monitor, even after the Marshal turned it off.

"Explanations?"

Mo shook her head and rechecked the time stamp. A car with her tag had left and returned to the compound over the weekend. Only it wasn't her driving.

"And if you think that's incriminating, I just received these photos from San Jose, Costa Rica."

Marshal Garrison leaned across the table so the two of them would be looking at the laptop's screen together. "Let's start with where you enter the country. This is a pretty clear picture of you, your passport and entry papers."

Mo's sharp intake of breath was not lost on the Marshal.

"Surprised? Do you know what's wrong with stupid, first-time criminals? They completely overlook the fact that cameras are everywhere—surveillance is a way of life today. Did you forget that you were probably being recorded?"

This last sounded pretty snide, Tim noted. The Marshal was enjoying a little game of gotcha. "Let's move on to when you try to leave. The Costa Rican authorities believe you were in the country just long enough to identify several costly, soon-to-be-extinct, orchid specimens and turn them over to operatives, who then flew them out of the country. You were suspect and put under surveillance because of your affiliation with the University's botanical project and your obvious knowledge."

Mo leaned forward. She followed the woman in the white-blond occipital haircut in a Goodwill castoff as the Marshal moved through the images.

"I've seen enough. I want a lawyer." Mo pushed back from the table.

Tim Foley tried to catch Mo's eye but she was stoically sitting ram-rod stiff, staring in front of her. And as clichéd as it sounded, it looked as if she'd seen a ghost.

Chapter Forty-one

The lawyer, Lindsey Grant, proved to be a real go-getter. One of those fresh graduates with a lot to prove and the energy to make things happen. Mo liked her immediately. A woman's advocate, instantly on Mo's side and ready to take action. And she believed Mo—believed in her enough to meet with the duty judge before a formal hearing to set bail and to call Marjorie to make bail—that was hustle. All this before lunch.

Then she ordered the warrant. Yes, a warrant to search and confiscate proof of occupancy—in this case the camera surveillance tapes that would prove exactly where Mo had spent the weekend. Thank God she had taken the time to fix the camera in the greenhouse. Little did she know at the time just how important her favor to Claire was going to be to her.

So, she was out. Marjorie had given her a hug on the building's front steps and whispered, "No need to say anything to Claire. She doesn't need to know I helped you with bail. Pick up your car and bring your things to my house. And, Sweetie, I just know you'll be able to prove you're entirely innocent."

Mo nodded, then kissed her mother on the cheek. "Thank you."

Lindsey dropped her off at Claire's. Mo needed to pick up her make-up bag and laptop—and be there when the officers served the warrant. The front door had been boarded up—quick work by the HOA probably. Mo went around to a side door on the garage. Open—Thank God. Hers was the only car on the property, proof that Claire was at work and Marty hadn't yet returned from Chicago. Looked like she'd be alone when the officers served the search warrant.

She left her car in the garage and walked into the kitchen. She guessed that Claire would go to her office on campus, so Mo would wait at the house. Claire would probably be home in an hour. There were just a few things to talk over. Yeah, right. More than a few things actually.

If she didn't know that Claire had been with her husband and mother in Chicago over the weekend, she'd swear that the woman at the entry gate in San Jose was dear old Claire. Dear old Claire pretending to be Mo—complete with stolen passport and bobbed platinum wig.

She thought of the Savannah presentation she would be missing. She had to take care of that bit of business. Mo emailed her presentation and slide show to an intern, who was thrilled at the opportunity to represent the labs and get some credit for it. Then she helped the young man check out a school vehicle, and called Savannah with the change in presenters. Now to wait.

Chapter Forty-two

Well, looks like the mother sprang for bail. Tough to convince a mom that her kid is a criminal."

"Because for starters, maybe she isn't."

"Ah, come on, Foley. What more has it got to take for you to admit the obvious?"

Tim was losing patience fast—new job or no new job. But he had to back off—the evidence looked conclusive. And his boss didn't know Mo like he did. Maybe if he tried to share some of his knowledge … No, this was better if it came from Ben. It would be tough to discount her psychologist. Tim checked his watch. Ben should be there in another thirty minutes.

"Are you familiar with the whole story?" he asked Garrison.

"Yeah, I am. Let's start with that debacle at the school. Kid brings a gun to class, points it at teacher, and pulls trigger. According to the aide who was less than twelve feet away, Ms. Beltzer did not follow protocol, in fact, acted like she knew the first chamber was empty, went out of her way to strong-arm the kid."

"Why? Does that make sense to you? What's the reasoning behind the action? What did Mo have to gain?"

"A lawsuit might have proved negligence on the school's part—a lack of protection. Or, in exchange, she might have been laid off with severance. It appeared she had a bargaining chip—at least a reason for doing it then."

"This was someone who had dedicated her life to teaching. What was so important about the timing?"

"The job at Whitney Labs had been advertised. She knew her sister would put in a good word. Maybe she already had a job waiting. The way I see it, Foley, it's all about money."

"Maureen Beltzer was traumatized by what happened in her class. She was seeing a shrink and trying to pull her life together. As I said, she'd never considered doing any other type of work—teaching was her life."

"Well, she didn't turn down the job with the labs. Within a week she was off to something new."

"Purely coincidental that the other job was open."

"Her aide has been really helpful at painting a realistic picture of Ms. Beltzer in the classroom. Not all roses, by any means."

"You do realize that her passport was stolen, or at least was not where it should have been, when we searched the house. I find it interesting that it showed up in Costa Rica."

"Did you ever follow up on that? Once she had a

chance to really look through the house, perhaps, she found she'd mislaid it?"

"No, I didn't follow up." Tim wasn't winning this one but the more his intuition was questioned, the more he dug in. "You know, we're overlooking that a child was kidnapped and held for over a month."

"Don't think we've gotten to the bottom of that either. Not proved that it was related to the incident in the classroom."

"But more than a little suspect. And then the bombing—"

"Totally unrelated. Some tree-huggers got carried away. Believe the government is raping our natural wetlands. No, I see an opportunist. Plain and simple. Someone who was smart enough to make some real money and maneuvered herself into position to take advantage."

"Well, whatever her lawyer told the judge, it was good enough to have a search warrant drawn up to be served this afternoon—on her sister's house. I think Mo has proof that she wasn't in Costa Rica over the weekend."

"I'll believe it when I see it."

"I'm going to check on that warrant and follow the officers over to the house when they serve it. I've asked Mo's shrink to join us. If I miss him, let him fill you in on what Mo's been through. I think the warrant is going to turn this case around. I'll let you know what's happening."

As luck would have it, Ben and Julie pulled into the parking lot just as Tim was getting into his car. Tim was praying Mo's evidence was absolutely conclusive and not open to any interpretation.

"Follow me. I'll explain when we get there."

Chapter Forty-three

Mo grabbed a Fat Tire from the fridge and drew a stool up to the Roth's butcher block island. She needed time to think before she confronted Claire. Claire. Was that really her sister in Mo's discarded plaid shirt going through customs in Costa Rica?

It couldn't have been. Claire and Marjorie and Marty Roth were in Chicago. Her mother would have said something if their plans had changed. But her car … how had someone stolen her car out of the garage? Unless they only borrowed the license plate and never moved her car.

A white 3-series Beemer was pretty generic. Would she have even heard someone in the garage? Doubtful. Probably an easy task to take the tag and return it. And a wig would duplicate the signature haircut. But she needed to hear it from Claire. She needed Claire to look her in the eye and swear she wasn't involved.

The greenhouse surveillance tapes were probably conclusive enough, but was there anything else to prove where she was over the weekend? Garbage. Why hadn't she thought of that before? Two and a half days' worth of empty dishes and paper plates—all those pre-packaged meals. She'd bagged the empties and put the sack in the city's roll-away. She quickly walked to the garage, down the two steps and threw back the lid—nothing!

The bag was gone. Only a pristine, and very empty container remained. Her heart was beginning to race—just a little but that unmistakable subliminal warning that maybe she was in danger quickened her breathing. Someone had set her up. Big time.

A plan, she needed a plan. She had no idea when the officers would serve the search warrant, but she needed to wait for them. Then, she was out of there. She could contact Claire later—hopefully in front of others. She'd put all of her stuff in the car and back it out of the garage. Easier for a get-a-way? Yeah, if need be.

She walked back into the house and headed to the downstairs guest bedroom to get her overnight bag. Wow. She'd totally forgotten that she'd tucked the .38 into the front pocket. Was she a perfect example of those who should not be trusted with a firearm? The ones a permit to carry was wasted on because they never carried?

She should have at least hidden it better—maybe asked to put it in Marty's safe.

She tucked it into the belt of her jeans. Was just touching a firearm in some kind of violation of her release from jail? After all, she was only out on bail. There were times when she wished she knew the law better, but she'd never been arrested before. A deep breath. She was certainly no Annie Oakley but just having a gun on her person seemed to quiet the case of nerves.

But now she needed to get her things into the car. She walked into the bathroom to collect makeup. And that's when she heard it. Muffled voices coming through the connecting vent in the ceiling.

She was beneath the master bedroom and bath on the second floor. Sound carried between the floors but not clearly enough to make out words. But this was anger— yelling punctuated by loud crashing, things being thrown. Was Marty home? There were no cars in the drive. Had someone broken in? She slipped the gun out of her waistband, held it by her side, took a second deep breath and headed toward the stairs.

As the voices got louder, she recognized Claire's. And she was pissed. Beyond angry, screaming obscenities. Mo had been on the receiving end of that before. But how embarrassing to burst in on a family quarrel. What in the world had Marty done to deserve Claire's wrath? The bedroom door was open about a foot—just enough for Mo to see Claire naked, with only a bath towel wrapped around her. And Marty? Mo inched forward to get a better look at the occupant on the bed. Yes, a man was sitting with his back against the headboard of the bed, but it wasn't Marty.

There, totally in the buff, was Dr. Geoffrey Mitchell. Hair dyed dark brown, cut short and curling around his ears. A scruffy beard dyed to match—but this didn't disguise him to her. No one needed to spell out what the argument was about.

Innocently telling Claire that Geoff Mitchell had been in love with her apparently was not popular. Claire and Geoff—obviously a twosome. They were the lovers ... and criminals. Two people who wanted her dead—tried to kill her more than once. Steal her identity and plunder rain forests to line their pockets.

Suddenly, in one of those flashes of insight, it was all clear. A wash of anger superseded any other emotion. Mo pushed the door open with her foot and stood in a shooter's stance, gun pointed into the room.

"Hello, Mo. You can put the gun down now. I think Claire and I can make you a deal you can't refuse." Geoffrey swung his legs over the side of the bed and stood.

"I don't think I'd count on it." Mo knew who had the control, and nothing they would say could sway her. "Stay where you are."

"Cut the melodrama, Maureen. Geoff told me how he only tolerated you because of the project. How you embarrassed him with your neediness, the clinging, begging for sex, walking into the bathroom while he was showering, taking your clothes off—"

"If that's what you choose to believe, I can't change you. I really don't care, Claire. What I do care about is how you set a child up to kill me, then had the child kidnapped—did you think he knew too much? After I shared with your boyfriend here over dinner that Toby said the person in the Buckley suit was a woman? And the burglary at my house—was I supposed to die then, too? Or was that just more of setting me up? But the bombing—two women killed, more injured, lives shattered ... and who gave his life so that Dr. Mitchell could escape to become an international high-end poacher?"

She hadn't taken her eyes off Geoffrey nor slackened her stance, so when he lunged, she got off a good, clean, unobstructed shot. He jerked backwards, then crumpled, folding up, grabbing his thigh as the grey-white carpet turned crimson underneath him. Claire stood, glaring at her, took a step forward but thought better of advancing any further. She dropped to the floor beside Geoff then looked up at Mo. "You won't get away with this."

"I think I can say the same thing to you, Claire."

"Place the gun in front of you on the floor." The loud command made her jump. Two men in uniform pushed into the room followed by Marshal Foley.

The officers serving the search warrant—all with guns drawn. They must have heard the gunshot and come racing up the stairs. Mo lowered her gun and placed it on the floor. Talk about perfect timing. Only then did she realize she was shaking.

"I left Ben and Julie in the kitchen downstairs. Didn't want them involved in crossfire, but they are really concerned." Tim Foley gave her a hug. "It's okay. You're with friends. Let's go downstairs."

The second officer knelt beside Geoffrey putting pressure on the wound. "An ambulance is on the way."

Chapter Forty-four

For the second time in a little under seventy-two hours, Mo was riding with a federal agent, but this time not shackled and handcuffed and not in the back seat of a squad car. Tim Foley was driving. She'd been allowed a phone call and her lawyer would meet them at the station to sort out the paperwork. The enormity of what had taken place, of what she'd found out hadn't fully sunk in. She wasn't allowing herself to dwell on the duplicity of one Dr. Mitchell.

And Claire? Her sister. She wasn't ready to go there. She only knew she felt sorry for her mother and Marty. It would be difficult on both of them because there was simply no way Claire and Geoff would escape prison time, if not something worse.

People died in that bombing at the Casa Monica. A bombing that was set up to throw authorities off the scent and free up Geoff to disappear, probably literally, into the jungle to collect priceless orchids. And then to live on the continent, maybe the two of them together—Claire and Geoff, the lovers, the co-conspirators—the killers. Two women attending the ceremony that night had been killed. That would, at least, be an accessory murder charge for Claire.

And kidnapping? Thank God there had been a happy ending. If nothing else, Claire again was guilty of aiding and abetting—the ever supportive accomplice to her lover's schemes. The lover who couldn't keep his pants zipped. The search warrant turned up the white-blond wig in her travel bag, and that kind of closed the door on Claire being an innocent bystander.

Chapter Forty-five

The arraignment was set for nine o'clock the next morning. In the meantime Tim Foley, Ben and Julie Pecos, and Lindsey Grant met with federal marshals and local law enforcement to compare notes and bring charges. And Mo had been released—now that there wasn't any need to prove her innocence. The criminals were caught. Claire in jail and Geoff guarded in his hospital bed.

Everyone's best guess was that a homeless person had forfeited his life—maybe even been paid to plant the bomb in the van that night in May at the Casa Monica—taking the place of Dr. Mitchell. But this could never be proved. No one had ever been reported missing. What parts of the remains had been found were cremated.

Already Geoffrey's very expensive lawyer was saying

the dead man was just a poor innocent off the street, unlucky enough to be in the wrong place at the wrong time. Really? Mo supposed it could be true. It certainly took life imprisonment and/or the death penalty off the table—for that murder but what about the two innocent women, unlucky enough to simply be in the hallway?

It seemed the lawyer was trying to make a case for Geoff Mitchell's not having anything to do with the bombing. Were they to believe it was just a lucky turn of fate that it allowed him the opportunity to disappear? Yeah, right.

In addition, the two of them were looking at the part of the Endangered Species Act Penalty Schedule, 16 U.S, C 1531 et seq. that read:

Possess, deliver, carry, transport, sell or ship illegally-taken threatened or endangered species in interstate or foreign commerce—statutory maximum, $13,000. Peanuts for either Geoff or Claire to come up with.

Prison time would have to be awarded through the court system for planning and attempting to carry out the death of one Maureen Beltzer, the kidnapping and retention of a child, and the killing of his captor, and possibly the deaths of two others. Those allegations, if proven, would mean prison time. Lots of it. Life, probably.

Mo sighed. Could she go through a lengthy court ordeal? Support Marjorie, continue to build and sustain the biopark's lab, travel to sister countries to help preserve what Claire was attempting to tear down and plunder?

She would help Marjorie find a house in St. Augustine if she wanted to move. But even that was just a 'maybe.' Marty Roth was being very generous to her mother, insisting that he wanted her to continue as his employee, complete with a retirement package that included paying off her house. How could she refuse?

"I just want to say I appreciate everyone's hard work in bringing this case to a close. Please excuse the handful of black feathers sticking out of my mouth here."

Marshal Garrison said this directly to Tim Foley. "Crow's not my usual lunch choice."

Tim laughed. "I understand."

"The son of the landscaper at the Roth's compound called local law enforcement this morning. Seems he accepted fifty dollars to switch car tags on the BMW then panicked when he saw all the police at the house today. Thought he better clear his conscience and his name."

"Did he describe who gave him the fifty?" Tim was curious. How big was this poaching ring? Did they have local backup?

"Scruffy man with a dark beard and curly hair. I think we have one of those in Flagler Hospital. And, I should add that a check of the airlines for last Saturday had Claire Roth flying to JAX from Chicago. Once she changed her identity to Mo Beltzer, she was picked up at the airport, taken to the compound so she could be shown driving *back* through the gate in a white BMW—a rental of the same model as Mo's. Later on, she was on camera parking the rental car at the airport and flying on to San Jose. On the trip back, she eluded Costa Rican authorities by becoming Claire Roth again, stopping in JAX to don the wig and be seen driving into her gated community in the BMW. We found the rental car abandoned a few blocks over. So, for the last leg of her trip, she had a ride back to the airport as Claire Roth who flew back to Chicago."

"But doesn't she have witnesses to the fact she was

at the conference? She wouldn't have left my mother by herself." Mo was having a hard time wrapping her mind around the complexity of Claire's plan.

"Seems like she did—under the pretense of having to spend the weekend in

Champagne-Urbana at the University of Illinois. She told folks she was cataloguing plants that were being sent to botanical gardens in the UK—filling in at the last minute for someone who had taken ill. There was no reason not to believe her."

"Wow. Things were pretty well planned, right down to seven prepared meals stacked in the fridge for me." She turned to Ben, "I keep meaning to ask, how's Toby Wolff?"

"I'm following up with counseling. He's doing well after his ordeal, but we still have some issues to address. His family is in total support."

"And the Miami *Herald* just bought my Florida article, *Poachers' Paradise*." Julie paused. "It's scheduled to come out next month."

"Am I going to recognize anyone? I mean is there a Maureen Beltzer in there somewhere?" Mo didn't need any more notoriety.

"Names will be changed to protect the innocent." Julie gave Mo a quick hug.

Mo never thought she would be so happy to hear that word in connection with her own name. Innocent.

+ + +

Thank you for taking the time to read *Under A Mulberry Moon*. If you enjoyed it, please consider telling your friends or posting a short review. Word of mouth is an author's best friend and is much appreciated. Thank you,

Susan Slater

+ + +

Get another Susan Slater book free! Visit Susan's website at http://susansslater.com to find out how, and to sign up for her free mystery newsletter and a chance to win some very cool stuff.

Contact Susan: susan@susansslater.com
Follow Susan on Facebook

Susan Slater lived in New Mexico for 39 years, where she began writing her internationally bestselling Ben Pecos series. When she retired from her career with a government contractor and moved to Florida to write full time, Ben and Julie moved with her. Susan also writes the Dan Mahoney mystery series, and has penned several standalone works as well.